Double Trouble

Double Trouble

Betty Sullivan La Pierre

ISBN 1-59109-216-7

Double Trouble

PROLOGUE

At three o'clock in the morning, a sharp rap vibrated the window of Tonia Stowell's bedroom. She moaned, rolled over and pulled the covers over her head. After the celebration of her twenty-eighth birthday at the Saddle Horn with a group of friends, she felt the agony of consuming too much champagne. When the second knock rattled the glass, she forced her eyes open and tried to raise her head.

"Tonia, wake up," called a harsh male voice.

"Who the hell?" She threw back the covers and struggled to get up. Glancing at the clock, she cursed. "Damn, I've only been asleep an hour."

She eased out of bed and clutched her head. Wrapping her robe around her nude body, she staggered toward the window and peered out.

"Dear God, what does he want?" she muttered, motioning for him to go around to the front door.

Her cat, Cyclone, leaped off the bed and followed Tonia into the living room where she opened the front door only as far as the chain allowed. "Drew Harland, do you know what time it is?"

His slate blue eyes met her stare. "Yeah, dammit. But I need your help."

She sighed, unlocked the safety chain and threw open the door. Folding her arms across her chest, she stepped back and glared at him as he entered, then slammed the door shut with her foot "This better be good, waking me at this ungodly hour."

"I'm in trouble. You've gotta help me."

Tonia marched over to the glass topped coffee table and picked up a pack of cigarettes. She sat down on the brocade velour couch and crossed her legs, revealing a shapely tanned thigh through the slit of her silk robe. After lighting her cigarette, she leaned back on the couch and blew a circle of smoke into the air. "What kind of trouble?"

Drew ran a nervous hand through his crop of blond hair. "Bad. Coty and I robbed The First National Bank on the edge of town and he killed the security guard."

She narrowed her jade eyes. "You fools!"

He ducked his head. "Yeah, I know. And to top it off, we noticed a damn video camera perched on the eaves, probably got the whole thing on tape. It'll only be a matter of time before the cops find us."

Tonia put her cigarette on the lip of the crystal ashtray and stepped into the kitchen. She mixed herself a stiff Jack Daniels and water, then carried it back into the living room. Sitting down, she flipped the ash from her cigarette. "How much did you get?"

"Close to a hundred grand."

A slight smile curled the edges of her mouth as she took a sip from the glass. "Where is it?"

He flopped down on an overstuffed chair opposite her and leaned forward, resting his elbows on his thighs. "In a safe-deposit box."

"So what the hell do you want me to do?"

He dug into his pocket, pulling out a gold-toned piece of metal. "I gotta get out of the state, but I'll give you a cut if you'll keep this key until the heat dies down."

Tonia crushed out her cigarette and stood. Untying her robe, she sauntered toward him, the silk material flowing open, revealing firm breasts and curved hips. He stood, his eyes wide as she took the key from his hand and slowly wrapped her arms around his neck. "Sugar, I'll keep this in a nice, safe place for you. Anything else you need?"

To my three sons, Kevin, Stan and Tom Acknowledgement: Thank you, Paul Musgrove for your great artistic ability in creating great covers for my books in print. Thanks to my critique group, WWS; Selma Rubler, Leila Anne Pina, Robert Warren and Sandra Skolnik for their time and patience.

CHAPTER ONE

Private Investigator, Tom Casey, better known as Hawkman to friends and family, hurried down the Medford court house steps and jumped into his truck. As he drove down the street, he loosened his bolo tie, undid the top button of his shirt and let out a sigh. Nice to breath freely again, he thought, turning into his usual parking space in front of the Donut Shop.

He bought a chocolate covered pastry, then sprinted up the narrow stairwell to his office. When he reached the door, he could hear the phone ringing while he fumbled for his key. By the time he stepped inside, the answering machine had already picked up and a sobbing female voice echoed throughout the room.

"Mr. Casey, my name's Nancy Gilbert. I need your help. My sister's been murdered."

Hawkman listened with interest while hanging up his suit coat and pouring himself a cup of coffee. He snapped up his eye-patch and rubbed his eyes with his fingers. The injury he'd received while working for the Agency was still sensitive to light. He flipped the patch back into place, turned on the desk light and punched the replay button, this time jotting down the information. Rolling his shoulders, he dialed the woman's number, then leaned back in his chair. "Nancy Gilbert?"

"Yes."

"Tom Casey returning your call."

He sensed a worried woman from the short silence that ensued. "Mr. Casey, I need to meet with you. Is there some place we can go other than your office?"

"Sure." Hawkman knew some first-time clients preferred meeting in a public place rather than a private investigator's office. "How about Rimmer's Coffee Shop in the Medford Center?"

"That's perfect. How will I know you?"

He studied the coat rack. "I'll have on a dark brown leather jacket and a cowboy hat. I have a black eye patch, so you won't have any trouble spotting me."

"I'll be there in thirty minutes," she said, and hung up.

Hawkman pulled open the bottom desk drawer and removed his shoulder holster with the Colt .45. He felt naked without it, but weapons weren't allowed in the court rooms. After buckling the holster around his large chest, he opened another drawer and removed a small recorder no bigger than a pager. He replaced the batteries then clipped it to his belt. Shrugging into his leather jacket, he plopped on his hat and left.

Fifteen minutes later, he strolled into the small coffee shop where the scent of brewed coffee and freshly baked pastries wafted through the air. After a quick survey of the patrons, satisfied that his prospective client hadn't arrived, he took an empty booth against the far wall.

He kept his eye on the door and it wasn't long before a tall, slender woman dressed in a blue suit entered the shop. Her blond hair had been artfully braided into a French roll and tendrils clung around her face, giving her an elegant appearance. She slipped off her sunglasses and glanced around the room. When she spotted him, he tipped his hat and watched her approach.

"Mrs. Gilbert?"

"Yes."

Hawkman stood as she slipped into the booth. He noticed that her chin quivered slightly and the perfectly applied make-up didn't conceal the ravages of recent tears. He wondered how emotional this encounter might be, especially after a ragged sigh escaped her lips. But before he had a chance to ask any questions, a waitress appeared.

Nancy clutched the purse in her lap, then glanced up at the woman. "Just black coffee, please."

Hawkman nodded. "Same here."

After the waitress left, he placed the small voice activated recorder on the table. "I hope you don't mind. I find this much easier than taking notes."

Her green eyes narrowed. "I don't want anyone else to know what I tell you."

"What is said between a client and myself is strictly confidential. But if it bothers you, I won't use it." He started to remove the recorder from the table, but she waved him off.

"No, it's okay. I'm just scared and nervous right now."

He studied her face. "Why are you scared?"

Tears filled her eyes. "I think my ex-husband killed my sister and is coming after me next."

Hawkman shifted in his seat. "Why don't you start at the beginning."

She dabbed her eyes with a tissue and took a deep breath. "Nine years ago I married a man named Drew Harland. Shortly afterwards, he robbed a bank and was convicted for armed robbery and sentenced to twelve years in prison. I divorced him." She paused a moment and stared blankly at the recorder. Then she took another ragged breath and continued. "He swore he'd kill me. Since that time, I've kept my whereabouts a secret."

Hawkman frowned, not understanding how any of this had a bearing on the murder. "That still doesn't explain why you think he killed your sister."

Nancy glanced at him. "I think he went to Tonia's house to find me. When she refused to tell him where I lived, he probably got angry and killed her." She shook her head and murmured. "He has a violent temper."

"When and where was your sister killed?"

"Last week, inside her home in Los Angeles."

He furrowed his brow. "How could your ex have done this if he's in jail?"

"He got out early on good behavior. I didn't know he'd been released until I flew down to Los Angles to make the positive identification of my sister's body. I found a note in her purse reminding herself to let me know." She rummaged through her own purse. "I have it here someplace." Her voice broke. "She was only thirty-seven years old."

Hawkman held up a hand. "You don't have to find it, I'll take your word. Do the police suspect your ex-husband?"

"No."

"Did you tell them about your suspicion?"

"No. because I hadn't discovered the note until after I talked with them. But putting together the information they gave me, I knew it had to be Drew."

Hawkman leaned forward and rested his elbows on the table. "How's that?"

"Her house had been methodically searched. He must have been looking for my address." She glanced at him. "But he'd never find it."

"Why not?"

"My letters to Tonia went to a Post Office box. After reading them, she destroyed any evidence of having heard from me and she never kept anything in her house that applied to my family, just in case Drew came looking."

"Then how did the authorities find you?"

"Tonia had given one of her neighbor's my husband's office phone number in case of an emergency. Then Jack relayed the message to me."

Hawkman again, shifted in his seat. "Mrs. Gilbert, while you were in Los Angeles, do you think your ex might have spotted you?"

She shot him a startled look. "Dear God, I didn't even think about that."

He rubbed his hand across his chin. "How long were you there?"

"Only a few hours. I flew down early in the morning and came back home that same afternoon."

"Did you make the funeral arrangements?"

She shook her head. "No. The police won't release her body for another week."

Hawkman leaned back and folded his arms across his chest. "Okay. So what is it you want of me?"

"Protection for my family. I fear for my husband, Jack and

our four year old daughter, Tracy. Drew is terribly jealous and very possessive. I felt safe with him behind bars, but now . . ." Her voice trailed as she dabbed her eyes.

He stared at her a moment, thinking how this situation would more than likely involve the police, which sometimes made things pretty damned complicated, especially working two states. "If I take the case, I'll need some background information. Also, if it means investigating your sister's murder, I'll need her full name."

"Tonia Sarah Stowell."

"Also, your ex-husband's full name."

"Drew Lawrence Harland."

The name struck a familiar cord and Hawkman tightened his jaw , trying to recall if he'd run into him on one of his many undercover jobs as an agent? He'd check into it later. "What type of employment did he hold before conviction?"

"Odd jobs. But most of the time he followed the rodeo circuit."

Hawkman jerked back in surprise. "The rodeo?"

"Yes. He competed in the bull riding events." Her eyes were cast downward as she twisted a strand of blond hair around her finger.

He nodded. "Interesting. How long were you married?"

"Five years of pure hell."

"You mentioned he had a violent temper."

She shuttered. "He'd beat me over nothing. It was a relief when he went to prison."

"He's had plenty of time to think things out. Maybe he's changed."

She folded her hands on the table and narrowed her eyes. "He isn't the forgiving sort."

"Tell me about your present family. What's your husband's name and his profession?"

"Jack Gilbert. He's a lawyer."

"No middle name?"

"No."

"And how long have you two been married?"

"Six years."

So now we have a lawyer and an ex-con. Quite an interesting combination, he thought. This could be intriguing. "I'd like to set up a meeting with you and your husband, so we can set up some surveillance strategy."

Nancy stiffened, her eyes wide. "Jack knows nothing about me wanting to hire a private investigator."

Hawkman raised a brow. "Mrs. Gilbert, this isn't going to be a pleasant situation if Drew comes looking for you. I think your husband should know."

The corners of her mouth drew down in a frown. "Why can't I hire you without Jack's knowing?" She opened her purse. "I'll give you a five thousand dollar retainer check today."

He held up his hands. "That's not the point. You can certainly hire me without Jack knowing. But I'd like his cooperation if I'm going to watch your house and especially your daughter. How do you think he'd react if he spotted some stranger tailing Tracy? Or himself, for that matter?"

"But. . ."

Sensing people were watching, Hawkman leaned forward and lowered his voice. "Look, things would be a lot less complicated if he's informed."

She wrote the check and slid it across the table. "I'll think about telling him."

Hawkman fingered the slip of paper and stared at her for a moment, wondering how much Jack Gilbert knew about her past. "Give me a call so I'll know how to proceed."

She slipped from the booth and stood for a moment as if she wanted to say more. Instead, she slowly turned and walked away.

Hawkman watched her go, then took a sip of his coffee, grimacing at the cold bitter taste. He set the cup down and drummed his fingers on the table, thinking about what she'd told him. So far as she knew, the LAPD didn't suspect her ex, but that would change after he talked to them.

He slipped the recorder into his pocket and picked up the tab. While walking across the parking lot toward his 4X4, he spotted Nancy Gilbert drive out the exit in a silver Mercedes.

While unlocking his truck, he fished out his cellular phone from his pocket, then climbed inside. He'd give Stan a call. See if he could get some information on Drew Lawrence Harland.

Stan Erwin and Kevin Louis were two retired police officers

Hawkman hired to assist him on complicated cases. They both volunteered at the police station and had access to their computers. He punched in the number. Stan's deep voice boomed in his ear.

"Stan, Hawkman here."

"Hey, good to hear from you. What's up?"

"I need you to run a check on Drew Lawrence Harland, released from prison sometime in the last two weeks."

"Okay, give me a second."

Hawkman could hear the drone of the computer going through its steps, then Stan came back on the line. "Okay, got it. Boy, looks like you're getting ready to tangle with a turkey. Got a rap sheet a mile long. Been in and out of jail on DUI's, public disturbances, wife battery charges, the list goes on. His last stretch was for armed robbery. Released early, a week ago Tuesday, for good behavior." Stan's tongue clicked in disgust. "Damn, can you beat that? So what's brewing with this character?"

Keeping his eye on the road, Hawkman weaved through the traffic with his cellular to his ear. "Have a client who's involved with him. Thought I recognized the name but still can't place him. How old is he?"

"Thirty-eight. Six foot, blond hair, blue eyes, 180 pounds and missing most of the little finger on his left hand."

"Fax that info along with his picture. Maybe that will stir my memory."

"It's on the way."

"Thanks, Stan."

When Hawkman reached his office, he immediately retrieved the fax and studied the face. The man looked familiar, but he still couldn't place him. He put it aside, hoping the memory would come to him eventually.

⊹×⊹×⊹×⊹×⊹×⊹

In a dimly lit bar, two brothers sat in a booth facing one another.

"You just got out of jail, for Christ sakes. Don't be stupid. Don't do this."

"Then help me, David. I've got to find Nancy."

"Call Tonia. She'd know."

"I already did. The bitch wouldn't tell me anything." Drew leaned back in his seat and looked around. "Man, this seedy hole ain't changed in ten years. Same old red paint on the walls, same old hanging bar lights that look like they've got ten years of dirt on em. Doesn't look like they've done a damned thing to the joint since I was in here the last time." He snorted and took a big gulp of beer, then wiped his mouth with the back of his hand.

David's steel blue gaze narrowed on his brother. "You've been on edge for the last couple of days. What's eaten' at ya?"

"Nothin'." Drew wouldn't meet his brother's stare, instead he glanced around the room and raised a brow at one of the waitresses. "Wow, what a babe. Man oh man, bet she's somethin' in bed."

David sighed. "You ain't changed a bit."

Drew finally turned his eyes from the bosomy waitress. "Look, brother." He slammed his fist on the table. "I've gotta find Nancy."

"What the hell for? She's done with you. Can't you get that through your thick head?"

Drew laced his fingers behind his head and stretched back against the booth. "Hell no. She's still mine. She just don't know it."

David let out a disgusted breath. "You're crazy, man."

"So, you ain't gonna help me find her?"

"No way," David said emphatically and got up to leave. "I want no part of it."

CHAPTER TWO

Hawkman found the traffic light on south Interstate Five and the Hornbrook turn-off loomed up quickly. He slowed and proceeded toward Copco Lake on the rough road. When he crossed the bridge near his house, he saw his wife, Jennifer walking up the ramp that connected the fishing dock to their back porch. He honked. She glanced his way and flashed a big smile, then waved her fishing pole.

By the time he entered the house, she stood at the stove gazing out over the lake while stirring a big pot of stew with a wooden spoon. A low eating bar divided the kitchen from the living room. The whole house had been designed in such a fashion that it allowed a view of the lake from almost every room.

Hawkman smacked his lips. "Ah, that smells good." He leaned over her shoulder and planted a kiss on her cheek. Her soft hazel eyes that missed nothing, sparkled. "Sure is quiet around here. Where's Sam?"

"He's riding his motorcycle." She cocked her head. "As a matter of fact, I think I hear him coming now."

They'd adopted Sam, their fifteen year old son, five years ago.

Hawkman sat down on one of the bar stools and sifted through the mail. "Anything interesting happen around here today?"

Jennifer put the lid back on the pot and placed a loaf of French bread on the cutting board. "I wrote a proposal for a mystery series and sent it out to an editor. Then I took a break and did a little fishing, but nothing's biting. Guess they're hunkering at the bottom for the winter. What's new with you?"

Engrossed in the mail, he glanced at her. "Oh, huh. Got a new case."

She stopped slicing the bread, dropped the knife onto the counter and gave him her full attention. She stared at him for a few moments. "Well, tell me!"

He grinned. "Why, so you can use it in your books?"

Jennifer smiled. "You know I only use the juicy stuff. And so far, this lake community has provided more story plots than you've been able to give me as a private investigator."

He laughed, then told her about the meeting with Nancy Gilbert.

"You think this Harland guy is dangerous?"

"Hard to say. He's been in prison for nine years." I'll have to do some more checking before I can answer that question."

"What's my job?"

Hawkman's expression turned stern. "You'll stay home and do your writing. I don't want you in any danger."

Jennifer put her hands on her hips, her voice low and stubborn. "Look, you've taught me how to use a gun and I even saved your butt once. So I can handle anything you throw at me."

Hawkman threw his hands up in defense. "I have no doubts about that. I'll let you know if there's something you can do. Stan and Kevin will be on the case so I might not need you this time."

She narrowed her eyes and grew thoughtful. When she got that look, he knew to change the topic of conversation, so he hurried toward the sliding glass door before she could pull him into an argument. "How long before dinner? Sure smells good."

"A few minutes. I've got to make a salad yet. But we're not through discussing this, so don't go trying to change the subject."

He grinned. "Too late. I already did. Got to check the birds." He hurried onto the deck where he'd built an aviary Going inside the oversized cage, he examined two ailing hawks found in the wilderness by local residents. "Sure glad I've got you two out here," he whispered. "You're great excuses to keep me out of trouble."

After the birds recovered from their injuries or illness, Hawkman always returned them to the wild. Except for one, Pretty Boy, a falcon he'd found injured in the hills years ago. The hawk refused to leave him once he'd healed. He became Hawkman's close companion, and his nickname derived from that association. The bird had passed away a year ago of old age and he missed him.

Sam interrupted his reminiscing when he yelled out the sliding glass door. "You're wanted on the phone."

Hawkman locked up the aviary and scurried inside.

"Stan here. Sorry to call you at home, but I found some more information on Drew Harland. They had it cross referenced and I didn't notice it until I'd already faxed the other stuff. Think you'll find this interesting. Want me to fax it to the house?"

Glancing over his shoulder at Jennifer putting dinner on the table, he gave it a second thought. "No, send it to the office. I'll check it out first thing in the morning. Hey, while I've got you on the line, check out the Tonia Stowell murder case in Los Angeles. See if they've come up with anything and find out who's in charge. I'm going to have to get an okay to investigate that litigation in California."

"Will do."

"Thanks, Stan. Appreciate it."

After dinner, Hawkman picked up the phone and punched in the code to check his answering machine at the office.

"Mr. Casey, I've discussed the problem with my husband and we want to set up a meeting. If it's convenient for you, we'd like you to join us at the Lone Brand Restaurant for lunch at twelve o'clock tomorrow. We have a private booth, so tell the hostess you're joining the Gilberts. If I don't hear otherwise, I'll assume you'll be there."

Hawkman let out a heavy sigh when he hung up.

Jennifer glanced at him . "That sounded like relief."

"Mrs. Gilbert talked to her husband."

"Which means?"

"Things will be a lot less complicated."

The next day at eleven forty-five, Jack pulled into the driveway of his home and beeped the horn. Nancy ran out and slid into the passenger side of her husband's white Cadillac.

Once she closed the door, Jack threw the car into reverse and gunned out into the street. "I still don't understand why you didn't talk to me before hiring a private investigator."

"Jack, we've already discussed this. I told you Drew is my problem, but Mr. Casey thought you should know so he'd have your cooperation."

"This whole situation stinks. Tonia's murder and Drew's release from prison. I hope you realize your sordid past could ruin my chance for the Senate."

Nancy shot a disgusted look at her husband. "You knew about Drew when you married me. It didn't bother you then."

"I didn't have politics on my mind at that time. We have to be careful. I don't have a clean slate with Drew Harland in the picture."

Nancy frowned and stared out the window. Jack seemed more concerned about his damned political career than his family. This whole ordeal could ruin their marriage. "I'd like to will it away, Jack, but I don't think it's possible."

He scowled at his wife and remained silent the rest of the way to the restaurant.

⊹⊱⊰⊱⊰⊱⊰⊹

Hawkman arrived at the parking lot of the Lone Brand Restaurant fifteen minutes early. He backed into a parking spot at the rear of the lot so he could see the front entry. Soon, the Gilberts drove up in a new Cadillac Seville. Hawkman took down the license plate number and watched the couple walk into the restaurant.

Jack Gilbert, approximately six foot tall, had a full head of black hair and a muscular build with large shoulders that filled out his expensive suit. Hawkman figured he visited the gym regularly. Nancy looked elegant in her beige dress. They made a striking couple.

After a few minutes, Hawkman buttoned his jacket to conceal his weapon and walked into the restaurant. He removed his hat as he followed the hostess through a hallway with wagon wheel chandeliers and walls decorated with branding irons lashed with pieces of leather.

They crossed the large dining room to a booth at the far end. After Jack Gilbert introduced himself, Hawkman slid into the seat across from Nancy and casually placed the recorder on the table. Jack glanced at it suspiciously.

"It's easier than taking notes," Hawkman explained, watching Jack's jaw tighten.

A cocktail waitress delivered a glass of white wine to Nancy and a Scotch on the rocks to Jack. Hawkman declined the cocktail offer.

No sooner had she left than another waitress dressed in a square dance outfit arrived to take their food orders. Hawkman quickly viewed the menu while Nancy and Jack placed their orders, then gave his choice. Once they were left alone, Nancy broke the silence.

"I've told Jack everything."

Hawkman glanced his way.

Jack's stare bore into him like bullets. "I don't like this mess. It could greatly impede my race for the Senate."

Hawkman lifted a brow. "How's that?"

"The opposition would love to stick me with a scandal."

Hawkman nodded. "I see." Here's a man more interested in power than anything else, he thought. "We'll try and keep things quiet. But if Drew's determined to come after Nancy, then we'll have to involve the police. There might not be much control over what leaks to the news media."

Jack scowled. "Do you think he'll try to find her?"

"I don't know. He made the threat right after the divorce and a lot of time has gone by. We'll have to wait and see." Hawkman shrugged. "On the other hand, he may surprise us and not attempt to hunt her down at all."

"Let's hope for the latter," Jack said. "But from the horror stories Nancy's told me about her ex, he's mean and vicious."

"That's how she remembers him. He's had a lot of time to come to terms with himself and the divorce. Regardless, I'll find out as much as I can."

Jack still held his jaw taut. "I understand Nancy gave you a five thousand dollar retainer. Is that enough to get you started?"

"Yes. That's sufficient."

Hawkman had slipped a contract into his pocket before leaving the office and placed it on the table in front of them. While Jack read it, Hawkman turned to Nancy, "Tell me about your sister."

"She'd been divorced for years, lived alone and never had any children." Her eyes filled with tears and her voice caught. "She tended to spoil our Tracy rotten."

Hawkman continued his questioning without a pause in hopes of getting through the rough spots without causing Nancy tears. "Any men in her life?"

She took a sip of wine, her expression thoughtful. "Several. A woman that beautiful attracted them like flies. But, she never found another one that she wanted to marry."

"Do you happen to have a picture of her?"

Nancy dug through her purse and handed him a photo. "This was taken last year at her place."

Hawkman studied the picture of the brown-haired, green-eyed beauty, dressed in tight red shorts and a white mid-drift halter that displayed her shapely figure. "She was a lovely woman," he said, handing the snapshot back.

Nancy glanced at it, then quickly shoved the picture back into her purse.

Jack signed the contract and pushed it in front of her. "This has been a terrible tragedy and Drew should be hung for what he's done. I'm counting on you to put him back in jail where he belongs."

After their meal, Hawkman asked, "Mrs. Gilbert, do you have other relatives in the area?"

"No. My parents died years ago. Only Tonia and I were left." Her chin quivered, but she managed to fight back the tears as Jack put his arm around her shoulders.

Hawkman quickly changed the subject. "I'll need phone numbers where I can reach either of you at all times. Once I assemble the surveillance team, I'll contact you to meet them." He gave each of them one of his cards. "The number written on the back is an emergency number for after hours. The call will be automatically routed to my house. Call me day or night if anything suspicious happens."

Jack checked his watch and rose from his chair. "I've got to get back to the office." He handed Hawkman the signed contract. "No offense, Mr. Casey, but I hope this is over soon."

"I understand. And just call me, Casey."

"Okay, Casey." He smiled tightly, then turned and followed his wife out the door.

CHAPTER THREE

The next morning, Jennifer stood on the opposite side of the bar, sipping her coffee and tapping her foot impatiently. Putting her hand on her hip, she let out a loud sigh. "Well, I'm waiting."

Hawkman glanced up from the newspaper with a surprised expression. "Waiting for what?" But he knew full well what she wanted. Hoping to stall her, he returned his attention to the sports page.

She gently bent the top of the paper down, her hazel eyes narrowed with determination. "I want to know what my job will be on this new case."

He leaned back in his chair and met her stare. "You're not getting involved this time. It could be dangerous."

"And chasing after Dirk wasn't?"

"That was a long time ago. Both our lives were in danger then. Remember, I didn't purposely involve you."

"This case can't be near as dangerous. Besides, I wouldn't be interested in a dull insurance fraud or one of those follow the spouse deals." Her eyes twinkled. "But this one sounds exciting."

Hawkman knew she wouldn't let up. There must be something he could find that wouldn't put her life in danger. He remained silent for a moment, then snapped his fingers. "Okay, I've got it. You're in charge of the Gilbert's four year old daughter, Tracy. It will probably be boring, but I need someone to keep an eye on her in case Drew tries to use her as bait, like Dirk did with you. She goes to a child care center for most of the day while Mrs. Gilbert works at the Charity."

Jennifer thought it over then nodded. "No one will harm that little girl while I'm around." With that, she turned and flipped on the dishwasher.

Hawkman smiled and resumed reading the paper. "Hmm, there's a rodeo coming to Redding, California."

"So?"

"Remember, I told you about Drew Harland being a bull rider? Well, yesterday I talked with the warden of Soledad. He confirmed Harland's obsession with rodeos, stating that he joined the rodeo prison team and participated in the bull riding event. If he's still serious about this, here's an opportunity to get closer to Medford."

"But I thought you said he doesn't know where Nancy lives?"

"I don't know that for sure. I'm going on the assumption that he's found out."

"So what else did the warden have to say about him?"

Hawkman shrugged. "He had no complaints. Harland never caused any problems with the inmates. No gang affiliations. And spent a lot of time working out in the gym."

"Doesn't sound like you learned anything new."

Hawkman ripped out the newspaper article and took it to the dining room table where he'd been working on the Gilbert file. "True, it's all recorded in his prison file." He slipped the clipping inside the folder and glanced up at the kitchen clock. "Ready to go?"

She rinsed out her coffee cup and put it on the counter. "Yep."

On their way to Medford, Hawkman filled her in on what he'd discovered about Drew Harland's life before prison.

She wrinkled her nose when he'd finished. "What a jerk."

"Definitely no angel. We can hope he's changed, but I doubt it."

When they pulled up in front of the pastry shop in old town Medford, Stan and Kevin were waiting outside eating donuts. They all trooped up the stairs and found a place to sit down inside the small office. Hawkman called the Gilberts to come over in an hour to meet the team. Meantime, he briefed the crew and handed out pictures of Drew Lawrence Harland.

Hawkman purposely left extra photos of Drew on the desk, and observed the Gilberts' reactions when they arrived. A muscle ticked in Jack's jaw when he noticed the pictures. Nancy glanced at them, then turned away with fear in her eyes.

After the introductions, Nancy turned over a picture of Tracy with the address of the child care center written on the back. Hawkman explained the procedure he intended to use with the surveillance team and that he planned to start this coming Monday morning. After a few questions, the Gilberts left.

Hawkman continued with instructions to the team and handed out two-way radios and portable chargers to each one. Stan reported that he'd contacted the Los Angeles Police Department.

"No new evidence has surfaced on the Stowell murder case. The detective in charge is Dan Grolier."

"Thanks, Stan." Hawkman stood thoughtfully for a moment, rubbing his chin. "I need to get some background information on that case plus do some paperwork so I can investigate the murder. If I go down to Los Angeles for a couple of days, can you guys handle it here until I return?"

They nodded and he concluded the meeting.

<figure>◦⊹•⟨•⊹•⟨•⊹•⟨•⊹•⟨•⟩⟩</figure>

Hawkman discovered through a phone call that Detective Grolier would be working the graveyard shift, so he set up an appointment and flew into Los Angeles that night. He walked into the LAPD a few minutes before the scheduled meeting and had the officer in charge notify Grolier.

A man of medium height and stocky build came out of a door at the far end of the hall. He approached Hawkman with an extended hand. "Tom Casey?"

"Yes." The firm handshake told Hawkman that this man felt secure and comfortable in his job. The big blue eyes that twinkled under bushy, twitching eyebrows showed confidence.

The detective pointed to the bulge under Hawkman's jacket. "Got a California permit for that piece?"

"Sure do."

Grolier nodded his approval and checked his watch.

"Got the paperwork that you requested, but before we discuss that, let's run over to the Stowell house while things are quiet around here."

"Sounds good."

Grolier stopped at the front desk and reported their destination. Then Hawkman followed him out of the station into an unmarked car.

"The murder was committed in an area where there's little crime." Grolier commented while pulling out of the parking lot. "Neighborhood's still in shock,"

Hawkman took his small recorder out of his pocket. "Mind if I tape our conversation?"

Grolier grinned. "Bad memory?"

"Just don't want to miss anything," Hawkman chuckled.

"Sure, go ahead."

He flipped on the recorder and clipped it to his shirt pocket. "Who discovered the body?"

"The next door neighbor, Ellie Mae Williams, when she brought Stowell's cat home. The coroner's report states that Stowell hadn't been dead much over an hour by the time they got there. So Ms. Williams probably missed the killer by a matter of minutes."

"How was the murder committed?"

"Death caused by a blow to the back of the head. From the position of her body, it looked like she could have hit her head on the sharp corner of a glass coffee table."

"That sounds like an accident?"

Grolier shook his head and frowned. "No. There were bruises on her face, abrasions on the arms and her blood on the cordless phone."

"Maybe some sort of altercation."

"Yeah, possibly. At first, we thought she might have surprised a burglary in progress. But we found two hundred dollars in her purse. The jewelry box appeared untouched. The video camera, microwave oven, portable TV, things you'd think a burglar would nab, none had been disturbed. However, we later discovered that the house had been methodically searched."

"That's strange. Wonder what they were looking for?"

"Wish we knew. Might make this case easier." Grolier turned on Binkley street and pulled into a driveway, where the yellow tape surrounding the house fluttered in the breeze. Hawkman followed the detective onto the porch. When Grolier unlocked the front door and started to reach inside to turn on the lights, he abruptly stepped back, pulling his gun. "Cover me."

Hawkman stepped to the side of the door, slipping his Colt from the holster.

"Somebody's been here. Could still be inside," Grolier whispered over his shoulder as the two men carefully entered the living room.

Hawkman's gaze darted around the room. The couch and matching chairs had been turned over and the cloth on the bottoms slit from corner to corner. The desk drawers had been dumped in the middle of the floor.

The men carefully moved from room to room. Hawkman wondered why someone would go through this house again. This could be an act of vandalism, but something down deep told him that the murderer hadn't found what he was looking for the first time.

Mattresses in two bedrooms were cut open and the stuffing pulled out from the centers. Pillows were cut open and the innards scattered. More drawers dumped, clothes in the closet had pockets turned wrong side out and a couple of coats had their linings ripped open. Every box and storage bin had been raked from the closet shelves, their contents strewn about the room. The whole house had been thoroughly wrecked.

Finding no sign of the intruder, the two men wound their way back to the front door, then went outside and explored the perimeter of the house. After a thorough search and finding nothing, they holstered their guns and went back inside.

Hawkman stood with his fists on his hips, surveying the mess. "Wonder what the hell they were looking for?"

Grolier stared at the floor. "For a minute there, I thought our murderer had returned, but now I don't think so."

"Why's that?"

"Completely different M.O. This looks like the work of a madman."

Hawkman glanced at the detective. "You think he found what he wanted?"

Grolier scratched his chin. "Hard to say, but with every room hit like this. I'd say he's still searching." Stepping over the debris, he headed out the door toward his car. "I'd better get the technicians out here and see what they can find." Grolier slid under the steering wheel, leaving the car door open and put a call through to the station over the radio.

Hawkman leaned on the fender next to the driver side and waited for him to finish. "Were fingerprints lifted earlier?"

Grolier shook his head. "Only Stowell's. The perp either wore gloves or wiped everything clean. We found a pair of expensive driving gloves on the coffee table in the living room, but they could have been left by anyone. I'll show you the reports when we get back to the office."

"Any suspects?"

"Nope."

"How did the murderer enter the house?"

"No evidence of a forced entry. Makes me think the victim knew her killer."

"How'd the lady who discovered the body get in?"

"Back door left wide open."

"Is this the same lady who furnished Mr. Gilbert's office phone number?"

Grolier nodded. "Yep. If it hadn't been for her, we'd still be looking for the next of kin."

"Mrs. Gilbert informed me her sister never kept anything in the house that would identify her or her family."

Grolier scratched his head. "Seems mighty peculiar if you ask me. Sounds like she had something to hide."

"I'll shed some light on that." Hawkman then told him about Drew Harland and Nancy's suspicions.

Grolier raised his massive eyebrows. "I'll definitely check him out."

Hawkman walked to the edge of the garage and squinted into the darkness. "What's out back past the yards?"

"Nothing but a gravel alley."

The technician's van soon arrived and Grolier gave them instructions. Then he and Hawkman left the scene and returned to the detective's office. Grolier shrugged off his jacket and tossed it on an extra chair next to his desk. Pulling a folder from the filing cabinet, he handed it to Hawkman. "Take a look at the Stowell file while I get us some coffee. You'll see what I mean about this last trashing being a different type of M.O."

Hawkman pulled a chair up to the desk and began examining the papers. A few minutes later, Grolier entered with two steaming mugs of coffee, setting one in from of Hawkman. He then settled into his chair in front of the computer. "Any questions?"

"No. Looks pretty complete," Hawkman said, blowing on the hot brew.

"Good." Grolier shuffled some papers on his desk then handed Hawkman a set. "Let's get you legal in California before I forget. Fill these out and take your copy."

After Hawkman completed and signed the forms, he gave them back to Grolier, who stashed them in his outgoing desk tray. He then pulled the computer keyboard toward himself, picked up his cold cigar from the ashtray and placed it between his teeth. "Okay, let's see what we can find out about Drew Harland."

Hawkman concealed a smile as he watched the man's eyebrows furrow like the brim of a hat, while two stubby index fingers flew over the keyboard. Grolier worked the cigar between his teeth while he mumbled and studied the computer print.

"Bad guy we're dealing with. Long rap sheet." Suddenly his face lit up. "Ah ha, Harry Foster's his parole officer. I'll give him a call." He rolled his chair toward the phone.

Hawkman listened while Grolier questioned Foster.

After the detective hung up, he swiveled his chair around and handed Hawkman a piece of paper. "Harland's supposed to be at this address. He's allowed free movement as long as he checks in at his appointed times. Foster doesn't expect to hear from him again until next week. But he's going to try and contact him, then he'll get back to me." Grolier ran his hand over his face. "Boy, he sure didn't seem too happy about me calling."

Hawkman glanced at his watch and grinned. "Can't blame him. It's three in the morning."

Grolier raised both eyebrows in tall arches and put a hand over his eyes. "Oh hell, no wonder he's ticked off. I better make a note to myself to take him to lunch." He scribbled something on a piece of paper and attached it to the calendar on his desk. "I lose all track of time when I work graveyard." He swirled his chair back toward

Hawkman. "Here's Foster's phone number, but don't tell him I gave it to you."

"Thanks," Hawkman clipped the paper to his notes. "Is there a chance I can get a copy of the Stowell report?"

Looking thoughtful, Grolier tapped his forefinger on the desk. "Not supposed to give it out." He picked up the file and headed out of the office, his voice trailing behind him. "But what the hell, this isn't a high-profile case. . ."

He returned shortly and handed Hawkman a parcel of papers. "You owe me one." Picking up his unlit cigar, he put it between his teeth and grumbled. "Damn no smoking laws."

Hawkman's mouth twitched at the corners while he tucked the copies into his briefcase. He then gave the detective his card. "If anything comes up, give me a call."

Grolier dropped it into his desk drawer. "Will do. You do the same."

The two men shook hands and Hawkman walked out of the station into the muted light of a new day. Feeling the hunger pangs gnawing at his stomach, he decided to have a bite to eat before searching for Harland's place.

After breakfast. he merged into commute traffic and found his way to a seedy run-down apartment complex. Beer cans, empty liquor bottles and broken down cars laced the streets. He frowned. "Sure don't like the looks of this place."

Hawkman maneuvered his way through the trash and pushed open the grimy front door. He hesitated a moment, letting his sight adjust to the dimly lit interior, then stepped inside. Spotting a stairway at the far end, he hurried toward it and ran up the concrete stairs. He grimaced as the stench of urine invaded his nostrils.

He quickly found apartment number twenty and knocked. No answer. He glanced up and down the hall. Seeing no one, he turned the knob and the warped door swung open. Cautiously, he poked his head inside and called in a low voice. "Harland."

"He don't live there no more."

Startled by the voice, Hawkman whirled around, coming face to face with a young punk standing behind him. "How do you know?"

The youth pushed his dirty long hair out of his face. "Saw him leavin' last night with a suitcase."

Hawkman stared into hollow eyes. "Did he say where he was going?"

"Naw. He just left like most do."

He watched as the youth swaggered down the hall and disappeared into a room, slamming the door. He surveyed the hallway once again, then stepped inside the vacant room, softly closing the door. He searched the closet and the drawers of a rickety dresser but nothing indicated that Harland had ever been here. Then he noticed the small garbage can and dumped the contents on the unmade bed. A crumpled instruction brochure on how to enter the Redding rodeo competition caught his eye. He stuffed it into his pocket. After making one final inspection of the apartment, he bounded down the stairs into the sunshine, grateful for a whiff of fresh air.

Glad to be back in the car, he spread the Los Angeles street map on the passenger seat and tracked the fastest route back to Tonia Stowell's place. He folded the map, made a U-turn and headed toward the freeway.

He parked in front of Stowell's house and studied the neighboring homes, wondering which neighbor had discovered the body. Checking his watch, he felt eight o'clock, a bit too early in the morning to go knocking on people's doors.

He pushed back the car seat and unfolded the newspaper he'd bought at the restaurant. But before he could read the headlines, a movement caught his eye at the front room window of the house next door. The drape peeled back revealing 'the little old lady that keeps watch over the neighborhood'. He smiled to himself, placed the paper on the seat and strolled toward the house, feeling his every move being calculated.

When he climbed the porch steps, the drape fluttered back into its original position. That's when he took advantage of the moment and flipped on the recorder clipped to his belt. The door opened before he had a chance to knock and he found himself staring into a pair of clear blue eyes. The woman appeared to be in her eighties, holding a black and white cat in her arms.

He took off his cowboy hat and showed her his badge. "Good morning, ma'am, are you Ms. Ellie Mae Williams?"

"Sure am. Are you a detective?"

"No, I'm Tom Casey, a private investigator. I'm here on behalf of my client, Nancy Gilbert. She's hired me to investigate the murder of her sister, Tonia Stowell. I'd like to ask you some questions if you have the time."

A purple splotched hand reached up and unlatched the screen door, then waved him inside with an impatient flick of her wrist. "Come in, come in, don't just stand there. My, such a horrible thing done to Tonia. Nice person. Never harmed a soul."

Hawkman followed the bent over woman into the living room where she gestured toward the sofa. "Sit, sit."

He took a seat on the end cushion of the couch, his nose twitching at the odor of a house seldom aired. Reminded him of his own folks complaining of how chilled they got if he opened the windows or doors to let in fresh air.

Ellie Mae took the chair across the room and continiued holding the cat in her lap. "Now tell me your name again."

"Tom Casey, but you can call me Casey."

Her face broke into a wreath of smile wrinkles. "I like that, sounds like a cowboy. You can call me Ellie Mae." She stared at him for a moment then abruptly took one hand from around the cat and pointed at the black patch covering Hawkman's left eye. "What happened to your eye, young man? Is it gone completely?"

Amused by her blunt question, Hawkman grinned. "I injured it about ten years ago. I have sight, but it's sensitive to light so I wear a patch."

"Well, at least you still got your eye and not just a hole in your head." Then she immediately changed the subject. "This here's Cyclone, Tonia's cat." She dropped the animal to the floor and brushed the hairs from her apron. "He's quite a corker. If the door's left open just a crack, he'll run out faster than a tornado. That's why Tonia named him Cyclone."

Hawkman leaped at the opening. "Did you know Tonia well?"

"'Bout as well as anyone, I guess. She worked long hours, so she didn't have much time to socialize with the neighbors, but she never did no one any harm. She always waved at me when I was in the yard." Ellie Mae shook her head. "Such a shame this happened."

"I understand you found her?"

She covered her face with both hands. "Oh, yes. Such a terrible sight."

"I know it's not easy to talk about. But did you see or hear anything unusual at her place that night?"

"No. Like I told the police. I ate my supper and had the television on when Cyclone scratched on my screen door for his treat. I'd seen Tonia pull into her garage earlier and she usually lets him out for a romp after she gets home from work. I let him come inside for a few minutes then I figured I'd better get him home because she always went out on Wednesday night and she never left the cat outside."

He raised a brow? "She went out every Wednesday night?"

Ellie Mae nodded. "Every Wednesday night."

"Where did she go?"

She shrugged. "Don't know. Never asked her either, cause it was none of my business."

Hawkman took a mental note to check on this. "So when you returned the cat, which door did you use?"

"I went to the front door, but she didn't answer the bell. So I went around to the back, figuring she might be looking for Cyclone. I didn't find her outside, but the back door was open, so I poked my head inside and hollered. When I still didn't get an answer, I stepped into the kitchen." She pointed a crooked finger in the air. "Now mind you, I'm still calling her name. I wouldn't think of just walking into someone's home, especially hers, without letting her know I'm there. Never knew if she might have a man friend inside."

Hawkman's interest piqued, he leaned forward. "I understand. Did Ms. Stowell have many male friends?"

"A beautiful thing like her," she harrumped. "You bet she did."

"Did you know any of them?"

Again she shook her head. "No. None of my business."

He nodded. "So what happened after you got inside the house?"

She raised her hands, then let them drop into her lap. "I found her on the living room floor in a puddle of blood." Her eyes rimmed with tears. She sniffed and wiped her eyes with the corner of her apron. "I knew she was dead the minute I saw her. I didn't want to touch anything so I hurried home and called the police. How could anyone have done that to her? She wasn't a bad person."

"I don't know, Ellie Mae, but we're trying to find out. Did you see anyone loitering about the house?"

"No. Thought I heard someone running on that gravel out back, but must have been my imagination as I didn't see a soul anywhere. Sure wish I had." She smacked a frail fist into her lap and her voice trembled. "My eyesight's real good too."

Hawkman stood and handed her his card. "Ellie Mae, I really appreciate you taking the time to talk to me. If you see anything suspicious or if you remember something that might help, call me collect at this number."

She took the card and placed it beside her phone. "I'll certainly do that." Then she looked up at him with wide blue eyes. "Will you be talking to Tonia's sister soon?"

"More than likely. Is there something you'd like me to tell her?"

"Yes. That I have Cyclone and what I should do about him?"

Hawkman patted Ellie Mae's shoulder. "I'll have her get in touch with you. Does she have your phone number?"

"I'm not sure. Let me write it down."

She wrote in a clear and steady hand, then gave the paper to Hawkman. He stuck it into his pocket and stepped out on the porch. Still holding the screen door open, he pointed toward the back yard. "I'd like to check the area behind the houses. How's the best way to get around there?"

Grabbing the cat from the floor, Ellie Mae followed Hawkman onto the porch. She pointed a crooked arthritic finger toward the hedge. "See that opening between the bushes? Go through there. It leads to the back alley."

"Thanks, Ellie Mae." He waved as he wound his way around the shrubs, his gaze traveling across the ground in case the police had missed something. When he reached the alley, he headed toward the dented blue dumpster, but the sound of crunching gravel caused him to stop and jerk his head around.

CHAPTER FOUR

Hawkman stood glued to the ground watching an old man jostle a wobbly three wheeled bicycle across the gravel strewn alley. Now what's that old fellow doing riding behind this private property? His question was soon answered.

The old man's matted gray beard bounced on his chest, while his dirty, ragged jacket flapped in the breeze. He came to an abrupt halt in front the garbage container, leaped off the bike and threw back the lid of the receptacle, banging it loudly against the side. Immediately, he began digging in the rubbish and tossing aluminum cans into a basket between the back wheels of his bike.

Hawkman reached down at his belt and flipped on the recorder as he stepped out from behind the dumpster. The stocking cap adorned head slowly rose above the brim of the trash container, his eyes wide as he stared at Hawkman. "Who are ya?"

"Tom Casey, private investigator."

"What you investigatin'?"

"A murder."

"Who got killed?"

Hawkman pointed toward Tonia's house. "The lady who lived there."

The old fellow dropped a can into his bag, then straddled the bike. "Well, I didn't do it."

Hawkman suppressed a smile and stepped in front of the bike.

"I didn't say you did. But, maybe you saw something that might be helpful."

"I ain't seen nothin'."

"Do you collect cans here regularly?"

He shrugged and eyed Hawkman suspiciously. "Every day. I don't always come at the same time though. Sometimes I come in the evenin'. Sometimes I come in the mornin'."

"Do you remember what time you were here last Wednesday?"

The fellow closed one bleary eye and cocked his head upward. "Let me think a minute. Evenin'. Yeah, evenin'. I remember, cause I had me a good haul that night. In fact, I had to make two trips cause my bag got so full."

"Did you see or hear anything out of the ordinary that night?"

The old man scratched his temple and looked thoughtful. "Yeah. A car was parked over there." He pointed a finger at an area behind Hawkman.

"Why would that be unusual?"

He raked his fingers through his bushy beard and shrugged one shoulder. "Cause people don't usually park back here. Could get a ticket. I just figured it belonged to somebody visitin'. They were gone before I got back."

"What time did you return?"

"Couldn't have been much past seven."

"Do you remember what kind of a car?"

The old man shook his head. "No."

"Big, little or medium size?"

Taking off a greasy stocking cap, the old man scratched his head, then pushed the hair out of his face before slipping the cap back on. "No, it weren't no big Cadillac or Lincoln but it weren't no sports car either. Somewhere in the middle, if you know what I mean."

"What color?"

"Black or a real dark green. Had a sticker on the window with those funny marks like they put on all the food in the grocery stores nowadays." He made gestures in the air with his finger.

Hawkman smiled. "You mean a bar code?"

The old fellow nodded enthusiastically and snorted. "Yeah, yeah. That's what they call it. This new fangled computin' talk, sounds like a foreign language."

Must have been a rental, Hawkman thought. "What's your name?"

Still straddling the bike, the old fellow stood tall and threw back his shoulders. "Elliot Cleaver Washington," he said, proudly.

"You live around here?"

He pointed east. "A couple blocks down."

"Thanks for your time and help, Mr. Washington. I won't keep you from your work any longer." Hawkman placed a ten dollar bill in his hand.

Washington's eyes lit up with a big toothless grin as he pocketed the bill. "Anytime."

Hawkman retraced his steps to the front of the house in hopes of questioning more of the neighbors. After an hour of trooping from house to house, he gave up. No one had seen nor heard anything that night, just as Grolier had reported.

He opened the car door and let the heat escape while he shed his jacket. Driving back toward the airport, he thought about his day's work. He'd found out very little that wasn't in the crime report. He still didn't know if Drew Harland had anything to do with Tonia's murder, however, he did have a better insight on Tonia Stowell. She obviously had her share of male visitors and went out every Wednesday night. That's interesting, he thought Could it have a bearing on the murder?

He removed the recorder from his belt and spoke into it, reminding himself to ask Grolier if he'd had the chance to look into Tonia's Wednesday night escapades. Also, he needed copies of her phone bills from the past few months. He frowned after clipping the recorder back onto his belt. If he were still in the Agency he could have secured those phone bills without having to ask the detective to get them with a warrant. There were a few disadvantages of being a private investigator.

He turned in the rented car at the airport, then waited on stand-by. Soon after he boarded and settled in his seat, a wave of fatigue swept over him and he slept.

The next morning, Jennifer and Hawkman headed for Medford in separate cars, communicating through two-way radios.

"I know this hasn't been very exciting for you, but you're doing a great job." Hawkman said.

Jennifer laughed. "Well, I admit it's boring." But then her voice softened. "But I couldn't bear the thought of Drew getting his hands on little Tracy."

"I couldn't either."

"Well, here's my street. Talk to ya later." She waved and turned off.

Hawkman returned his radio to the charger and continued down the road. Entering his office, he grimaced at the room's stuffiness and opened the window. He glanced up at the dove's nest perched on the eaves and shook his head. Doves had to be the worst nest builders and he marveled that the eggs hadn't rolled off the few twigs and smashed onto the sidewalk below.

He shrugged off his jacket, grabbed a pencil from the decorated tin can Sam had made for him several years ago, then pushed the play button on his answering machine.

"Mr. Casey, this is Ellie Mae Williams. I need to talk to you."

Rummaging through his notes, he found the piece of paper where she'd written down her number for Nancy. He hit the speaker phone and keyed it in.

"Hello Ellie Mae. Tom Casey returning your call."

"Mr. Casey, you told me to call if anything unusual happened."

He leaned back in his chair, holding a pencil between his index fingers. "That's right."

"While I was weeding my flower beds early this morning. A man stopped his car in front of my place and called to me. He appeared real upset. Said he was Tonia's cousin from out of town and just heard about her murder. He asked me how he could get a hold of her sister."

Hawkman came forward resting his elbows on the desk. "What did you tell him?"

"I told him he'd probably find Nancy in Medford."

He snapped the pencil in two. Damn, he thought. Ellie Mae's been sucked in. But by whom? Drew? "What else did this cousin want?"

"He asked for her phone number, but since I didn't have Nancy's home phone, I gave him Mr. Gilbert's office ."

He tossed the broken pencil aside and snatched another from the can. "What'd this guy look like?"

"Nice looking fellow. Had the strangest color blue eyes I've ever seen. Sandy blond hair and a crooked, like it had been broken at one time. He seemed like a nice young man."

Hawkman's jaw tightened. "Anyone with him?"

"No. I didn't see anybody else."

He rapidly jotted notes. "What kind of a car?"

"I don't know. A medium size."

"Color?"

"Dark green."

He traced around 'dark green car' several times and put exclamation marks beside it. "Ellie Mae, the next time anyone comes around asking question, don't tell them anything. But get their license plate number. If they're persistent, refer them to me."

She gasped. "Did I do something wrong?"

"You did right in calling me. He might be legit, but he also might be a scam artist."

Hawkman heard her let out another gasp.

"You don't think he might be the killer?"

"I doubt the killer would ask for Tonia's sister. But do call me when someone comes around asking questions."

"Oh my, I will. Next time I won't tell them one thing. By the way, did you tell Nancy I had Tonia's cat?"

"I'll tell her today." He hung up, muttering. "Things are going to get sticky now." He pushed the speaker button and keyed in a number. "Grolier, Hawkman here. Got a piece of information you might be interested in." He told Grolier about the call from Ellie Mae and how she described a man that fit Drew's profile. "Also, there's an old fellow who collects cans from the local dumpsters. He saw a medium sized, green car parked in that alley about the time of the murder. It sounded like a rental with bar codes on the window. Ellie Mae described a similar car driven by this so called relative. It might be worth checking into."

"You bet it is. I'll get right on it."

"One more thing. Have you checked out Tonia's male friends?"

"Yeah, the ones we could find. They all had alibis for the night of the murder."

"Well, that's a dead end."

After Hawkman hung up from Grolier, he called Nancy.

"Mrs. Gilbert, I've just talked with Ellie Mae Williams, your sister's neighbor in Los Angeles. A man of Drew's description paid her a visit this morning claiming to be an out-of-town relative. She innocently gave him your last name and Jack's office phone number. I'm advising you to stay close to home and screen your calls."

A moment of silence elapsed. "Dear God, he's really out there," she whispered, then let out a long sigh. "Mr. Casey, Tonia's body has being released. I've made reservations to fly down and receive her ashes tomorrow. Jack will pick up Tracy later than usual from the child center."

"I'll pass the word to Jennifer." He thoughtfully tapped his pencil on the desk. "So Jack's not going with you?"

"No. He's too busy."

"I don't like it. Drew might be watching Tonia's house." He heard Nancy suck in her breath.

"But, why would he go there? Do murderers return to the scene of the crime?"

"Sometimes, but let's not jump the gun. We don't know for a fact that he murdered your sister."

"I can't think of anyone else who would commit such a horrible act," Nancy cried.

"Try to stay calm."

She sniffed. "I'm sorry."

"I don't want you going to Los Angeles alone. Get another reservation and I'll go with you."

"Thank you. I'll get right on it."

"Also, call Ellie Mae Williams. She's wondering what to do about your sister's cat. Confidentially, I think she'd like to keep it."

"She can have the cat. I certainly don't want that animal."

⟨•⟩•⟨•⟩•⟨•⟩•⟨•⟩•⟨•⟩

Jack stood in the doorway of the kitchen with his hands stuffed deep in his pockets, listening to Nancy's conversation. After she hung up, her hand rested on the phone a moment before she turned and glanced at him.

His lips were drawn tight across his teeth. "Well, this really puts a monkey wrench into our lives. Everything had been going so smoothly. Now, I might as well kiss the senate seat good-bye. My opponents will make sure that the paper gets this story."

With a flourishing wave of her hand, Nancy glared at him. "So your political career takes priority over Tracy and me?"

He walked over and took hold of her shoulders. "I'm sorry, honey, I just made a comment without thinking. You and Tracy are my world."

She turned away. "I'm not so sure I believe you anymore."

"Honey, how can you say that? You know all my future plans involve us as a family."

Nancy faced him and put her arms around his neck. "I'm sorry Jack. I'm so upset over everything, I'm not thinking straight. I want Drew out of our life as much as you do. But I'm afraid that's not going to happen until he's dead."

He kissed her passionately, caressing her back, then letting his hands slip down over her slim hips, pulling her against him.

She tried to push away. "I need to call the airlines and pick up Tracy from the center."

"Not yet, he said, continuing to kiss her ears and neck. His hands fondled her breast and he slowly led her into the bedroom. He pushed her gently down on the bed, running his hands up her thighs until she closed her eyes and moaned. "I guess those things can wait a few minutes."

CHAPTER FIVE

Drew Harland sat alone in his brother's apartment with the phone to his ear. Suddenly, he slammed down the receiver. "Why the hell won't the police tell me which mortuary has Tonia's body? No one can harm her now. So what's the big deal?" He paced the small living room for a few moments, then sat down and grabbed the phone book. "I'll show them," he hissed, and started dialing funeral homes nearest the morgue.

On the fifth call, he reached the Jones Family Mortuary. "I'm a cousin of Tonia Stowell. I wondered when her service is scheduled?"

"We have nothing scheduled here, sir. But her sister will be picking up the ashes later this morning. Maybe you should contact her."

Drew's body relaxed and a sly grin creased his face. "I'll do that. Thanks."

He hung up and copied down the address. "Good thing I took David to work so I'd have his wheels today." He crammed the piece of paper into his pocket and dashed out the door.

The funeral home only had a small parking lot, so he drove around the block looking for a more secluded place where he could still see the front of the building. After a futile search, he finally decided on the alley across the street and backed into it. Figuring he'd have time to spare, he'd purchased a six pack of beer and cracked open one of the cans. He crunched down in the seat and let his mind drift back to that day in prison when he'd received the paperwork on his divorce. It made him angry every time he thought about it. But not for long, Nancy, baby. Have I got news for you. Just wait until you find out you're still mine whether you want to be or not. He snickered when he thought about her reaction.

Taking a big draw of beer, he suddenly stiffened. Damn, caught up in his reminiscing, he'd nearly missed Nancy's arrival. She climbed out of a car that had just parked in the mortuary lot and stood waiting for the other person. He eyed her every move and muttered. "Still has a great bod."

Then his attention darted to the cowboy who walked up beside her and took her arm. "Now, who the hell is that? Jack Gilbert ain't that big and sure as hell ain't got no patch over his eye." Drew's mouth twitched as he crushed the empty beer can between his hands. A burning jealous rage surged through him. "Got yourself a lover, Nancy?"

⊹∗⊹∗⊹∗⊹∗⊹

Hawkman noticed the dark green car parked in the alley across the street. From what he could see of the blond haired man slumped behind the wheel, he'd bet it was Drew Harland. Taking Nancy's arm, he guided her through the door and whispered in her ear. "Remember, act as though I'm your husband."

She nodded, her eyes focusing straight ahead but welling with tears. He knew this had to be a difficult experience for her. They were met by one of the employees and led into a small office where they were handed several forms. Hawkman took care of filling out the address section, substituting his office and phone number in place of the Gilbert's residence. He then handed the papers to Nancy for her signature.

While signing the papers for Tonia's ashes, she sobbed. "I'm cheating her of any sort of memorial and I feel wretched."

When she finally finished all the paperwork, Hawkman handed the sheets back to the person in charge. "We don't want the names or addresses of the family given out for any reason."

"This information is strictly confidential," the woman assured them. "However, one call did come in this morning from one of Ms.

Stowell's cousins, wanting to know what time the services were being held."

Hawkman shot a look at her. "Did you get a name?"

"No sir. I just told him to contact Mrs. Gilbert." She walked from behind the counter and motioned for Nancy to follow. "Now, come with me and I'll show you where you can pick out an urn for your sister's ashes."

"You go ahead. I'll wait in here," Hawkman said, wanting to remain where he could keep an eye on the car across the street. After she left the room, he glanced out the window. Drew had gotten out of the car and stood on the curb facing the funeral home. Hawkman's hand slid inside his jacket and rested on the butt of his gun.

But at that moment, a black and white happened to cruise by. Drew stepped back, hesitating for only a moment, before he scurried back to the car. Hawkman breathed a sigh of relief. Thank God for street patrols. He wouldn't have wanted an altercation here.

It surprised him that Drew had the ingenious to figure out which mortuary had Tonia's body. Hawkman knew that information wouldn't be given out by the police morgue. He watched Drew settle back into his car, then chanced a glance down the hallway where Nancy had disappeared. This whole process seemed to be taking much too long.

She finally returned to the office area and paid her bill. It wasn't long before a woman came from the rear of the building and handed her an urn. Anxious to get out of there, Hawkman guided Nancy out of the building to the car, his eye on the vehicle parked in the alley.

When he pulled out of the lot, Hawkman checked his rear view mirror. Sure enough, he spotted Harland two cars behind them. He tried shaking him by making several quick turns. Nancy glanced at him with a puzzled expression, then twisted around to look out the rear window. "Is someone following us?"

"Drew."

Her face paled as she crunched down in the seat. "Oh my God."

"Hold on." He hit the accelerator, knowing he couldn't relax until they were on the plane and into the air.

At the terminal, Hawkman quickly turned in the rental car at the curb and hustled Nancy inside. They all but ran to the gate and onto the jet. Once settled in their seat, he touched her arm. "You okay?"

She nodded and stared out the window. Tears trickled down her cheeks while she clung to the urn. He'd never seen anyone cry so much.

Once they arrived in Medford and only after he got Nancy home safely, did Hawkman breath a sigh of relief. He swung by his office where he found a note from Jennifer on his desk: "Another uneventful day. I took down your phone messages and am heading home. See you later. Love ya, Jennifer"

He sat down and reviewed the calls. Seeing nothing urgent, he opened the Gilbert file and stared at the papers in front him. His gut told him he had overlooked something.

He leaned back, flipped up his eye-patch and rubbed his eyes. His gaze swept over the wall where Jennifer had hung a picture of him and Tom Broadwell, his old boss at the Agency. It took him back to the days they'd worked together. Tom had always told him that he had the ability to analyze sticky situations and act accordingly. If that's true, why am I now drawing nothing but blanks? He sat forward in his chair and picked up the phone.

"Grolier, Tom Casey. Glad I caught you."

"What's up?"

"Harland's not at that address anymore."

"I know. Spoke with his parole officer, Harry Foster today. He's moved in with his brother."

"Did you find out his whereabouts on the night of the murder?"

"Yep, and you're just going to love this. His brother threw a big party in his honor that night. Lots of witnesses."

Hawkman ran a hand over his jaw. "You're putting me on."

"Nope, I've got the guest list and have a man on it right now. So far he looks clean."

"Damn."

"I hear ya, pal. Bout the only thing we can do now is get him for parole violation if he leaves the state. So far our leads have bounced off a brick wall. Another one that's gone sour is the car parked in the alley the night of the murder. I even talked with your Mr. Washington. He told me the same thing he told you. Plus I checked the neighborhood and no one had company that night nor did they see the green car."

Hawkman frowned as he listened. "Talk to Foster. Tell him if Harland leaves the state and comes to Oregon just to hold off on reporting him. I'd like the chance to observe his movements up here. That would for sure tell us he's really after Nancy and not just interested in the Redding rodeo. As far as the car thing, I'll check the rental agencies and see what I can come up with."

"You better let me handle that, they'll require a warrant."

"Thanks." Hawkman leaned back in his chair and tapped his pencil on the desk. "You know, even though Harland has an alibi, it just seems odd to me that Tonia Stowell was murdered shortly after he got out of prison. Think I'll do some checking on her. See if there's a connection between those two. I hate to ask Mrs. Gilbert any questions along that line right now. She's so overcome by grief that just mentioning Tonia's name brings on the tears. You think you could help me out?"

"Sure. What do you need?"

"Ellie Mae told me Tonia went out every Wednesday night. I'd like to know where. Also, I'd like to see her phone bills for the past two or three months."

"Got those here. I'll fax them to your office."

"Great."

"I'll get a man on her Wednesday night capers and get back to you."

"Thanks, Grolier. Really appreciate your help."

Hawkman hung up and tapped the top of the phone with his pencil. If Harland didn't murder Tonia Stowell, then who did, and why? The timing of Drew's release might be a damned coincidence. He stretched, tossed his pencil on the desk and went home.

Later that evening, Hawkman fixed after dinner cocktails for himself and Jennifer. When they retired to the living room, he glanced at her with a twinkle in his eye. "I have a little shocking tidbit of news that I've been saving for you."

She leaned forward in her chair. "What?"

"You know how we were all so sure Drew murdered Tonia. Well, it turns out he has an air-tight alibi the night of the murder."

She stared at him with wide eyes. "No! I don't believe it."

"Yep. He attended a big party thrown in his honor the night of the murder. Grolier's got a man checking out the guest list and so far Harland looks clean."

Jennifer waved a hand in the air. "This is incredible. Then who do you think murdered her?"

"I don't know, but I'm going to find out. You know, ever since Ellie Mae's call, I've had my doubts about Harland. Things just aren't fitting together. It's like having a picture puzzle with a box full of the wrong pieces.

That night, Drew pulled on a black hooded sweat suit and sneaked out in his brother's car. He parked on the street within two blocks of the Jones Family Mortuary then hiked the rest of the way to the building. He ducked into the shadowed alley that wound around to the rear of the structure. After he searched the exterior and found no evidence of an alarm system, he tried the back windows until he discovered one he could pry open. Climbing through, he snickered, "Guess they don't worry about body snatchers anymore."

He dropped to his feet inside a very cool room, causing goose bumps to form on his arms. The strong smell of embalming fluid made him wince. He took a pen flashlight from his pocket and cautiously directed the beam around the room, but froze when the light fell on a sheeted lumpy table. It took him a few seconds to realize it was nothing more than a table piled high with linens. He sighed in relief and continued to shine the beam over the walls until it landed on a door on the opposite side of the room. He wound around several tables before reaching it, then slowly turned the knob. Peeking down a narrow hallway sprinkled with doors on both sides, he stepped out of the cold room and proceeded down the fairly long hallway.

He opened the door at the end, which emptied into what appeared to be a formal waiting chamber. The street light sent a soft white glow through the window so he flipped off the flashlight and stuck it into his pocket. He noticed a draped opening at the other end and hurried toward it. When he glanced through the slit in the curtains, he smiled. He'd come upon the front office. The filing cabinet sat in the far corner behind the receptionist's desk.

He had no trouble finding Tonia Stowell's folder and wrote down all the information he needed. Retracing his steps down the hallway, he returned to the cold room, climbed out the window and disappeared into the shadows.

⸙⸙⸙⸙⸙

Jennifer left Hawkman's office and headed for the child care center in her van. It had been over a week since Hawkman had spotted Drew in Los Angeles. They all wondered why there had been no sign of him here. Maybe he'd decided to forget about Nancy.

As she idled at the stop light, her thoughts wandered. Today was Saturday, so Nancy would pick up Tracy at noon. giving Jennifer the rest of the day to finish shopping. Her gaze traveled to a small seedy motel directly across the street and suddenly, she became alert. A familiar looking man stood on the second floor landing with a pair of binoculars trained on the building across the street. Nervously, she threw on her signal, made a right turn and drove around the block, approaching the motel from the side. Her heart lurched when she looked up and recognized Drew Harland leaning against the railing.

Trying to remain incognito, she steered slowly past the motel. But once out of Harland's view, she hit the accelerator and sped back across the street. She jumped from the van and ran up the stairs to Hawkman's office.

Holding the phone to his ear, he glanced up in surprise. She motioned for him to hang up and darted across the room to the window. When he joined her, she pointed across the street. "Drew Harland's at that motel. I just spotted him on the landing."

"You're sure it's him?"

"Yep. I drove right in front of the parking lot. He's spying on you with a pair of binoculars."

Hawkman took his own pair from the top of the file cabinet, put them to his eyes and fiddled with the focus. A big grin spread across his face. "I'll be damned. You're right. There he stands staring right at me."

She wrinkled her forehead and gazed at Hawkman with concern. "How would he know that Nancy had hired a private investigator?"

"He doesn't. He thinks Nancy lives here. I substituted this

address and phone number on the forms at the mortuary. Looks like he found a way to get those confidential papers."

Jennifer walked over and leaned against the desk. "Why don't you have him arrested for breaking his parole? He's not supposed to be out of California."

He lowered the binoculars and looked thoughtful. Then he shook his head. "No."

She put a hand on her hip and glared at him. "Why not? I don't understand. It would certainly solve Nancy's problems if he went back to jail."

Hawkman looked at her, determination lining his face. "Maybe. But I want to find out why he's so interested in Nancy after all these years. And also, he might hold the key as to why Tonia was killed. Because my gut tells me, he didn't do it."

CHAPTER SIX

Monday morning, Hawkman shoved open his office door and grabbed the ringing phone before the answering machine picked up.

"Grolier, what's up?"

"Have something I thought you'd like."

"Yeah, what's that?"

"Drew Harland's name kept sticking in my craw, so I looked back in the files. Guess what I found?"

"What?"

"I was the goddamned detective on that robbery case."

Hawkman threw back his head and laughed. "Memory going?"

"Yeah," Grolier chuckled. "After reviewing the file, it all came back. How I thought Harland and Coty were a couple of bad apples. Also, which I thought interesting, we never recovered the money they stole."

"How much?"

"Close to a hundred grand."

Hawkman let out a whistle. "You think Harland stashed it?"

"There hasn't been a trace of it all these years. Since it's bank money, I'm sure the Feds will start moving in. They'll want to keep an eye on him. If he still has it, we'll get it back."

Hawkman sat on the edge of his desk. "This case is getting more complicated every day."

"You got that right. Just keep me informed on our boy's whereabouts."

"Will do."

Hawkman hung up, glanced at his watch and figured he'd better get to work. He picked up the morning paper on his way down the steps and checked his mail. From his 4X4, he called the team. "I'm taking the first shift, be ready to take over."

When he reached the motel, he maneuvered into a parking place that afforded a full view of Harland's room. Shoving back the seat, he stretched out his long legs and opened the paper. He didn't have to wait long before Drew came plodding down the stairs, crossed in front of his truck and entered the small mom and pop eatery.

Hawkman picked up his radio. "Stan, Drew just went into the diner across the street from the motel. I'm going in. Be out front in twenty minutes."

"I'll be there."

Hawkman slipped off his eye-patch, winced and quickly put on his Ray-Ban sunglasses to block the light. He then shrugged into a Levi jacket that he'd pulled from the duffel bag, tucked the newspaper under his arm and strolled into the small cafe. Harland slouched in a booth next to a window, so he took a stool at the counter and opened his paper.

Mildred, the waitress, winked at Hawkman. "Want the usual."

"Yes, ma'am."

She poured a cup of coffee and placed it in front of him. Pretending to wipe a stubborn spot off the counter, she leaned over and whispered. "You tailing somebody?"

Hiding his hand under the paper, he pointed toward Harland.

Mildred gave a slight smile and nodded.

Turning a page, Hawkman pretended to be engrossed in reading, but all his senses were focused on the man in the booth. He hoped Harland hadn't recognized him from the mortuary.

Mildred swished around the corner of the counter with a tray containing a hamburger, fries and soft drink, and placed it before Drew. "Will that be all, sir?"

He rubbed his hands together and smacked his lips. "Yeah, thanks." Then he grabbed her arm before she could turn around. "Oh, wait. Maybe you can help me."

Mildred glanced down at his hand and pulled her arm away. "I'll try, what do you need?"

"I'm looking for my cousin, Nancy Gilbert. Wonder if you might know her?"

Hawkman's attention perked.

"Nancy Gilbert, hmm." Mildred shook her head. "No, sorry. I don't know anyone by that name." She left Harland and winked at Hawkman on her way back around the counter.

After Drew ate and slurped his soda dry, he left. Hawkman slid off the stool and peered out the window. He spotted Stan's car parked in front of his truck and turned back to the counter sliding a five dollar bill to Mildred. "Thanks, see ya later."

He left the diner and passed his team member but gave no sign of recognition. When he pulled out into the street, he glanced up toward Drew's room and saw him leaving once again. Hawkman drove around the corner before he contacted Stan. "Keep a close eye on him. He's asking questions. Won't be long before he finds out the Gilbert's address."

⊰•⊱•⊰•⊱•⊰•⊱

Jennifer kept her two-way radio on so she wouldn't miss anything while keeping surveillance at the child care center. Engrossed in Stan and Hawkman's conversation, she spotted Nancy coming to pick up Tracy. The two soon left and Jennifer headed for town. She interrupted the men's talk. "Where are you Stan?"

"I'm at Bear Creek Plaza, following this guy from store to store. Don't know what the hell he's looking for. Shit!"

Jennifer heard the squeal of tires. "Stan, you okay? What's happened?"

"Some jack ass just cut me off and now I'm stuck at the red light. Harland's long gone. Damn," he swore again.

"Is he in an old gray Chevy?" Jennifer asked.

"Yeah."

"Got him."

Suddenly, Hawkman's voice butted in. "Jennifer, what are you doing in town?"

"Nancy picked up Tracy early. I'll stay with Harland until Stan catches up. Talk to you later." She flipped the switch on her radio and stuck it into her purse, cutting off Hawkman's protest.

She stayed three cars behind Drew as they traveled down Interstate Five, but she soon closed the gap when she saw him swerving off the Stewart exit. She followed him into The Plaza parking lot and waited a few moments before trailing him into a sporting goods store. Inside, she hovered near the knife counter while scanning the aisles looking for him.

A clerk approached. "Can I help you?"

Not wanting to look conspicuous, she smiled and rattled off the first thing that came to her mind. "I'm looking for a small pocket knife to carry on my key chain." She held up her thumb and forefinger about three inches apart. "One that has the small pair of scissors."

While the clerk selected a tray from beneath the counter, Jennifer continued glancing around the store and suddenly spotted Harland walking straight toward her. Her heart pounded. She averted her eyes, fearful he might suspect she was following him.

When he reached the counter, he leaned against it and stared at her with slate blue eyes. Smiling, he tipped his hat. "What's a pretty gal like you doin' lookin' at knives?"

Before she could answer, the clerk placed a tray in front of her and turned toward Harland. "Can I help you, sir?"

He pointed to a sheathed knife inside the glass display counter. "Let me see that one."

Jennifer pretended to study the pocketknives while keeping an eye on him. He picked up the knife the clerk had placed on the counter top and removed the sheath. Holding it up to the light, he gave it a twist. The shiny seven inch plus blade reflected in his pale blue eyes.

"Now this is the top of the line."

Jennifer narrowed her gaze but kept her attention on the small Swiss Army knife that she held in her hand. She recognized the Buck M9 Field knife that Drew held. Hawkman wore one just like it on his belt when he worked in the field.

After paying for his purchase, Drew strolled by Jennifer. He touched her arm and pointed to the tray of knives. "That little red one is the best."

Her eyes followed him out the door. She told the clerk she'd be back later and hurried outside. Her gaze immediately went to the gray Chevy, but no sign of Harland. She stepped off the curb and hastened toward the van, her eyes checking the lot. Finally, she spotted him at a pay phone near the corner of the buildings. He appeared to be thumbing through the telephone directory.

Breathing a sigh of relief, she climbed into her car and pulled the two-way radio from her purse. "Hawkman, I'm checking in."

"Jennifer, where the hell are you?" Hawkman responded angrily. "Don't ever turn your radio off on me again."

She knew he'd been worried. He always worried, but sometimes his protectiveness drove her crazy. "Cool down, Hawkman. I'm fine. I'm at The Plaza watching Drew. He bought a M9 Field Knife at the sporting goods store. Now he's ripping up the yellow pages of a phone book. Probably looking for Jack's office."

"So, he bought a knife. That's just great." he grumbled.

"I'm going to stay with him for a while, but my cover is probably blown because he saw me inside. I'll see where he's heading. If it's toward Jack's office, you can pick him up there. I promise to keep my radio on if you won't lecture me."

She heard him let out a long breath and felt proud of him. Ever since the time she'd been taken hostage out of revenge against him, he seemed to have a hard time letting go of his fear and his need to protect.

"Okay, but I'm not happy about this. Stay in touch."

"I will."

She turned her attention back to Drew who stood in front of the phone, emptying his pockets of loose change. While he had his back to her, Jennifer quickly brushed her hair out of its pony tail, slipped on a pair of sunglasses and slapped on one of Sam's ball caps he'd left in the van.

After a few minutes on the phone, Drew hung up and dashed into the drug store. When he came out he had a map which he spread out on the hood of his car. After a few minutes of studying it, he jumped into the gray Chevy and left the shopping center, leaving a smoke cloud in his wake.

Jennifer followed and when he headed in the direction of Jack's office, she called in. "Hawkman, you ready? Looks like he's on his way."

"Yep. When you get within a block of here, disappear."

⸬⸬⸬⸬⸬

When Jack's secretary announced a Mr. Drew Harland on the phone. Jack felt the muscle in his jaw twitch.

"Put him through." He took a deep breath and picked up the phone.

"Hey buddy, remember me? Drew Harland?"

Jack stiffened in his chair. "Only too well. What do you want?"

"I want my wife. You and I both know you're not legally married. Don't you think that news will blow Nancy away when she finds out she's had a kid out of wedlock?"

Jack felt rage surge through him like a living thing. His eyes narrowed to slits. "I'm warning you, Drew. If you know what's good for you, you'll stay away from her."

"So what are you going to do. Sic the police on me? Then I'll blow the whistle on you. What will that do to your career?"

Jack heard a cynical laugh before the line went dead.

⸬⸬⸬⸬⸬

Hawkman signed off. The idea of Jennifer tailing Drew sat like lead in his belly. Just an unpleasant reminder of the time Dirk Henderson used her to get to him. In his dreams, he still saw Dirk with his arm around her neck, holding a gun to her head. There were times like today that he regretted letting his wife get involved in his work. But she had a strong will and insisted they be partners.

He sighed. At least she knew how to use a gun and defend herself. He'd seen to that. But his biggest fear for her and Sam lay in the fact that his past as an Agent might catch up with him.

He dumped the disguise items that he carried in his duffel bag onto the passenger seat. Throwing a hooded sweatshirt over his head, he whipped off his eye-patch, put on his Ray-Ban sunglasses, grabbed a western paperback and jumped from the truck. He crossed the street diagonally to the bus stop in front of Jack's office and sat down on the wooden bench where he opened his book.

The Chevy soon rounded the corner. He watched Drew crane his neck to see the addresses printed on the business fronts. His hand automatically went up to his holster and released the flap.

Drew passed Jack's office and went a block before he stopped in the middle of the road and made an illegal U-turn. He sped back, pulled into the complex and parked.

Slumping his shoulders and faking a limp, Hawkman hobbled over to Jack's office and went inside.

A young woman glanced up from her reception desk. "May I help you?"

"Tell Jack that Tom Casey's here to see him."

"He's with a client right now."

"It's important. I'll only take a moment."

"I'm not supposed to interrupt."

"He'll see me."

The young woman sighed and disappeared around the corner. She returned a few moments later, followed by her boss.

Jack's face showed concern as he approached Hawkman. "What is it?"

Hawkman took him by the arm and walked him over to the window. See that gray car out there? That's Drew Harland. He's going to try and follow you home."

Jack jerked his head around and stared at Hawkman. "Can't you stop him?"

"I'll try. And I'll have my team maneuver between him and you to slow him at the lights. But keep your eyes pealed."

Jack nodded.

Hawkman strolled back to his truck where he called Kevin and Stan, giving them instructions. Then he waited. When Jack came out of his office at closing time, Hawkman fired up the 4X4 and drove into the parking lot directly behind Drew's car where he deliberately stalled his engine. Jumping out of the truck, he raised the hood.

Drew poked his head out the car window. "Hey, you gotta move that damn thing. I can't get out."

Hawkman raised his hands in mock despair. "Sorry, pal, don't know what's wrong." With that, he ducked his head under the hood and pretended to be working on the engine.

Meanwhile, Jack quickly drove away. Drew opened his car door and yelled. "Hey, I gotta get out of here. Ain't you got that piece of junk fixed yet?"

Hawkman saw Kevin drive up, so he slammed down the hood and jumped into the cab. He slowly eased the 4X4 out of the way.

Drew hit the accelerator, leaving a puff of gray smoke and squealed out of the parking lot. Kevin picked up right behind him. Hawkman listened on the radio as Kevin and Stan played car tag.

"Hell, Stan, he's headed back to the motel," Kevin said.

"Damn, we just got started. He's no fun."

"Stan, he just made a quick right turn. You got him?"

Hawkman cut in. "Where are you guys?"

"Just turned right on Bishop and ooh shit," Kevin swore.

"What's the matter?" Hawkman asked.

Stan cut in. "Big accident up ahead. We've just been stopped by a black and white."

"Do you see Harland."

"Yep. He's right behind Jack's white Cadillac. Jack must have been stopped and Drew squeezed through before the police closed this end of the street."

Kevin hit the steering wheel with his hand. "Damn. Jack should have been long gone by now."

Hawkman sped around the congested area and prayed that Jack would notice the gray car behind him.

⟨·⟨·⟩·⟨·⟩·⟨·⟩·⟨·⟩·⟨·⟩⟩

Jack felt sweat bead upon his forehead. His eyes darted around at the different cars stalled in the traffic jam. So far he hadn't seen the son-of-a-bitch. Then the officer ahead began directing the traffic around the accident. He'd no more made his way past the scene when he glanced up in his rear view mirror and saw the gray Chevy on his tail. He ground his teeth, put both hands on the steering wheel and drove the accelerator to the floor. Surely that pile of junk couldn't compete against the Cadillac.

Only a few blocks from the Interstate, he squealed around the corners and hit the on-ramp without getting stopped by the cops. He opened it up and fled south, keeping his eyes glued to his mirrors.

When he no longer saw the gray car behind him, he took an off-ramp, made a turn-about and headed back north. Checking each car coming from the opposite direction, he breathed a sigh of relief when there was no sign of the gray car. He felt pretty smug that he'd lost him and headed home.

What he didn't realize is that Drew knew his car couldn't keep up with the high-powered Caddy and he'd pulled off the Interstate into a tree-covered rest area and waited until he saw the white Cadillac head back toward town. He kept his distance this time and followed Jack down the freeway.

When Jack pulled into his driveway, he glanced into his rear view mirror. His face paled when he saw Drew Harland pass his house.

◆┊◆┊◆┊◆┊◆┊◆

By the time Hawkman got there, Jack had closed his garage door. He spotted Drew down the block, making a U-turn, so he pulled into a neighboring driveway. Drew passed by without even noticing and turned the corner. Hawkman followed him back to the motel.

Once Drew disappeared into his room, Hawkman went into the manager's office. A man sitting at a desk behind a low counter, raised his head and stared at him with bloodshot eyes. "Can I help you?"

"Do you have any vacancies? I'm interested in renting a room.

The man opened a ledger. "Yep. Any preferences and for how many days?"

"A week and I'd like room eleven on the second floor," Hawkman said, purposely asking for the room next to Drew's.

The man swiveled his chair around and took a key out of one of the cubby holes that lined the wall.

Hawkman paid for the room, then checked it out. It didn't take long to examine the simple interior. At least the place is clean, he thought, putting his hand on the knob to leave. But when the door of the next unit banged shut, he stepped back and watched Drew's shadow pass the window. Hawkman waited until he crossed the street and entered the diner before taking advantage of the moment.

He left his door slightly ajar and quickly moved to Drew's unit, opening it with his pick set. This room appeared almost identical to the one he'd just rented. The place would be a cinch to bug. He did a quick search but found nothing of interest except a paper indicating that rodeo competitors were to report to the board day after tomorrow.

He picked up the garbage can, found the receipt for the field knife and stuck it into his pocket. Glancing out the window before stepping out of the room, he spotted Drew crossing the street toward the motel with a can of soda in his hand.

CHAPTER SEVEN

Hawkman watched Drew tread slowly through the parking lot sipping his soda. "Come on," he mumbled, "get under the landing."

When Drew's head disappeared under the stairwell, Hawkman quickly slipped out of the room and stepped into the next unit. Drew's boots clumped loudly on the wooden planks as he passed the window. The minute Hawkman heard the blast of the television being turned on, he eased out and softly closed the door. Back in his truck, he wiped his forehead. "Just a bit too close for comfort," he muttered.

Sunday morning, Hawkman tailed Drew south on Interstate Five for several miles before he picked up his radio off the seat. "Looks like Harland's on his way to Redding. Everyone can relax for a while. I'm heading back."

"Do you think one of us should follow?" Kevin asked.

"Don't think it's necessary. I'll check on the competition through the newspaper and that should give me an idea of how long he'll be there. If he doesn't make the finals, he'll be back in the area before Sunday. I'll keep everyone informed."

"Sounds good," Stan said.

After signing off with the team, Hawkman pulled his cell phone from his pocket and called Nancy. "Mrs. Gilbert, looks like Drew will be out of town most of this week. Now would be a good time for you to go to Los Angeles and wrap up your sister's estate."

"Where did he go?"

"Redding. Big rodeo."

"Sounds just like him. Thanks for letting me know. I'll get down to Los Angeles as soon as I can get a flight."

For the next few days, Hawkman wrapped up a couple of other cases and brought the Gilbert file up-to-date.

Friday morning, he opened the paper to the rodeo competition results. D. Harland had made the finals. He placed a call to the detective.

"Grolier, thought I'd give you a run down of what's been happening."

"Our boy in trouble?"

"No, he's at the rodeo in Redding, competing in the bull riding event."

Grolier chuckled. "So he's back in California?"

"Yep and he's doing damned well. He's made the finals."

"That should give him a few bucks to stay on and pester Nancy."

Hawkman laughed. "Anything new on the Stowell case?"

"Nope. Been classified as a mystery now."

After speaking with Grolier, Hawkman contacted the team and alerted them that Drew would more than likely be back in town on Sunday. He stood and stretched, then started for the door to head for home, when the phone rang. He glanced over at the pesky machine and decided he better answer it.

"Mr. Casey, Nancy Gilbert. I'm glad I caught you before you left for the day. I just returned from Los Angeles and wondered if you could drop by the house on your way home."

"Sure." This would give him a chance to review the case with them.

Hawkman arrived at the Gilbert home with the file tucked under his arm. Nancy led him into the living room where Jack sat at a small desk in the corner of the room. He glanced up and nodded.

"Can I fix you a drink?" Nancy offered.

"Got a beer?" Hawkman asked, sitting down on the couch.

Nancy came from the kitchen with an Anchor Steam and handed it to him. "You'll be happy to know that I spoke with Ellie Mae and gave her the cat, Cyclone. She seemed thrilled."

Hawkman smiled. "I figured she wanted that animal, but she had too much pride to ask."

"I've also arranged for Tonia's house to go on the market. Also I'm having the furniture and miscellaneous items shipped here. They should arrive next week."

"Sounds like you've gotten everything taken care of."

Nancy let out a sigh. "It took some doing, but now it's done and I'm relieved."

Hawkman opened the file and began bringing them up to date on Drew's movements, but Jack never turned around and seemed preoccupied with other thoughts. Hawkman stopped and closed the file. "What's troubling you, Mr. Gilbert?"

Jack tossed his pencil down. "I planned on leaving Sunday for a law convention in New York. I'd rearranged all my appointments and have a colleague covering for me." He slammed his fist down on a stack of papers. "Now this bastard has put a monkey wrench into my plans."

Hawkman noticed the Hertz car rental packet and plane tickets lying under his hand. "Take Nancy and Tracy along."

Jack abruptly stood and looked out the living room window. "It's too late to get them accommodations."

Nancy raised her hands in a helpless gesture. "I couldn't leave anyway with the movers bringing Tonia's things next week. Tracy and I will be all right with your team watching out for us. Anyway, Drew doesn't know where we live."

Hawkman glanced at her in surprise. "I'm afraid he does. Didn't Jack tell you he followed him home."

Nancy gasped, narrowing her eyes at her husband. "No, he didn't."

Jack raked his fingers through his hair, not meeting her stare. "I didn't want to worry you."

She clenched her hands at her side and marched toward him. "How could you keep that from me. I've let Tracy run around in the front yard, not dreaming Drew would have been anywhere near."

Jack waved a hand in the air. "Forget it, Nancy. Nothing happened."

Hawkman glanced from one to the other, realizing it would be futile to talk to them at this point. He stood. "Thanks for the beer.

I'm outta here." Neither of them glanced his way as he stepped out the front door.

⋅⊱⋅†⋅⊰⋅†⋅⊱⋅†⋅⊰⋅†⋅⊱⋅†⋅⊰⋅

Over the weekend, Hawkman had set up the schedule so that Kevin would start the surveillance shift Sunday and Stan take over at midnight. Monday morning, he checked in with Stan before leaving home. "Anything to report?"

"Nope. It's been a quiet night. That bull-riding must have tuckered him out. He never left his room."

"I'm getting ready to leave, so I'll get back with you later once I get into town."

Jennifer stood at the kitchen counter filling her travel mug with coffee. "Want me to fill yours?"

Hawkman shook his head. "No thanks, I've had enough for now. By the way, I'd like to switch cars with you today. That is, unless you need the van."

"That's fine. But grab your duffel bag out of the truck.

Hawkman slapped on his cowboy hat. "Will do. See ya later."

He snatched the bag from his truck and tossed it into the front seat of Jennifer's pale blue Dodge Caravan. When he reached Medford, he drove by the motel and noted Drew's car still parked in the lot. Suddenly, Kevin's urgent voice came over the radio.

"Hawkman, there's something fishy going on at the Gilberts."

He grabbed the radio. "What do you mean?"

"There's a strange car cruising the block."

Hawkman lifted his brows and wondered if the Feds were already making a move. "You're sure he's interested in their house?"

"Positive."

"I'm on my way."

Stan's voice interrupted. "Harland's left the motel. I'm right behind him. Looks like we're headed in your direction, Kevin."

Approaching the turn-off, Hawkman noted that traffic had backed up and come to a stop. He glanced ahead and spotted the problem; a big moving truck attempting to maneuver around the corner. Both Drew's and Stan's cars were stuck in the line of vehicles. The eighteen wheeler finally made the turn and by the time

Hawkman rounded the corner, the semi had stopped in front of the Gilbert's home.

"Stan, where are you?"

"I'm following Drew around the block. One of you take over before he catches onto me."

Hawkman surveyed the area. "Okay. But first I want to check out this other guy? Where is he?"

"He's circled for the past hour, so he should be coming into view any minute. There he is, stopping next to Drew's car."

Suddenly, a shot rang out. Harland gunned his car and sped around the corner. The sedan made a screeching U-turn and followed him.

"What the hell's going on?" Hawkman yelled into the radio. "Stan, keep an eye on the Gilberts. Kevin, take the sedan. I'll follow Drew."

The sedan's dark tinted windows made it impossible to see the occupant. The license plate couldn't be read as it was covered with mud. The cars squealed down the street. Hawkman unbuttoned his jacket and lifted the flap on his holster. This was no Fed.

The sedan veered off with Kevin on his tail. Drew's gray beast still had guts and hit seventy plus when he hopped onto south Interstate Five. Hawkman kept him in view, but then Drew abruptly exited the freeway, circled underneath the over-pass and jumped back on the Interstate going the opposite direction.

Hawkman grabbed the radio. "Stan, hop on north Interstate Five, Harland did a turn around and I got cut off."

Within minutes, Stan reported. "Got the bastard. He's headed back to the motel."

Then Kevin's voice broke in. "I lost the sedan. Got sandwiched between lights and he disappeared. I've covered the area several times, but can't find the son-of-a-bitch."

Hawkman hit his fist on the steering wheel. "Damn, this is turning into a three ring circus. Why the hell is someone shooting at Harland?"

"Beats me," Kevin said.

"Stan, stay with Drew. Kevin, meet me back at the Gilbert's. Maybe the sedan will show again."

Hawkman arrived first and parked in front of the large moving truck. Nancy stood at the garage entrance directing two men where to stack boxes and furniture. When she spotted Hawkman, she left the workmen and met him in the middle of the yard.

"Mr. Casey, what happened?" She lowered her voice. "I'd swear I heard a gun shot."

"You did." Hawkman frowned. "You mean to tell me that you didn't recognize Drew?

She gasped and stepped back. "No." Her wide eyed gaze shifted to the street. "Did he shoot at the house?"

"No. Someone tried to kill him."

Her hand went to her mouth. "Oh dear God. Why?"

He stared into her fear filled face. "I wish I knew."

CHAPTER EIGHT

Hawkman stood with his fist on his hips speaking with Nancy when suddenly, Stan's booming voice echoed across the yard. "Hawkman, where the hell are you." He jerked his head around and dashed across the yard to the van. Reaching through the window he grabbed the radio off the seat. "What's up?"

"Drew's running scared. He stopped at a used car lot and traded that gray beast in for a tan colored Chevy truck."

"Where is he now?"

"Back here at the motel. But I bet he's poked his head out that door at least a dozen times. He must be looking for that black sedan."

"Has it showed?"

"Not a sign."

"At which used car lot did he make the trade?"

"Off McAndrews Road, near Bear Creek Plaza. A little place tucked in between a couple of buildings. You can't miss it."

"Okay, check with you later."

Hawkman glanced back where he'd left Nancy, but she'd returned to the garage to direct the movers. He jumped into the van and took off.

He cruised McAndrews Road and spotted the used car lot immediately. The gray bomb sat in all its glory on the back row. Hawkman parked on the side street and headed for the car. He'd no more opened the door on the driver's side when a salesman appeared at his heels.

"Sir, this car just came in and we haven't had a chance to clean it up. Can I show you something else? We have some very nice vehicles that are ready to drive off the lot." The man rattled on, a fake grin twitching his lips.

Hawkman glared at the salesman, flipped open his wallet and flashed his badge at the man's nose.

He stepped back with wide eyes. "What's wrong? This car ain't stolen is it? We're strictly a clean business."

"Nothing's wrong. Just want to look it over." Hawkman jerked his thumb toward a couple of young men looking at a white Ford. "Go take care of your other customers."

The man nodded and walked rapidly away.

Hawkman slipped under the steering wheel, glad he'd gotten to the car before they'd spruced it up. He flipped open the glove compartment and rummaged through napkins, straws and packets of condiments, grimacing when his hand came in contact with an open catsup packet. Wiping it off with one of the napkins, he continued his search.

On the passenger side floor, he raked through the clutter of empty fast food sacks, rodeo programs, beer cans and miscellaneous trash. He sat back against the seat and tried to visualize the incident in front of the Gilbert home, then ran his hand around the window casings. When his fingers reached the right corner of the metal frame above the windshield, he felt the small hole. He worked his little finger into the cavity, rubbing the edge of what he figured to be the bullet. Opening the small blade of his pocket knife, he carefully worked around the outer border so as not to scar any markings. Finally, the slug popped out. He wrapped it in one of the loose napkins and stuck it into his pocket. Envisioning the angle in which the bullet traveled, it amazed him that Drew escaped getting hit.

Back at his office, he sat down at his desk and pulled the Gilbert file toward him. The case just seemed to get more complicated and more baffling. Too many pieces of the puzzle just didn't fit together.

Kevin's observation point allowed him to see inside the Gilberts' garage. Nancy and Jack were sorting through stacks of boxes. Kevin became very attentive when he heard Jack's shouting.

"What are you going to do with this?"

Kevin squinted, trying to make out what Jack held up in his hand.

"I thought I'd hang it in the hallway," Nancy said, reaching toward the item that Jack held out of her reach.

"Like hell you will!" He threw it down on the concrete floor and stormed into the house.

Nancy knelt down and proceeded to pick up the pieces, then gently wrapped it in a towel. She glanced at her watch and hurriedly placed the item into a secluded box in the far corner, then she jumped into her car and took off.

Kevin picked up the radio. "Nancy's on her way to pick up Tracy."

"She's late," Jennifer said.

"Yeah, I think she realizes it. Lot's of stuff going down."

"Oh really?"

"Yeah. Keep your radio on."

She laughed. "I never turn it off."

"Hawkman, checking in. Nancy and Jack just had a good fight."

"Oh yeah. How do you know?"

"They were in the garage going through Tonia's boxes when Jack found a picture he didn't like."

"Any idea of who it was?"

"No, but he threw it down on the garage floor and stomped into the house. Nancy rescued it and stored it in a box."

"That's interesting. Any sign of the sedan?"

"Nope. And where the hell is Drew? I expected him to show up."

"Stan just called. He's laying low at the motel. But first, traded that gray bomb for a truck."

"Oh Lord," Kevin murmured.

"I had a chance to examine the car before they cleaned it up and found the bullet embedded in the metal over the windshield. Drew had a close call. No wonder he's running scared."

"You come up with any ideas of why someone's after him?"

"None," Hawkman said.

"I'll ask around to some of my contacts. Maybe they'll know something."

"Good idea. Let me know if you find out anything"

Hawkman signed off and opened the Gilbert file to enter the latest data, when Jennifer entered. She flopped down in the chair in front of his desk and let out an audible sigh.

"Hey, you don't look too happy."

"It's very boring watching a little girl play." Then she sat up straight, her eyes glistening. "Why don't I trade with one of the guys tomorrow?"

Hawkman leaned back in his chair and looked at her thoughtfully. No way would he ever put her in a dangerous situation again. "We've got some added problems now and I don't want you in the cross-fire."

Jennifer's eyes twinkled. "I know. Someone's gunning for Drew. I heard you guys talking."

"Do you listen to us all the time?"

She grinned. "Yeah. It's more fun than watching kids play."

"It's better to have a woman at the preschool site. A man might set off their alarms. So I want you to keep your position."

Her shoulders slumped. "You're probably right. But is there really a need to watch the preschool? No one can take Tracy without their parent's consent."

"That's not the full purpose of your being there. I want to know if Drew even goes near the place."

Wanting to change the subject, he picked up the phone and made a quick call. After hanging up, he glanced at Jennifer. "I need to go to the Gilberts. Want to go with me?"

"Sure."

"I'll tell you more on the way over."

When Hawkman pulled in front of the house, they found Nancy working in the garage. She had unloaded a box of clothes and had them sorted in piles. Hawkman noticed a picture sitting on the washer and picked it up . He could barely make out the photo of Tonia Stowell and Tracy Gilbert through the shattered glass.

Nancy glanced at him, then casually removed the picture from his hands and slid it into a box out of sight. "It got broken in the move and I'm just sick. I'm afraid it's ruined now."

Jennifer shot a look at Hawkman.

Shoving her hair behind her ears, Nancy massaged the small of her back with her curled fist. "I'm about ready to call it a day." She picked up her portable phone and headed inside. "Come on in and let me fix you a drink before we talk."

"A beer will be fine," Hawkman said.

"Me, too," Jennifer said.

Nancy smiled. "Well, I'm having something stronger." She handed both of them a cold bottle from the refrigerator, then fixed herself a Scotch and water. Leading them into the living room, she motioned toward the couch. "Have a seat and tell me what you need to know."

Hawkman leaned forward, his forearms on his knees. "Can you describe the contents of Tonia's safe-deposit box?"

"Sure. Better yet, I'll show you." Nancy went to a large oak hutch and removed a box about the size of a ream of paper. She handed it to him. "There isn't much there."

He slipped off the lid and fingered through the items which consisted mostly of snapshots of Tracy, Tonia and Nancy. A couple of personal letters and a copy of the will. Some costume jewelry littered the bottom.

Hawkman held up one of the gaudy pieces. "What are these?"

Nancy's eyes rimmed with tears. "Tracy always shopped for something she thought her Auntie Tonia would like. She'd wrap them in colorful paper and we'd send them to her. They're just trinkets," she sniffed. "But Tonia always made a big deal out of the small gifts. It made Tracy feel wonderful."

Hawkman nodded and dropped it back into the box. "Most of these pictures looks like they were taken at Tonia's place. Didn't you ever take pictures here?"

"Very few. Jack hated our snapping a camera around him, so we'd wait until he went to work or when the three of us went someplace together."

Hawkman put the lid back on the box and set it beside him. He folded his hands together and studied Nancy's face. "Did Tonia ever mention being frightened?"

Nancy gazed at him with a questioning frown. "Never."

"Did she fear her ex-husband?"

"No. He ran off with some young gal and she washed her hands of him."

"What about her male friends?"

She again shook her head. "No man frightened that girl. If anything, she intimidated them."

"Did she owe anyone money?"

"I've been through her books. She doesn't owe a dime to anyone."

Hawkman raised a brow. "What about the mortgage on that lovely home?"

"No. It's free and clear. Along with her car."

Hawkman raised both his brows. "Doesn't it make you wonder where she got the money to pay off those high-priced items?"

She shrugged. "I never questioned it. Tonia always managed her money well. She could squeeze a dime out of a penny."

"You know, of course, that the second time Tonia's house got ransacked, valuables were stolen?"

Nancy took a deep breath. "I suspect vandals that time."

Hawkman leaned forward and looked Nancy in the eye. "Mrs. Gilbert, I don't believe Harland killed Tonia."

She stiffened and stared at him. "What do you mean?"

"He has an air tight alibi with lots of witnesses on the night of the murder."

Her lips twitched. "If he didn't do it, then who did?"

"I don't know, but I'm going to find out. Right now, we've got this other problem. Someone's out to get Drew. What bothers me the most, is that whoever it is, has connected him with you and Jack."

Fear crept into Nancy's eyes. "What makes you think that?"

"He circled your block for at least an hour before Drew ever came into the picture. He obviously knew Drew would show up here eventually."

She wrung her hands and her chin quivered. "That scares me."

Jennifer went to her side and put an arm around Nancy's shoulder. "We're not going to let anything happen to you or your family."

Hawkman rubbed a hand over his chin. "When Jack returns from the convention in New York, have him search through his files and see if he's handled any criminal cases that might have involved Drew Harland, either in the past or lately."

"Surely, he would have mentioned it."

"There's a remote chance that he didn't realize his client was connected to Drew. If anything looks suspicious, have him call me and we'll do some background research. Also, I want you to explore your memory for any enemies, especially while married to Drew. Call me immediately if you come up with anything."

"You sound just like that FBI Agent."

Hawkman looked at her with surprise. "What agent?"

"Oh dear, I can't remember his name, but he left a card." She hurried into the kitchen and returned within a few seconds.

He stared at the title, 'Frank Collins, Agent, Federal Bureau of Investigation'. "What did he want?"

"After several preliminary questions, he asked if I knew where Drew and Coty stashed the money. Can you imagine him thinking I'd know anything like that?"

Hawkman took a deep breath and stood. "Well, I think you've had enough questions for now."

Nancy accompanied them to the door. But before Jennifer stepped over the threshold to follow Hawkman to the van, Nancy touched her arm. "You know the one thing I can't find is my mother's Bible. When Tonia turned sixteen, mom gave it to her. I thought it would be in the safe-deposit box."

"Maybe you'll run across it in her things," Jennifer said, patting her shoulder. "How nice to have something like that handed down from your mother. I'm sure you'll find it." She waved and headed for the van. When she climbed inside, Hawkman had removed the recorder from his belt and had it on the seat.

"I know, you didn't know I had it going."

Jennifer snapped her seat belt. "What's bothering you?"

"A lot. One thing is we now have to contend with the FBI. Another thing that's puzzling me. Did Tonia know about the stash?"

"Grolier warned you that the Feds would get involved." She scooted her leg up on the seat and turned toward him. "What if Drew invested the money and is receiving dividends?"

"The Feds would have traced it. And besides, I don't think Drew is smart enough, plus he didn't have enough time before he got caught. Unless, he turned it over to someone else. And I pretty much rule out Nancy. I can't phantom her doing anything like that. But what I don't understand, is Drew's interest in her." Hawkman slapped the steering wheel. "Damn!" My gut tells me that she knows something that's the key to this whole mess."

Jennifer put her hands palms up. "How? She hasn't had contact with Drew for years."

He shook his head. "I'm not sure. But things don't fit. For instance, why would she lie about how the picture got smashed, when she knows Kevin saw the whole thing? They were right out in the open. And why would Jack be upset over a picture of Tonia and Tracy? They're not leveling with me."

Jennifer reached over and gave his arm a loving squeeze. "Well, you know that old saying about one never knows what goes on behind closed doors. These people are so used to putting up a front, they do it naturally. But I thought it odd, that Jack wasn't in one of those snapshots."

"Yeah, I noticed that too. But Nancy said he doesn't like his picture taken. Lots of men are like that, so it probably doesn't mean a thing."

"Well, it doesn't make sense if you're going into politics to be camera shy."

He laughed and patted her leg. "You've got a point."

"I don't mean to be rude and change the subject, but I noticed Kevin's still at the Gilberts. Who's relieving him? I bet he's exhausted."

"Me. After I take you back to your car."

"I should have known," she said grinning.

CHAPTER NINE

Hawkman circled the block of the Gilbert home, then flashed his bright lights at Kevin, signaling his arrival. Hawkman positioned himself so he could easily view the front and side area of the property, then shoved his seat back and opened the pastry box that Jennifer had scolded him for bringing. He poured himself a cup of coffee and settled in for a long night. Shortly after midnight, a county sheriff's spotlight splashed onto his windshield. He shaded his eyes from the bright beam.

"Casey, that you?"

Hawkman recognized the officer's voice. "Yeah, Schroeder. Kill the damn light."

"Sorry, buddy. One of the neighbors called and reported that some strange cars had been parking on this road the past few nights. So you and your boys got a job out here?"

"Yeah, a little surveillance going on for a couple of weeks. Just tell the complaining neighbors we're taking care of official business and won't bother them." Hawkman held the pastry box out the window toward Schroeder. "Want a donut?"

"Don't mind if I do," said the officer, reaching into the box for a jelly filled roll. "Thanks. I'll radio the station and let them know you have business out here in case they get anymore calls."

"Appreciate it."

Once the black and white pulled away. Hawkman extended his

long legs, poured another cup of coffee and started to reach into the box for another donut, but withdrew his hand and closed the lid. "Jennifer will kill me if I eat anymore," he mumbled. He tried for several minutes to find a comfortable position, but gave up and decided to stretch his legs.

After a quick trek around the block, he headed back to his vehicle. The moment he reached for the door handle, he heard the low rumble of a truck engine. He ducked behind the fender and watched a pick-up with no lights slowly pass him. Looked like Drew's trade-in. Hawkman quietly slipped into his 4X4, thankful he'd disengaged the interior lights and started the engine. He'd no more eased out of his parking spot with his lights off, when Stan's voice echoed over the radio clipped to his belt.

"Hawkman, you there?"

"Yeah, where are you?"

"My damn car died and Drew's on the loose."

"He's nosing around here. Uh oh, looks like he's planning a midnight visit to the Gilberts. I'll get back to you later."

He rolled out of his parking spot, eased up alongside Drew and aimed his portable spot light into the cab.

Drew jerked around, throwing his arm up to protect his eyes from the bright light. "What the hell," he yelled, flipping on his head lights and gunning forward. He squealed around the corner, but Hawkman stayed on his tail all the way to the motel. When Drew parked and before he had a chance to yell, Hawkman yanked him out of the truck by the scuff of his collar and slammed him against the fender.

"Who the hell are you?" Drew growled, trying to shove Hawkman away.

"I'm the Gilberts' bodyguard. What were you doing driving around their house at this hour without any lights?"

"I have business with Mrs. Gilbert."

"Yeah? Well, most people make those types of calls during the day. If I ever catch you around any of them, I'll have your ass arrested for parole violation. Got that?"

Drew glared at Hawkman and twisted out of his grip. "Okay, okay." He yanked his shirt down and stomped up the stairs.

Hawkman watched until he slammed into his room. How the

hell did he think he'd get Nancy out of her house at midnight? He went back to his 4X4 and called the room next to Drew's. "Stan, you see that?"

"Hell, yes. Who could help but. Then I put the head phones on just as he slammed the door. Almost broke my ear drums."

"If he leaves again, let me know. I'm going back to the Gilberts. We still don't know what's going on with that sedan. Get that car of yours fixed tomorrow."

"Will do."

His adrenalin surging after the encounter with Drew, he went back to the house and resumed his watch. He had no problem staying awake the rest of the night, but the minutes dragged like hours. At four in the morning, the cellular phone rang.

"Kevin, what are you doing still up?"

"I grabbed a few winks then went down to the station. Thought you'd be interested to know the police found the black sedan."

Hawkman straightened, the doldrums disappearing. "Where?"

"In an alley, not far from the Gilberts' house. The driver had been shot through the back of the head. No sign of a struggle. The car has been reported as stolen from somewhere in southern California."

"Who's the guy?"

"No ID on the body. They're running his prints through the computer, but haven't come up with anything yet."

"How long do they figure he'd been dead?" Hawkman asked, wondering if Drew had time to kill the guy before he got to the Gilberts.

"Too early for any definite information, but from the rigor mortis, the coroner guessed several hours."

"Interesting. Keep me informed."

"Will do. See ya at noon."

Hawkman rubbed the stubble on his chin and wondered about a connection between the corpse and Drew. He picked up his thermos and fingered the pastry box lid, lifting it just enough to send the aroma of donuts wafting through the air. He let out a sigh, patted his belly and continued to sip his coffee.

Soft streaks of light finally flickered across the sky and dimmed the stars. He tried to enjoy the miracle of a dawning new day, but the faces of Drew Harland and Jack Gilbert kept floating across his mind, disturbing the image.

He picked up his clipboard from the seat and started writing down everything he knew about the case, then jotted questions that had plagued his mind during the long night. He drew a triangle and put Nancy in the middle and at each apex put the names, Tonia, Jack and Drew. Somehow, he knew they were all connected in this scheme, but how? He studied the drawing. By eight o'clock he'd filled nearly three pages. He set the notes aside and called Stan on the two-way.

"Anything happening?"

"Nope. He never left his room after your confrontation. And these walls are paper thin. I can hear him snoring like a motor boat."

Hawkman then related Kevin's news.

"Do you think Drew murdered him?" Stan asked.

"Not sure. How many minutes elapsed from when you discovered your car problem and the call to me?"

"Couldn't have been much over five."

"That wouldn't have given him enough time to get to the alley, kill someone, then make it over here. I'll run a stop-watch on it as soon as Kevin relieves me."

"Seems like there's a hell of a lot more involved in this case than an ex-con trying to find his ex-wife," Stan said.

"You're right. I just wish I knew what."

"Uh oh. Drew's heading out and my car isn't ready."

"I'll get him," Hawkman said, tossing the radio onto the seat.

Taking the fastest route from the Gilberts', he sped toward the motel. Within a few seconds, Hawkman spotted Drew's truck coming toward him. He turned off a block away, u-turned and waited for Drew to pass, then followed him to the vicinity of the Gilbert's home. Hawkman parked on the side street and watched Drew make two passes in front of the house, before he parked a half block away.

Now, what the hell is he up to? Hawkman wondered.

Jennifer's concerned voice came over the radio. "Hawkman?"

"Yeah, over."

"Tracy isn't at school yet. Is something wrong?"

He put the binoculars to his eyes. "Hmm, house seems pretty quiet. Maybe I'd better check." But just as he started to turn on the ignition, the Gilbert's garage door slid open. "Looks like they're running late. Nancy's leaving right now."

When the Mercedes pulled out of the driveway, the Chevy truck roared to life. He grabbed the radio. "Okay everyone, heads up. Drew's going after Nancy."

He put a death grip on the steering wheel as he roared onto the street. Would Drew actually try to kidnap the child? Maybe that's what he had on his mind last night. The thought made the adrenalin surge through Hawkman's veins.

He had both Drew and Nancy in his sights when she stopped at the day care center. He breathed a sigh of relief when Drew continued on down the road. As much as he hated to, he called Jennifer. "Pick up on Drew, see where he's going. But by no means try to stop him."

He pulled behind the Mercedes and jumped out. "Mrs. Gilbert, wait a moment, I need to talk to you."

She whirled around, her eyes filled with concern. "Mr. Casey, what is it?"

He kept his voice low and calm to avoid frightening the child. "Drew followed you here."

"She took Tracy's hand and frantically looked toward the street. "Where is he? Why didn't you stop him?"

"I can't stop a man for driving down the street."

Fear in her eyes, she snatched up the little girl and held her tightly. "I'm taking Tracy home."

"She's safe here," Hawkman stated. "Only authorized adults could take her out. Also, I have Jennifer on watch."

"No," she stated emphatically. "I want her with me." She carried the girl back to the car and left.

Hawkman called Jennifer while trailing Nancy back home. "Where's Drew?"

"Back at the motel."

"I'd like to know what he's up to."

"Do you think he's going to attempt to kidnap little Tracy?"

"We'll keep our guard up. Nancy brought her home. Don't think she'll be taking her back, at least not for a while."

Jennifer sighed. "Well, looks like my job's over."

"Unless they change their minds. But, don't go home just yet. Wait at the office until I contact you.

"Okay. I'll work on your books. God knows you're not a bookkeeper."

⊹»⊹»⊹»⊹»⊹»⊹

Drew Harland barreled into his room and slammed the door. "I can't even get close to Nancy with all those goddamned bodyguards," he grumbled, snatching up the phone.

"David."

"Sister called yesterday. Call her. Feds are asking questions."

Drew dropped the phone back into the cradle and felt his chest tighten with fear. 'Sister called yesterday' was the code he and David had used since they were kids to warn each other of trouble. David must have feared the call could be traced. Damn. Time was running out. He needed to get that money fast so he could get far away from here.

⊹»⊹»⊹»⊹»⊹»⊹

Hawkman sat in the Gilberts' living room facing Nancy. "I know it's hard to understand why we're not arresting Drew on parole violation. But the Feds want to recover the bank money and he can't lead them to it if he's in jail."

Nancy paced in front of him, rubbing her hands up and down her sleeves. "I don't care if the Feds never find the money. I don't want my daughter kidnapped or used as a hostage." She stopped and looked upward, shaking her head. "I don't need this."

"Drew's getting frustrated. Soon he'll make a wrong move," Hawkman assured her. "But there's something else I want to discuss with you."

She slumped down in a chair with a sigh. "What now?"

"The police found the guy who took the pot-shot at Drew, he'd been murdered in his car. I don't feel Drew is responsible, since he wasn't out of our sight long enough to commit the crime. Have you thought of anyone who might have a grudge against him?"

"No. But, like I told you, I know nothing about the people he met in prison."

"I understand. Has Jack checked his files?"

"Yes. He didn't find anything."

Hawkman let out a long breath. "Keep searching for anything that may put some light on things."

"I will," she nodded. "How are you going to keep a stake out on Drew, now that he knows what you look like?"

Hawkman smiled. "My presence will only make him nervous." He paused and looked into her face. "Was there, by some chance, a connection between your sister and Drew?"

Nancy thought a moment. "Just through his brother, David."

"How?"

"She dated him."

Hawkman stiffened and raised his brows. "Tonia? Even knowing how Drew treated you."

Nancy shrugged, "I know. I could hardly believe it myself. But she said even though they looked alike, they were as different as night and day."

"Has David ever been in trouble with the law?"

She gave a wave of her hand. "Heavens, no. He's as straight as an arrow. He has a much cooler head than Drew."

"Do the two brothers get along?"

"Oh yes," Nancy nodded. "They're very loyal to one another."

"You said they looked alike. What's their age difference?"

"They're identical twins."

Hawkman slapped his forehead with the palm of his hand. "Drew has a twin brother?"

"Yes, the only way you can tell them apart is Drew's little finger on his left hand is partially missing due to an accident when they were children."

"Why didn't you tell me this before?"

She shrugged her shoulders. "I didn't think it important."

Hawkman rubbed his hand over his face. "Do you think David would help Drew?"

"I doubt it. David's never approved of Drew's behavior, especially of his beating up on me."

"Boy. This could have put my whole team in jeopardy."

Nancy ducked her head at Hawkman's reprimand. "I'm sorry, I never thought of it that way."

"Is there anything else about his family I should know?"

"No. There are no more brothers or sisters and his parents are dead."

"Well, let's hope David doesn't get involved in Drew's shenanigans. But, first I've got to get on the horn and notify my team. So if you'll excuse me, I've got a lot to do."

When Hawkman left the house, he didn't see Drew anywhere, so he called Stan.

"Drew still at the motel?"

"Yeah. But where the hell have you been? I've tried to reach you for the past hour."

"What's up?"

"Drew made a call to his brother, but they've got some sort of a code between them. David said something about his sister called yesterday. They don't have a sister, do they?"

"No."

"I didn't think so. The only bit of information David gave him was that the Feds had been there. I've got it on tape."

"Are you ready for this? I just found out David and Drew are identical twins."

"You're putting me on,"Stan said.

"The only way you can tell them apart is the little finger on Drew's left hands is partially missing."

"Wasn't that on his rap sheet?"

"Yeah, now that you mentioned it, I just didn't give it that much significance," Hawkman said.

"You know, if David decides to help Drew, we could have a real problem."

"That's true. However, Nancy doesn't think he'll get involved. He disapproves of Drew's lifestyle. But who knows. We'll just have to stay alert."

"I'll check his hand the next time he's outside. Make sure we're watching the right guy."

"Also, keep close tabs on those phone calls. Any little code word that might indicate David is joining him, we'll need to know immediately."

"Will do. Car's fixed. I'm ready for anything. Over and out."

Hawkman placed the radio in the charger and rubbed his chin thoughtfully. "Twins usually think and act alike. Why would these two be any different?" he mumbled. "We could be in for a heap of double trouble."

CHAPTER TEN

Stan spotted Drew coming out of the mom and pop eatery, heading back toward the motel, so he stepped back from the window. He figured the man knew they were watching him. But he probably had no idea they were right next door.

When Harland started up the stairs, Stan twisted the blinds closed, turned on the television and flopped down in the overstuffed chair with his back to the window. His ears were alert to every step of Drew's cowboy boots, down to the jingling of the keys in the lock. When Drew's door slammed, he put on the head gear and switched on the recorder. Within a few minutes, he heard Drew dialing.

"David, call me back from a pay telephone."

In less than fifteen minutes, Drew's phone rang.

"Hey man, anymore from the Feds?"

"No. But they're after the stash and I told them I didn't know nothin' about it and that as far as I knew, you were in Redding at the rodeo. They're waiting for you to lead them to the loot. Otherwise they'd have arrested your butt for parole violation. You can bet your life they know damn well where you are. If you hid that loot somewhere you better forget it."

"Leave me alone, David. Has anyone else been around?"

"Yeah. Some detective."

"What'd he want?"

"A list of the people who came to the party. They're going to question everyone."

"Damn. They're trying to pin Tonia's murder on me too, but there's no way in hell I'm going to let that happen."

"I hear ya. I told em' you weren't anywhere near her place that night, but I'm not sure they believe me. Look, Drew, why the hell don't you get home before they send you back to prison?"

"I've got to talk to Nancy, but I can't get near her."

"How come?"

"There's bodyguards around her house. Not only that, some dude in a big black sedan took a pot shot at me. It's dangerous as hell around her place."

"Why don't you just call her?"

"She's got an unlisted number. They won't put you through even if it's an emergency."

"Then leave her alone."

"I don't have a choice." Drew said, his voice serious. "Look, if Foster calls, cover for me."

David groaned. "Drew, get your butt home and take care of your own damn business. I don't want any part of it."

"Goddammit, David, it won't hurt you for once to help me out."

"I'll be glad when this is all over," David said, letting out an exhausted breath. "Is the old car giving you any trouble?"

"I got rid of it. I didn't want to be seen in it any more so I traded it for a honey of a Chevy truck along with a hunk of cash from my rodeo winnings."

"Well, that old car guzzled too much gas. Just as well you got rid of it."

"Come on up here and help me, David."

"Absolutely not."

The line went dead. Then Stan heard Drew's temper go off like a time bomb. He shouted obscenities and kicked what Stan figured to be a metal waste basket, bouncing it off the dividing wall. He waited until things quieted down, then called Hawkman, informing him of the twin brothers' conversation.

Hawkman sighed with relief. "Glad to hear David will stay clear of Drew. It would be quite a challenge to keep track of identical twins."

⋅⊰⋅✴⋅⊰⋅✴⋅⊰⋅✴⋅⊰⋅

Hawkman eyed the motorcycle parts strewn across the garage floor forcing him to park in the driveway. He hoped Sam didn't have a major problem. Inside the front door, he hung his jacket on one of the wooden pegs in the entry. Sam lounged on the couch, engrossed in a hunting magazine.

"What's wrong with your bike, Sam?"

The boy glanced up. "Oh, sorry about the mess in the garage. There's nothing wrong. It just needed a good cleaning. Lots of dust inside."

"Good, glad that's all it is. Are you through for the night?"

"No, Jennifer called me in for dinner. Thought I'd finish up after we eat."

"Okay, I'll leave the garage door open."

Jennifer came from the back of the house, heading for the kitchen.

"Any calls?" Hawkman asked.

"No. You expecting one?"

"Yeah, Detective Grolier." He put his arms around her and gave her a peck on the cheek, then whispered into her ear. "Wait until I tell you the latest. You're not going to believe it."

"Are you guys going to get mushy in there or are we going to eat?" Sam hollered from the living room.

Jennifer laughed. "No, we're going to eat first, then we'll get mushy while you're out in the garage working on your bike."

He let out a long sigh. "Good."

After dinner, Sam excused himself, leaving Hawkman and Jennifer at the table relating the day's events.

"So Drew has an identical twin?" Jennifer shook her head in disbelief. "It's odd Nancy didn't mention it earlier."

"She didn't seem to think it important."

When the phone rang, Jennifer answered, then handed it to Hawkman. "Detective Grolier."

"Understand you've got some breaking news on the case," said the detective.

Hawkman advised Grolier about Drew's identical twin.

"That certainly puts a new twist on things," Grolier said. "Maybe Drew wasn't at that party the whole night. A lot of people might have been fooled. We better do some deeper checking."

"Can't hurt," Hawkman said. "But how the hell do we prove which one was there? A sharp lawyer could tear us apart."

A thoughtful pause ensued on the other end of the line. "Let me see if we can match any hair or tissue to the Harland brothers from those leather gloves we found at Stowell's place. If we do, we at least have a start of a case."

"Another thing, did you talk to Foster about delaying the report of Drew being out of state?"

"The Feds have already alerted him about the situation. So, no problem there."

"Great. Thanks Grolier."

⊹⊱✶⊰⊹⊱✶⊰⊹⊱✶⊰⊹

Thursday morning, Drew rolled over in bed and opened his eyes. It took him a moment to realize the room didn't have concrete walls. Something he hadn't gotten used to yet. But he sure enjoyed seeing that sun shine through dirty windows and bent blinds. At least they weren't bars.

Emitting a loud yawn, he stretched his arms and ruffled his blond hair with his fingers. He climbed out of bed and went into the small bathroom where he took a long hot shower. After drying his lean body, he dropped the towel onto the floor and took out a clean set of clothes from his duffel bag. He flipped on the television, sat down on the bed and pulled on his socks and boots.

Staring at the screen without actually seeing it, he wondered how he'd manage a visit with Nancy. He didn't really want to tangle with the big one-eyed cowboy again, but it might be necessary.

His slate blue eyes narrowed into slits when he thought of the grief he'd suffered in prison over the divorce. Then she had the gall to go get married again. "Who the hell does she think she is?" he hissed through gritted teeth. He slammed his fist into the mattress, his breath coming in ragged spurts, then grabbed his jacket from the floor. "We've got a few things to discuss, Nancy girl."

⊹⊱⊹⊱⊹⊱⊹⊱⊹

Since Stan feared Drew had become suspicious of his comings and goings, he and Kevin traded places. Kevin stood five foot eight with gray blond hair and looked the spitting image of Michael Douglas. They figured it would throw Drew off for a while.

Kevin sat in the motel room, pushing the earphones hard against his head, trying to understand Drew's mumbling. He vaguely caught something about 'who the hell' and 'we've got some talking to do'. He pulled off the earphones when Drew's door slammed, crossed over to the window and peeked around the edge of the blind. Drew was heading for his truck.

Kevin quickly flipped off the recorder, snatched his jeans jacket from the chair and stepped out on the landing into the morning brightness. He shoved on his shades and ambled nonchalantly down the stairs. Drew stood beside the Chevy patting out a rhythm on the metal while the radio blared the latest tunes. He glanced up when Kevin passed. "Mornin'," he greeted, smiling.

Kevin gave him a nod while observing Drew's left hand resting on the opened window frame. He immediately noticed the missing part of the little finger. Continuing across the parking lot. he turned down the side street where a few stores dotted the area. He spotted a dry cleaner two doors down, ducked inside and waited until Drew passed in his truck. Dashing back outside, he ran to the parking lot and jumped into his car.

He squealed out onto the street, casting glances left and right at each intersection until he finally spotted the truck. Keeping two cars between Drew and himself, he slapped on a baseball cap, shoving the bill down until it touched the rim of his sunglasses. Then he switched on the radio. "Drew's on the move."

"Give me your location," Hawkman stated.

"We're traveling south on Riverside. Looks like we could be heading for the Gilberts."

"Stan, you ready?"

"Yep."

Kevin followed Drew until he made the turn off. "He's all yours Stan."

Stan was parked in the shade of a large clump of trees situated a half block from the Gilbert's house. After Kevin's message, he hunkered down in the seat and adjusted his hat so that it partially covered his face, then feigned napping. When Drew's truck made the corner, he peeked from beneath the brim, but jerked upright. Drew had his truck aimed straight for the side of his car. He rolled to the passenger side and covered his head only to hear the screeching tires of the truck.

When Stan chanced a look, Drew had twisted the vehicle into a sharp U-turn, missing his car by inches. When he rose above the window, he found Drew glaring at him with a smirk across his face.

Stan grabbed his radio and started the car. "He's spotted me. I'm out of here."

Hawkman gunned his 4X4. "I'm on my way."

⊹≻⊹≻⊹≻⊹≻⊹

Drew parked in front of the Gilbert's house, and was so engrossed with the pleasure of seeing Stan drive off in a huff, that he failed to notice the big 4X4 pull up behind him. He watched Stan disappear around the corner, then attempted to open his door, but it wouldn't budge. When he glanced out the window, he jumped, finding himself looking square into the face of the big man with a black eye-patch. He felt the blood surge through his heart for a second then immediately composed himself. "What the hell are you doing here?"

"You got business at this house?" Hawkman asked.

"Yeah, I've come to see Nancy."

"Got an appointment?"

Drew pushed with all his might against the car door, but without success. "I don't need an appointment to visit a friend!"

"You do if you want to get past me. Either state your business or get the hell out of here." Hawkman stepped back and put his hand on the butt of his gun.

Drew twisted the key in the ignition and gunned the engine. "No goddamn bodyguard has the right to push me around. I'll get a hold of my wife one way or the other." He squealed away, leaving black tire marks half way down the street.

Fuming inside, he glanced into his rear view mirror and caught a glimpse of the dark blue Mustang he'd seen at Nancy's. He immediately swung into the left lane and made the turn against the red light.

⊹⊱⊰⊹⊱⊰⊹⊱⊰⊹

Stan gripped the steering wheel. "What the. . . ," he swore, watching the Chevy truck disappear down the side street. It seemed the light took forever before he had the green arrow. He sped through the motel parking lot but didn't see Drew's truck. Shooting back across the street, he spotted it parked in front of the donut shop below Hawkman's office. Harland was nowhere in sight. Suddenly, Stan screeched to a stop when he saw Jennifer's light blue van parked in front of the barber shop next door. "Oh my God, Jennifer's in the there." He shouted into the radio. "Hawkman, Jennifer's at your office. Drew's parked in front. I'm going in."

He threw down the radio, bounded from his car and headed for the stairwell, his gun drawn. People on the sidewalk scattered and headed for cover. Flattening his back against the wall at the bottom of the stairs, Stan wiped the sweat from his forehead with the back of his arm. He glanced up toward the closed office door and took a deep breath. Slowly, he inched up the stairs.

⊹⊱⊰⊹⊱⊰⊹⊱⊰⊹

Needing a change of pace from her novel writing, Jennifer decided to go into Medford and work on Hawkman's books. She opened the window of the stuffy office when she arrived and the aroma of those wonderful donuts wafted up to her nose. No wonder Hawkman has gained weight, she thought. Who could resist that heavenly fresh-baked smell. Before leaving the window, she glanced up and smiled at the dove hunched down firmly on her nest.

She strolled over to Hawkman's desk and sat down. Out of curiosity, she pulled the Gilbert file toward her and opened it. Suddenly, the office door flew open and banged against the wall.

Jennifer's head jerked up and she sucked in her breath. Drew Harland stood before her.

When she saw the knife glistening in his hand, she slowly rose from the chair. "Oh dear God," she whispered.

His gaze moved from her face to the stairwell. He partially closed the door and watched through the crack.

Jennifer's mouth went dry. She glanced around for her fanny pack, with her gun tucked inside. It lay just out of reach at the edge of the desk.

She cleared her throat. "May I help you?"

Drew shot a quick glance her way. "Shut up." Then he abruptly shut the door and dashed toward her. Shoving her down into the chair, he grabbed the large iron paper weight from the desk. In doing so, he knocked the fanny pack to the floor. Her heart pounded as she watched him head back to the entry and raise the weight above his head.

She screamed too late as Stan pushed through the door. Drew brought the weight crashing down on Stan's head and he crumpled to the floor.

Jennifer dashed toward him but Drew grabbed her arm and twisted it behind her back, forcing her body in front of his. He waved the knife at her nose and hissed into her ear. "Keep your mouth shut and don't try anything cute " Then he whirled her around and stared into her face. "I've seen you somewhere before."

Jennifer remained silent.

"Why I'll be a son-of-a-bitch, I remember now. You were looking at knives the same time I bought this one." He whirled it threateningly . "So you work for this snoop."

He grabbed her shoulder and gave it a stiff shake. "Hey, babe, cat got your tongue?" He picked up Stan's gun and pointed it at her as he shoved the knife back into the sheath at his waist. "Get the Gilbert file."

She picked up the folder from the desk and at the same time tried to rescue her fanny pack from the floor, but Drew reached down and snatched it from beneath her fingers and tossed it on the desk. He unzipped the pack with his left hand and dumped the contents.

His brows shot up. He glared at her with cold slate blue eyes.

"Well! Well! Well! So, you were tailing me that day? You're a female snoop, aren't you?" He picked up her gun and shoved it hard into her ribs.

"Yes," Jennifer whispered, relieved he didn't make the connection of her being the real snoop's wife. He pushed her gun into the belt of his jeans then rescued the extra clip that had fallen to the floor and tossed the empty pack across the room.

She winced when he grasped her arm in a wrenching hold and led her toward the door, where she deliberately tripped over Stan's limp body. Drew yanked her upright and kept her in front of him as they made their way down the stairs. Once they stepped into the open parking lot, he kept her close with the gun jammed into her side. "Stay near me and you won't get hurt,"

He guided her to the passenger side of his truck and pushed her inside. "You're gonna drive, so get behind the steering wheel." He climbed in behind her forcing her across the seat.

Drew grabbed the file from under her arm and dropped it to the floor beneath his feet. With the gun still aimed in her direction, he inserted the key into the ignition.

"Okay, drive."

"Where to?" Jennifer asked.

"Just move it out of here."

CHAPTER ELEVEN

Hawkman and Kevin roared into the parking lot from opposite directions. They leaped from their vehicles and hit the pavement running, reaching the stairwell at the same time. When Hawkman nodded, they pulled their guns, flattened their backs against the wall and crept up the stairs. When the two men reached the closed office door, Hawkman shoved it open with his foot. He stepped inside and almost stumbled over Stan who was struggling to sit up.

Hawkman grabbed his blood covered shoulders and pulled him into a sitting position. "What the hell happened?"

Kevin dashed past them to the desk where he called for an ambulance.

Stan fell against Hawkman's chest and moaned. "Harland's got Jennifer and my gun." His head lolled to the side and he fell into unconsciousness. Hawkman gently eased him to the floor, checked his vital signs and breathed a sigh of relief to find them strong.

Meanwhile, Kevin picked up Jennifer's empty fanny pack from the floor and held it out toward Hawkman. "Isn't this Jennifer's?"

"Oh my God." He took the pack and glanced at his desk, recognizing her possessions scattered across the surface. "After you've taken care of Stan, call for back-up and meet me at the Gilberts." He charged out of the office and down the stairs.

⊷⊹⊶⊹⊷⊹⊶⊹⊷⊹⊶

Jennifer noticed perspiration dripping down Drew's sideburns and sweat beads ringing his forehead. Good, she thought, he's nervous. Maybe that'll work to my advantage. "Where to?" she asked again.

He pointed the gun at the next street. "Turn here." Reaching down on the floor, he grabbed the Gilbert file and opened it. After a few seconds of flipping through the papers, he snatched a sheet from the file and crammed it into his pocket. Then he dropped the folder back to the floorboard.

Jennifer eyed him questionably. "What are you doing?"

"None of your business." Then he yanked the radio from her belt and studied it with a puzzled expression. "What the hell is this thing?"

Jennifer tried to smother a smirk. He's definitely been out of circulation. "It's a two-way radio. I call the other investigators on it."

He threw it to the floor and scowled. "That won't do me a damn bit of good."

She remained silent.

Drew slouched back in the seat and began to stare at Jennifer. His gaze ran from the top of her head to her toes. A sly grin curled the corners of his mouth. "My, you're a pretty lady. Too bad you work with that ugly one-eyed snoop." He scooted close to her and ran his hand up her thigh.

Jennifer smacked his wrist and hit the brake. The truck went into a sideways skid, throwing Drew against the opposite door.

He groped for the handle and yelped. "What the hell are you doing?"

She shot him a narrow eyed glare. "Keep your hands to yourself, if you want me to drive."

He stared back and pushed the gun hard against her ribs. "Lady, you're in no position to make any demands. Now, you make a nice, slow right turn at the next corner."

Careful, she thought. Don't push this psychopath over the edge or you might pay the consequences. She knew Drew wanted to get to the Gilberts' home, but played dumb and drove past the next turn. She hoped and prayed the delay would give Hawkman time to get there.

Drew jabbed the gun into the air. "Stop, bitch, Where the hell are you going now? Can't you follow directions?"

Jennifer again hit the brake hard slamming Drew against the dashboard.

His eyes glistened with rage.

She gripped the steering wheel and looked straight ahead. "You told me to stop."

"Lady, you pull any more stunts like that and you're dead," he hissed between his teeth. "Back this goddamn truck up and turn at that corner you just passed."

Once Jennifer brought the truck to a stop in front of the Gilberts' house, Drew grabbed her arm and jerked her across the seat to exit on the passenger's side. He shoved her in front of him and gouged the gun into her back, pushing her toward the entry.

He rang the bell and after a few moments, Nancy opened the door. Her face paled. He brandished the gun and pushed Jennifer inside. She stumbled to a stop alongside Nancy.

Jennifer glanced at her, then glared at Drew. "I'm sorry, but I had no choice."

"Shut up," Drew barked.

Nancy stared at him with fearful eyes. "Why are you doing this?"

"How the hell do you expect me to get in touch with you. Your phone number isn't listed and this place is swarming with snoops." He slammed the heavy front door shut with his foot and waved the gun impatiently. "We can't talk standing here."

Nancy hesitated for a moment then led the way into the living room.

Drew surveyed the area. "Wow, hell of a place you got here, Your old man must do pretty good."

She stopped in the middle of the room, her head bowed. Jennifer's fists were clenched at her side as she eyed Drew.

He dragged a chair away from the dining room table, turned it backwards in front of the two women and straddled it. He then pointed the gun toward the sofa. "You two sit on the couch." The gun dangled from his hand as he rested his arms on the chair's back. When the women were seated, he brought up the weapon and pointed it toward Nancy's head. She let out a gasp and sank deep into the couch.

Drew's slate blue eyes sparkled and he grinned maliciously. "What'sa matter, Nancy baby? Nervous? I just wanted to comment on your nice view." He pointed the gun toward the bay windows that overlooked the yard.

At that moment, Tracy ran into the room, but stopped abruptly when she saw the strange man. Never taking her eyes off him, she put a finger in her mouth and shied toward her mother. "Mommy, can I have some juice?"

Nancy wrapped her arms protectively around the child.

Drew stood and observed the child. "Get the kid some juice but no funny stuff." He then pointed the gun at Jennifer. "You stay right where you are."

Nancy took Tracy by the hand and Drew followed her into the kitchen, taking quick glances over his shoulder at Jennifer. He rested his back against the siding of the door, keeping an eye on both women. After giving Tracy some juice, Nancy sent her to her room to play. She then glared at Drew with hatred, folded her arms in front of her and walked slowly back into the living room taking her place next to Jennifer.

Drew again straddled the chair and narrowed his eyes on Nancy. "How come you never answered my letters?"

She wrinkled her forehead. "What letters?"

He slapped a hand against the chair back. "The ones I wrote you from jail. I sent them to Tonia's for her to forward them to you."

Nancy clasped her hands tightly in front of her. "She never sent them to me."

"You're lying'."

She raised her hands in despair. "Drew, I swear, I never received one piece of mail from you, ever."

He waved his hand and shook his head. "Okay, okay. I have something more important to talk about. But first I want your mama's Bible."

She looked perplexed. "Why do you want mama's Bible?"

"Just get it."

Nancy shrugged and put her palms up. "I don't have it."

He jumped up and kicked over the chair. "You're lying. Tonia had it and now you've got her stuff."

"Honest to God, Drew, I never found it in her things. I don't know what happened to mama's Bible."

His eyes flashed as he advanced toward her.

Nancy put up her hands in defense and ducked her head. "I'm telling you the truth. I don't know where it is."

Drew's mouth turned into a grimace and he pointed the gun at her.

When Jennifer came forward on the couch, Drew turned the gun on her. "You stay right where you are, snoop. This isn't any of your business."

He then slowly moved the gun back toward Nancy. She again put her hands up, shielding her face. "Drew don't point that thing at me."

"I've got some news for you. my sweet one." A smile curled the corners of his mouth. "We're still. . ."

At that moment, a shot rang through the room. Nancy screamed and collapsed on the couch, covering her head with her arms.

Jennifer dropped to the floor.

Drew pitched forward, the gun slipping from his hand. Jennifer quickly pushed it out of his reach as he fell to the rug clutching his chest and moaning.

Two police officers charged through the front door with guns drawn. They were followed by Hawkman and Kevin. The officers halted, their guns trained on the two women and Drew. "No one move."

Hawkman immediately went to Jennifer, who held a sobbing Nancy in her arms. "You all right?"

She nodded.

One of the officers stood guard over Drew lying on the floor in a puddle of blood. The other used his radio to send out an emergency call.

Hawkman spotted Jack standing in the doorway holding a smoking Smith & Wesson revolver. His eyes fixed on Drew. Hawkman approached him carefully and removed the gun from his hand. "Looks like you arrived home in the nick of time."

"He was going to kill my wife," Jack said, his voice catching.

Upon hearing her husband's voice, Nancy freed herself from

Jennifer's arms and stumbled toward him. He wrapped his arms around her.

⊹⊱⊰⊹⊱⊰⊹⊱⊰⊹

An hour later, Hawkman and Jennifer stood in Stan's hospital room.

Hawkman pointed at Stan's bandaged head. "Man, that's quite a gash you've got there."

Stan rolled his eyes. "You're damn right. However, other than a terrible headache, I feel fine, but the doc won't let me go home. Have to stay overnight."

Hawkman patted his shoulder. "Do what the doc says and you'll be up and out of here in the morning. Then I want you to take it easy for a day or two."

Stan hunkered down in the bed with a disgruntled look. "Oh sure, and miss more of the action, like tonight."

Hawkman smiled and bid him good night, thankful he'd be all right. He and Jennifer walked down the hall toward the surgery waiting room. They stopped at the receptionist's desk. "Any word on Drew Harland?" Hawkman asked.

"The woman referred to her notes and shook her head. "Nothing yet."

They went inside the waiting room where Hawkman leaned against the wall and thoughtfully studied Jennifer. If anything had happened to her, he'd never have forgiven myself for letting her get involved in this case. He cleared his throat. "Wonder how Nancy's doing?"

Jennifer took a deep breath and looked down at her feet. "You know, I don't think Drew would really have shot her. But he sure took pleasure in making her squirm. I could see it in his face. It makes me shudder to think about what kind of a life she had with him."

Hawkman put a comforting arm around her shoulders. She looked up into his face. "Do you have any idea why he wanted Nancy's mother's Bible?"

He furrowed his brow and looked at her. "What are you talking about?"

Jennifer pulled away from under his arm and faced him. "Don't you remember that day we were at Nancy's house and how upset she was because she hadn't found her mother's Bible in Tonia's things?"

"Hmm." Hawkman said, rubbing his chin. "No, I didn't hear that."

"Well, while Drew had us under gun point, he told Nancy to get the Bible."

"Did she?"

"No. She swore she hadn't found it. He got real angry and accused her of lying."

"That's very interesting." Hawkman said, pacing the waiting room. So the Bible must hold the answer to the hidden stash, he thought. And somehow Tonia's involved. Now, where the hell would she have hidden it?

A hospital aide with a coffee cart interrupted his thoughts. He and Jennifer carried their cups to some empty chairs lining the wall and sat down. An hour later, the doctor, still in his scrubs, came to the waiting room.

"Mr. Harland's prognosis looks good. He's very lucky that the bullet lodged in a rib. But he isn't out of danger."

Hawkman stood. "When can we see him?"

"He's still in recovery and won't be moved into a regular room for a couple of hours. We've contacted his brother and he'll be here as soon as he can get a flight out of Los Angeles."

"Thanks, doctor. By the way, what was the condition of the bullet?"

"Pretty mashed, doubt you'll get any ballistics, but I'll write a report and turn it over to the police."

Hawkman nodded and watched the doctor walk down the hall.

Jennifer took his arm. "I think we should head home. There's nothing more we can do here."

He pulled her hand through the crook in his arm and yawned. "I think you're right."

⟨╌⟩∗⟨╌⟩∗⟨╌⟩∗⟨╌⟩∗⟨╌⟩

The next morning, Hawkman stopped at the hospital only to find an officer posted at Drew's door. "I'm sorry sir, but you'll have to get a permit before I can allow you inside. However, if you want to check on Mr. Harland's condition, his brother's down the hall."

"Thanks," Hawkman said.

When he reached the small waiting room, he had no trouble spotting David Harland. If he hadn't known better, he'd have sworn that it was Drew sitting there staring into space.

"Hello, David."

He jerked up his head and stared at Hawkman. "Who are you?"

"I'm Tom Casey, private investigator."

"What do you have to do with my brother?"

"Nancy Gilbert hired me."

David nodded. "Figures." He took a deep ragged breath. "Can you tell me exactly what happened?"

Hawkman pulled up a chair next to him. "What is it you want to know?

"Why and how my brother got shot?"

Hawkman leaned forward putting his elbows on his thighs and clasped his hands in front of him. "Drew threatened Nancy with a gun at her home. Her husband, Jack shot him."

David raised his brows and stared at Hawkman. "Where did Drew get a gun?"

"He knocked out one of my men, stole his gun, then kidnapped my wife so he could get inside Nancy's house."

David dropped his head into his hands. "Oh my God. Now he'll go back to jail for sure."

"Yep, I'm afraid so."

David let out a low moan. "Will he never learn?"

"Can you tell me why Drew was so intent on finding Nancy?"

David slapped his hands on his thighs. "I really don't know. I tried to talk him out of it. You'll have to ask him."

"How's he doing this morning?"

He glanced down the hall toward Drew's room. "He's still out of it, and he looks terrible. I don't think he even recognized me. I'm worried he's not going to make it."

"The doctor thinks he'll be fine, but he isn't out of the woods yet."

The two men remained silent for a few moments before Hawkman tried another avenue. "I understand you threw a big party for Drew after his release?"

"Yeah, I had some people over."

"Can you give me an idea on the time frame?"

David ran his fingers through his hair. "Oh, man, people started showing up at three in the afternoon and the last person didn't leave until three the next morning."

"Drew there the whole time?".

"Yeah, except for about fifteen minutes when he went to the liquor store."

"Do you remember what time he left?"

"Look, I don't want to answer any more questions. I've been hounded by the police and the Feds. I'm tired of it."

Hawkman nodded. "I understand, but Nancy thinks Drew killed her sister."

David turned and looked at Hawkman. "Drew mentioned they were trying to pin that murder on him. But there's no way he could have done it."

"How can you be so sure?"

"For one thing, my place is too far from Tonia's house. He couldn't have made it over and back in the short time it took him to go to the liquor store. The people at the party can verify that. Maybe you should talk to them."

"I will." Hawkman stood. "Think I'll come back later when Drew is feeling better."

He left the hospital and went to his office. A message from Stan awaited on his answering machine. "Call me at the station. Need to advise you about something."

Hawkman shook his head, a slight grin on his lips. Couldn't stay at home and rest, could you, Stan? He picked up the phone and punched the auto-memory button. "What are you doing back at the station?"

"I got bored. My head's a little sore, but I'm fine. By the way, what the hell did he hit me with?"

Hawkman chuckled. "An old antique iron that belonged to my great-grandmother. You know the kind they used to heat up on the old wood stove. I had it on my desk as a paper weight."

Stan managed a short laugh. "Oh God, no wonder I hurt."

"What'd you have to tell me?"

"Got the identity of the guy in the black sedan. Alphonso

Vernandos, from Los Angeles. A low life, worked off the street."

Hawkman propped his feet on the desk. A look of concern crossed his face as Stan relayed the information. "Doesn't make sense that someone would come all the way from Los Angeles just to shoot Harland."

"Big money talks."

Hawkman dropped his feet to the floor and leaned forward on his elbows. "Fax me that report."

After hanging up, he opened the Gilbert file that he'd retrieved from Drew's truck and shuffled the pieces for the hundredth time. Who had enough money to hire a hit man from Los Angeles? He felt he'd overlooked something. Somewhere, there was a connection between Tonia Stowell's murder, the Gilberts, the man in the black sedan and Drew Harland.

And now that Drew no longer posed a threat, the Gilberts would probably terminate his services. But there were too many loose ends. He wouldn't give up this case just yet.

CHAPTER TWELVE

Saturday morning, Hawkman dropped by the Gilberts and found Nancy in the garage busily going through more boxes. When he cleared his throat, she whirled around putting both hands to her throat.

He stepped back. "Sorry, I didn't mean to startle you."

"You scared me to death." She blew some loose strands of hair from her eyes and dusted off the front of her designer jeans. "What can I do for you?"

"Now that Drew won't be bothering you anymore, thought I'd drop by with the final charges on that part of the case."

"Oh, thanks. I planned on getting in touch with you about that next week."

"You'll still have to testify at Drew's trial, but that's down the road a ways. Also, I'd suggest you change your phone number because he got it from the file."

Nancy closed her eyes and shook her head. "I know it's terrible of me, but I wish Jack's bullet had killed him."

Hawkman shifted his feet and changed the subject. "Do you want me to continue my investigation of Tonia's murder?"

"No. We're going to let the police handle it from here on. But I do want to thank you for all that you've done."

Hawkman expected that answer, and had decided that he wouldn't tell her he planned on continuing the investigation on his own time. He handed her the bill. "You can either write me a check today or send it in the mail."

"I'll get it for you now." She disappeared into the house and returned a few minutes later with the signed check.

Hawkman started to walk away but then turned back. "Oh, I meant to ask you something. Jennifer mentioned that Drew wanted your mother's Bible. Why?"

She put her hand on her hip. "You know, that really puzzles me. I haven't the vaguest idea why."

"Have you found it yet?"

"No. But I still have a few more boxes to go through." She waved her hand at a stack. "I pray it's in one of them."

"When you find it, would you mind if I took a look?"

"Not at all. I'll give you a call."

"Thanks." He tipped his cowboy hat and left.

He'd received authorization from Captain Brogan to visit Drew, so he stopped by the hospital. When he entered the room, Drew appeared to be asleep, so he quietly sat down in a chair at the foot of the bed. As if sensing his presence, Drew's eyes sprang open and he looked angrily at Hawkman.

"What the hell do you want?"

"I'd like to ask you some questions."

"You're a damn snoop."

"That's right."

"Well, I don't have to answer any of your questions."

"True, you don't." Hawkman sat back and waited.

Drew continued to stare at him. "Did you shoot me?"

Hawkman grinned. "I don't have to answer your questions either."

Drew shifted his position and let out a moan. "Okay, okay. I'll play the game."

Hawkman leaned forward. "No, I didn't put that bullet in you. Jack Gilbert did because you threatened Nancy with a gun."

Drew's eyes shifted to his hands. "I only wanted to scare her."

Yeah, you scared a lot of people, Hawkman thought. "I don't understand why you'd want to frighten her like that when you were so intent on finding her."

"That's none of your damned business," Drew snarled.

Seeing he wasn't getting very far on this subject, Hawkman got up and moved to the foot of the bed, placing his hands on the railing. "Did you recognize the man in the sedan who took a shot at you in front of the Gilbert's home?"

Drew shook his head. "I only saw the reflection off that gun barrel. If I hadn't ducked, I'd be dead meat."

"The man came from Los Angeles. Do you think he followed you up here?"

He shrugged. "I have no idea."

"Does the name Alfonso Vernandos mean anything to you?"

"Nope. Never heard of him."

"Is there a reason someone might want you out of the picture?"

"Beats me."

"What about Coty? Maybe he doesn't want you to have all the loot."

Drew shot him a fearful look and clenched his fist. "I don't know what you're talking about. Why don't you butt out of my business?"

"I'm making it my business because the woman you kidnapped happened to be my wife."

Drew let out a sarcastic laugh. "I didn't kidnap her. She came with me willingly."

Hawkman glared at him. "Right, with a gun at her back." He watched Drew finger the sheet covering his body. "Why is Nancy's mother's Bible so important?"

Drew snapped up his head, a cynical grin curling the corners of his mouth. "Cause I wanted to get some religion."

"I see," Hawkman said, rubbing his chin. "Well, I thought you'd be more cooperative but it looks like you're going back to jail and live happily ever after."

Glaring at Hawkman, Drew narrowed his eyes. "Get the hell out of here."

⊹⊱⊹⊱⊹⊱⊹⊱⊹

On Tuesday at noon Hawkman finally got away from the court house and arrived at his office. He changed into comfortable clothes and placed his suit on a wooden hanger. When he punched on his messages, he suddenly heard Nancy Gilbert's voice.

"Mr. Casey, call me as soon as you can."

Puzzled and curious, he dialed her number. When she answered the phone, she rattled on about some charity work. He couldn't make heads or tails out of her conversation. Finally, it dawned on him that she couldn't talk openly, so he interrupted her. "Would you like to meet at Rimmers?"

"Yes, three would be fine." And she hung up.

He stared at the phone for a moment and muttered. "What the hell is this all about?"

He finished listening to the rest of his messages, then set to work on another case. Time passed rapidly and when he glanced at his watch, he jumped up and grabbed his jacket. He had fifteen minutes to meet Nancy.

The wall clock hanging in the coffee shop read straight up three when he entered. Nancy hadn't arrived, so he sat down in his regular booth and caught his breath. When she came through the door, he tried to hide his shock at her appearance. Not only did she look exhausted with dark circles under her eyes, but she had her hair tied back with an off-color scarf and loose strands of straight blond hair fell around her face. Her brown slacks and tee shirt were dirty and rumpled. She practically collapsed into the booth.

"You look all tuckered out. What's the matter?" he asked.

"I'm worn out. Jack's complained because his car has to sit outside, so I've worked hours getting Tonia's stuff out of my garage. My goal is to finish by this coming weekend before the Charity Flea market."

"I think you'd better slow down before you overdo it."

She pushed loose strands of hair out of her face. "I know. I'm almost done."

"Your message sounded urgent. What did you want to see me about?"

She rummaged through her purse and pulled out a key. "I found this in one of Tonia's coat pockets."

"Looks like a key to a safe-deposit box."

"It is. I checked. Turns out she had a box at two banks."

"That's interesting. Normally, one would suffice."

Nancy shrugged. "This was probably a free one and I suspect it's empty, but I want it closed out. I'm giving you Power of Attorney to go do that for me."

He raised an eyebrow. "Can't you take care of that yourself?"

She pulled the document from her purse and scooted it across the table. "I don't want to go back down there. It upsets me too much." Taking another slip of paper from her purse, she placed it alongside the Power of Attorney. "Here's the bank's address. I'll call them as soon as you let me know when you're going."

"Why can't Jack take care of this while he's on one of his business trips?"

She sighed. "I haven't told him. He's about had it with this whole mess, so I'm not going to bother him with it. I'll pay your fees out of the estate fund."

"I'm not sure how soon I can get away."

"There's no big hurry. Just let me know a day or two ahead of time."

"Do you think your mama's Bible might be in it?"

"No, sadly I'm afraid it's lost." She stood, ready to leave.

"I'll advise you as soon as I can go."

Nancy started to walk away then turned around. "Oh, by the way, if there is anything in that box, don't bring it to the house. Keep it at your office and I'll pick it up. As I mentioned, this whole thing upsets Jack."

Hawkman raised his eyebrows. "Okay."

When the waitress came to take their order, he shrugged and placed a couple of dollars on the table. He then slipped the key, the Power of Attorney and the check into his pocket. When he passed the cashier's counter, he grabbed a toothpick and stuck it between his teeth. Outside, he stood for a moment and watched the Mercedes drive out of the parking lot. *She's actually worried about what's in that safe-deposit box,* he thought. *And I'm also very curious. Maybe it's the money.*

CHAPTER THIRTEEN

The next morning at the office, Hawkman opened the Gilbert file and studied the Stowell murder case. He went through it page by page. In looking over Tonia's telephone bills, he discovered a Medford phone number that didn't match any he had on file. It had been used twice on the statement he had. It's probably nothing, he thought, but won't hurt to check it out. He keyed in the number and leaned back in the chair, but immediately sat forward when he heard: "Jack Gilbert's answering service"

He hung up and wondered why the hell Tonia would be calling Jack. Funny, neither of the Gilberts mentioned this service when he asked for phone numbers. Was it Jack's private line or did he give it out to his clients? Does Nancy know about it?

Before jumping to conclusions, he faxed a letter off to Detective Grolier, asking him to secure copies of Stowell's phone bills for the past six months. He also requested her financial statements from both banks, plus her employment records. If possible, he'd like all rental car schedules in that area stemming from a week before to a day after Tonia's death.

When he turned his attention back to the file, his arm brushed against some of the papers, causing them to float to the floor. He leaned over to retrieve them and Jack's business card caught his eye. It read; "Attorneys at Law, Jack Gilbert and Associate". Hawkman knitted his brows. Strange, how'd I miss this? Jack never mentioned an associate. He flipped open the phone book to the attorney section and found the Gilbert's lawyer service. Jack's name was the only one listed. He thoughtfully closed the book and placed the card back into the file, clipping it to one of the papers so it wouldn't fall out again. Tomorrow he'd do some checking. Placing the bulky file into his briefcase, he plopped on his hat and left the office.

❖❖❖❖❖

Harland's eyelids fluttered slightly when the doctor came in and checked the intravenous bag. "What time is it?" he mumbled, as the doctor emptied a syringe of what he thought to be medication into the tube leading to the needle inserted in the top of his hand.

The doctor smiled and patted his shoulder. "Little after midnight. Don't fret, you'll get a good night's sleep."

Shortly after he left, one of the technicians monitoring vital signs on the computer, quickly put out an emergency alert.

Harland's room filled with doctors and nurses within seconds. They tried to revive him with CPR. When that failed, they applied an electric current to his chest. Suddenly, a seizure shook his body so hard that the medical staff had a hard time holding him on the bed. Then, his body stiffened and the line on the monitor went flat. They quickly injected his heart with a strong medication, but nothing helped. The whole room became silent when the attending doctor pronounced Drew Harland dead.

❖❖❖❖❖

The next morning, Jennifer kissed Hawkman good-bye and gave him a loving pat on his belly. "Those donuts are showing."

When Hawkman climbed out of his truck and started for the stairs to his office, the aroma of the newly made pastries twirled around his nose. He sucked in his gut and mustered his self-discipline as he passed the door of the shop. Stepping up the first couple of stairs, he came to an abrupt halt when he noticed a shaft of light penetrating the normally dark and dim stairwell.

He pulled his gun and flattened his back against the wall as he silently advanced toward the partially opened entry. Bringing his weapon into position, he lifted his boot and swiftly kicked the door. It wobbled to a lopsided standstill and hung precariously by one hinge.

Hawkman froze to the spot as he tried to digest the disaster before him. His gun hand dropped to his side. "What the hell?"

His gaze traveled over the littered floor. The fax machine and computer lay on their sides alongside the broken lamp. The cushions of the small couch and matching chair were slashed in an "X" design, exposing their stuffing. He let out an audible sigh and holstered his gun. Not wanting to touch anything, he went downstairs and called 911 from the donut shop.

He bought a jelly roll and paced in front of the building until the police finished their investigation. When the last officer finally ventured down the steps with a clipboard full of papers, Hawkman slowly made his way up to the office. He stood in the doorway for several minutes surveying the mess before stepping inside.

He mustered up his energy and set to work cleaning the place. It relieved him somewhat to find the phone still worked. He up righted the desk and placed the instrument on top, then proceeded to pick up the loose files scattered across the floor. Questions entered his mind when he noticed the only files disturbed were the "G's" and "H's". They obviously didn't find the ones they wanted as all were accounted for. All those except the Gilberts' and Harland files, which Hawkman carried with him at all times. The culprit showed his anger and frustration by taking it out on the rest of the room.

Hawkman then turned his attention to the lopsided door. He managed to fix it temporarily so that he could at least get it shut and locked. While picking up as much of the debris as he could stuff into the wastebasket, his mind kept questioning about who would be that interested in either Gilbert or Harland? And what did they expect to find? At that moment, the phone rang, interrupting his thoughts as he placed the last folder into the filing cabinet.

"Hawkman, Detective Grolier. Do I have your fax number right? I've tried several times to send this stuff to you, but nothing's happening."

"Somebody made a big mess out of my office and it's going to take me a few days to get things back in shape." He maneuvered his office chair around and sat down on the riddled seat.

"Robbery?" Grolier asked.

"So far it looks like they just trashed it. I haven't found anything missing yet."

"Someone out to get you?"

Hawkman glanced around the room and nodded to himself. "Sure looks that way."

"Sorry to hear it. Want me to over-night the Stowell items you requested?"

"I'd appreciate it."

"I'll get them out this afternoon. Let me know when you're back in business."

He no more replaced the receiver than it rang again. This time a sobbing almost hysterical male voice came over the line. "Mr. Casey, this is David Harland. Someone has killed my brother."

"Hold on, David. What do you mean?"

Hawkman heard the man sniff, then take a deep breath. "Drew died last night."

He frowned at the sudden turn of events. "I'm sorry, David. The doctor gave me the impression that he was doing okay."

David's voice quivered. "That's what I thought last night. He seemed fine. I think they gave him the wrong medication, because something's just not right."

"I'll check into it. Try to remain calm."

Hawkman hung up and immediately called the hospital. They confirmed Drew Harland's death, but wouldn't divulge any information until after the autopsy. He started to call Nancy, but on second thought, decided it would be better if he dropped by in person.

Nancy opened the door and showed surprise. "My goodness what brings you out this morning?"

He studied her face a moment before speaking. "You obviously haven't heard about Drew?"

"Oh, please! I don't think I can stomach hearing anymore about him. I know I've still got the trial to go through, but I don't want to think about it right now."

"There won't be a trial."

She wrinkled her forehead in question. "What do you mean?"

"Drew died last night."

Her hand flew to her mouth. "Oh dear God!" Her eyes glistened with tears. "I wished him dead, but I didn't really mean it."

Hawkman nodded. "I know."

❖·❖·❖·❖·❖·❖·❖

Early the next morning, Hawkman's office buzzed with activity. A new fax and computer were brought in and hooked up. By the time the couch and chair arrived, the carpenter had finished hanging the new steel door which supported a double dead bolt. Hawkman stood back and eyed the new purchase. He nodded his approval and figured this is the only good thing that came out of this whole mess.

After the workman left, Hawkman faxed a note to Detective Grolier, informing him things were back in working order. He also conveyed the news of Drew's untimely death and strange circumstances. What would the Feds do now? Would they continue the search?

The package from Grolier arrived at noon and Hawkman immediately cleared off the center of his desk, anxious to look over the information. After an hour of going through the information, he leaned thoughtfully back in his chair and picked up the phone.

A female voice with a thick southern drawl answered. "Jack Gilbert and Associate."

"Jack Gilbert please."

"He's with a client right now. Can I help you."

"Have him call Tom Casey."

It was late afternoon, when Jack finally returned the call. His voice sounded curt and impatient.

"Mr. Casey, Jack Gilbert returning your call."

"Thank you, Mr. Gilbert. I'm curious about a couple of things. Your business card states you have an associate in your law firm. You never mentioned such a person, nor is he or she listed in the phone book."

"That's because I just took Mr. Damon McElroy on six months ago, fresh out of law school. A very talented young man and I predict we'll eventually become partners."

Hawkman jotted down the name. "My next question is about the answering service you didn't tell me about."

A slight pause before Jack answered. "Why are you asking me these questions? You're not in my service anymore."

"I'm investigating Tonia Stowell's murder and thought it odd that she called your answering service once or twice a month."

Another moment of silence, then Jack cleared his throat, his voice biting. "That's confidential."

"Mr. Gilbert, the police are going to question those calls and the nature of your business with Tonia Stowell."

"She had some legal questions."

"What about?" Hawkman asked.

"That's none of your business."

"The police will make it their business."

"When that time comes, I'll disclose the problem only if a warrant is issued. And, I've answered all the questions I'm going to."

"For the time being, Mr. Gilbert, that's sufficient."

Hawkman hung up and leaned back in his chair, tapping his fingers together across his chest. Every time you call a lawyer, there's a charge for the time you keep him on the phone. Funny, there were no receipts or canceled checks in Tonia's records indicating she'd used the legal services of Jack Gilbert. He either gave her free service or he was lying. Now, why would he lie?

Checking his watch, he decided he had time to make the courthouse before the sessions ended. He inquired about the new lawyer in town and found him conducting proceedings in one of the courtrooms. Hawkman slipped into one of the back rows and immediately recognized Counselor McElroy as the man who'd limped out of the lawyer's office the day that Drew Harland followed Jack home. The outline of the leg brace showed through his slacks. Hawkman listened a few minutes and left impressed with McElroy's arguments in the case he defended.

The next day, while studying more of Tonia Stowell's records, Hawkman received a phone call from Kevin.

"Somebody got to Harland all right."

"What do you mean?" Hawkman asked.

"He died from an overdose of heroin. They found it in his blood and traces of the drug inside the intravenous tube. They suspect foul play because Harland's blood showed clean when they brought him in on emergency."

"How did the culprit get past the guard?" Hawkman asked. "Unless, they posed as a doctor or nurse."

"The police are questioning the guard right now."

"Keep me informed."

He knew in his gut that Drew hadn't died from that gunshot wound. Another kink in this case that didn't make any sense. Frustrated, he took a deep breath and jotted down the information, then called Detective Grolier. Not finding him in, he left a message to return his call.

Getting back to the papers he'd been working on, he did some figuring with the calculator. When he finished, he tapped his chin with the pencil. The bank statements showed Tonia had one account where her pay checks were direct-deposited. But in the other bank, she had a non-interest checking account showing cash deposits only. His tally showed she had more money than she'd earned and her tax forms revealed she'd not reported the extra income.

Her work records disclosed regular deposits into the company's savings plan but no withdrawals. All her accounts were quite substantial. Where the hell did she get all that extra money?

He decided to take a breather from the financial statements and moved to the Hertz rental car documents. Scanning down the list of names from the downtown office, he saw nothing of interest. But looking at the list from the airport branch, he suddenly sat forward and snapped off the cap of the high-lighter. He stroked across Damon McElroy's name in two places, then picked up the phone.

"Kevin, get Captain Brogan to get a subpoena from the judge. I need records of the airlines' booked flights to and from Los Angeles covering Monday, September fourth through Thursday, September seventh."

"This on the Stowell case?"

"Yeah."

"You on to something?"

"Not sure yet."

"I'll see what I can do."

After hanging up, Hawkman glanced at his watch. Past time to go home, he thought, rolling his shoulders to ease the tension. He slid the Gilbert file into his briefcase and shrugged on his jacket.

When he closed the new steel door, his ear caught the solid thud of security behind him. He nodded and grinned, giving a thumbs up to the air.

Driving out of the parking lot, he glanced into his rear view mirror and spotted a dark brown pick-up turning into the lane of traffic two cars behind him. Instinct, honed to perfection in the Agency, shot him a warning.

Keeping his eye on the mirror, he exited onto Stewart Avenue, then went through a maze of right and left turns before he returned to his office. The truck had stayed on his tail. Definitely a novice, Hawkman thought, hurrying up the office stairs. Inside, he went straight to the window with his binoculars and focused on the pick-up. The truck had parked a couple of spots down from his 4X4. The front license plate hung by one screw, so twisted it couldn't be read.

Then, he moved to the man. Now who in the hell is this guy? Hawkman wondered, studying him through the glasses. He appeared to be a migrant worker wearing a broad rimmed straw hat that hid most of his face. The man seemed nervous as he glanced around the parking lot. Now why would this guy be interested in Hawkman?

He must have finally decided it would be safe to get out of his pick-up. Hawkman watched him stroll over to his 4X4 and peek in the window. Then he boldly tried the doors. "Hell, he's going to steal my truck," Hawkman yelled, dropping the binoculars onto the desk and dashing down the stairs. He circled behind his own truck and grabbed the man by the collar, whirling him around to face him. The worker let out a startled cry and stared out from under the brim of his straw hat with big frightened brown eyes.

"What are you doing nosing around my truck?" Hawkman demanded.

The man gestured with his hands toward the 4X4 and attempted a jittery snaggle-toothed grin. "Very nice truck. You want to sell it?"

"You couldn't afford it," Hawkman said, glaring at him. "What's your name?"

"Alvero Rodreges."

"Why did you follow me?"

The grin faded. "I not follow you. I just wanta see inside very nice truck. I do something wrong?"

Hawkman freed his hand from the man's collar with a jerk. "I don't want to see you around here anymore, Rodreges. Do you understand?"

The man nodded and backed away.

"Now get out of here."

Alvero turned and hurried toward his own truck, glancing fearfully over his shoulder.

Taking note of which direction he went, Hawkman dashed back into his office, grabbed the briefcase and ran back down the stairs. He jumped into his 4X4 and sped down the street, checking each intersection until he spotted the truck making a turn onto Interstate Five. He followed it to a local dive on the outskirts of town which was known for catering to migrant workers. Hawkman pulled to the side of the freeway and watched Alvero go inside. Who hired an amateur and why? It didn't make sense.

He drove to the next exit and back tracked to the bar. He circled the parking lot, but saw no familiar cars or anything unusual to give him a clue of why the man had tailed him. Hopping back on south Interstate Five, he headed home. He'd call Stan tomorrow and see if Alvero Rodreges had a record.

CHAPTER FOURTEEN

Midmorning of the next day, Hawkman started up the stairs to his office, only to meet Kevin coming down.

"Figured you were at the court house," Kevin said.

"Not today. Had a few things to do. Come on up."

Kevin placed the airline passenger lists on the desk while Hawkman shrugged off his jacket and hung up his cowboy hat. "How much trouble have I caused you this time?"

"No problem. Got everything with minimum hassle."

"That's great," Hawkman said, glancing at the papers.

"Lot of hubbub going down about Harland's death," Kevin said, tapping his fingers on the desk.

"Oh, yeah," Hawkman said, glancing at him.

"Frank Collins, the Fed agent, questioned the guard on duty that night."

"Did he find out anything new?"

Kevin shook his head. "No. He swore no one went inside Drew's room other than the doctors and nurses. But the word is circulating that Jack Gilbert might be charged."

"It won't stick. Harland's death wasn't the result of the gun shot wound. He died of an overdose." Hawkman reached up into the small cabinet above the coffee urn and took out a stack of Styrofoam cups. "Got time for some coffee?"

"I'll take it with me. I've got some work to do at home."

Hawkman filled him a cup, then took a time card out of the desk drawer and handed it to him.

Kevin stuck it in his pocket. "I'll fill this out and get it back to you later."

After he left, Hawkman sat down and started reviewing the airline lists. In the midst of his concentration, the phone rang. Without looking up, he hit the speaker-phone.

"Hawkman, Stan. No record on the migrant worker, Alvero Rodreges. But it doesn't matter, he's a dead end."

The pencil Hawkman held in his hand snapped in half. "What happened?"

"They found him beside his truck on a country road not far from that bar. Shot through the head."

Hawkman slumped back in his chair. "Damn. Someone wanted to make sure he didn't talk."

"I took a run out to that dive and talked to a couple of men who had worked with him. They said he told big tales and had bragged to them last night that he would get a couple hundred dollars for following some guy who looked like a pirate." Stan chuckled. "I figured that one out real fast."

"Thanks," Hawkman grinned to himself. "Did they know who hired him?"

"No. I don't think they took him seriously."

Hawkman grabbed another pencil from the tin and tapped it on the desk. "Get me a copy of the ballistics report as soon as it's completed?"

"Sure. You got any ideas?"

"Not yet, but I'm working on them."

After saying goodbye to Stan, he poured himself another cup of coffee and walked over to the window in deep thought. *Why would someone be so interested in my movements that he'd commit murder?* He shook his head and glanced up at the bird's nest. A baby dove peeked his head out from underneath his mother's wing and stared at him. Hawkman laughed. "By gum, you made it, you little rascal. Now don't get too rambunctious and fall out of that nest. Enjoy a week of your mama's warmth before she kicks you out to be on your own in this cold cruel world."

Sipping his coffee, he glanced out over the the parking lot. His gaze rested on a familiar looking white Cadillac parked at the far corner. Snatching his binoculars from the top of the filing cabinet, he focused on the driver. Jack Gilbert came in sharp and clear.

He scanned the area just in time to spot Nancy scurrying out the doorway of the party store across the street. She headed in the opposite direction and climbed into her own car. A few moments after she drove off, Jack followed.

"Now, what's that all about?" Hawkman murmured, lowering the binoculars.

Pondering the situation, he went back to his desk and made a quick note of his observation in the Gilbert file. He then turned his attention back to the airline list. Running his finger down the names of the passengers, he felt his jaw grow taut when Damon McElroy's and Jack Gilbert's names popped up twice. The dates revealed they were in Los Angeles at the time of Tonia's murder.

He leaned back in his chair. "Think I'll have a little talk with Mr. McElroy," he stated aloud.

Suddenly, the door banged open. Hawkman's fingers automatically grasped his gun. But when Nancy Gilbert appeared from the other side, he pushed the weapon back into the holster.

She flew straight to his desk and slammed both hands down on the surface. "Do you know what that son-of-a-bitch is doing?" she hissed through her teeth, her green eyes flashing.

Hawkman leaned back in his chair and stared at her. "Who?"

She reached into her purse and threw a tape cassette in front of him. "These past few days, I've noticed strange clicking noises on my phone. At first, I thought I had a loose connection. When I checked it out, I found a damn recording device rigged to the line." Her face flushed with anger. "He's been eavesdropping on my conversations."

Hawkman shook his head and asked again. "Who?"

She narrowed her eyes and glared at him. "My husband! That's who."

Hawkman fingered the mini-tape on his desk. "Did you confront him?"

She folded her arms across her chest. "You bet I did. But he gave me this song and dance about a weird client who might try to harass me over the phone. He wanted to make sure he had taped evidence." She threw her hands up in frustration. "I just had our unlisted phone number changed. What does he think I am? Some sort of a dummy. He just out-right lied to me."

She paced the office, hugging herself.

Hawkman watched in silence.

Suddenly, she whirled around in the center of the room, her hands on her hips, her eyes like green fire. "Know what else he's doing?"

Before Hawkman could respond, she continued. "He's following me. Everywhere I go. I can't believe it."

"Why would he do that?"

She dropped her arms to her side in disgust. "This time he gave me this sad story about now that Drew's dead, David will probably come after me." Her breath came in short spurts. "I tell you, the more he talked, the madder I got."

"Did you ever get a straight answer?"

"He finally admitted that it had upset him because I hadn't talked to him first before hiring you to go to Los Angeles. I tried to explain that I thought it a waste of his time, instead of thanking me, he blamed me for throwing money away. He said he could have done it on his next trip."

Hawkman raised a brow. "I see."

"I told him I didn't think he wanted to get involved with any more of the problems dealing with Tonia's death."

"How'd he take it?"

"Not well." She walked over to the window, her arms still crossed in front of her. Then Hawkman noticed her back stiffen. She dropped her arms to her side and clenched her fists. "He's down there now." Turning from the window, she marched to the door. With her hand on he knob, she glanced at him. "I've got to go." Hesitating for a moment, she gnawed her lower lip, but left without speaking.

Hawkman hurried to the window and peered out. Sure enough, when she pulled out into the street, the white Cadillac followed close behind.

He rubbed his chin, puzzled by Jack's behavior. Maybe he'd better get to Los Angeles before Jack changed her mind. He went to the phone and called Detective Grolier.

"I'm flying down tomorrow morning. When's a good time to see you?"

"You got something?" Grolier asked.

"Not sure, but I'm going to need your help."

"Come on down. I'll make the time."

Hanging up, Hawkman decided the interview with Damon McElroy would have to wait. He wanted to get to that safe-deposit box before Jack.

⸭⸭⸭⸭⸭

That night, Jennifer noticed that Hawkman appeared abnormally quiet and preoccupied. She walked up behind him as he sat at the kitchen bar twirling a key. Sliding her arms around him, she kissed his cheek. "What's wrong? You're awfully quiet."

He patted her arm. "I'm flying to Los Angeles tomorrow. Want to come?"

Her eyes lit up. "I'd love to. There's an editor down there I'd like to show my mystery series to."

"Is it too late for you to set up an appointment?"

"I've got her after hours number. Let me see what I can do."

Jennifer sat down at the phone and after a few minutes, announced, "I have an appointment tomorrow at four." Then she frowned. "Is that too late?"

"No, not at all."

She gave him a hug. "This is going to be great." Then she pointed to the key in his hand. "That looks like it belongs to a safe-deposit box."

"It does. Nancy Gilbert found it in her sister's things. Turns out Tonia has another box at a different bank."

Jennifer stared at him, her brows furrowed. "Nancy Gilbert? I thought she'd paid you off and you'd closed the case?"

"I did, but she's reopened Tonia's part. She wants me to check this box, bring back the contents, if any, then close it out. One thing about it, this will certainly make it easier for me to continue my investigation."

He then told her about Nancy charging into his office. "I've never seen a woman so angry and upset."

Jennifer scooted onto the stool next to him. "Why would her

own husband follow her around? Does he think she's cheating on him?"

Hawkman shrugged, then piled the key, check, Power of Attorney and bank address on the counter in front of her.

She traced around the key with her finger. "This all seems a bit bizarre."

His jaw tightened and he nodded. "Yep. There're a lot of strange things going on. But I do know one thing."

"What's that?"

"I want to get to Los Angeles before Jack has a chance to change Nancy's mind about me opening that box. Because, he sure as hell doesn't like the fact that I'm back in the picture."

◦⊹⊱◦⊹◦⊹◦⊱⊹◦

Hawkman called Nancy early the next morning to inform her that he had the opportunity to go to Los Angeles and would take care of her business while there. She assured him that she'd make arrangements with the bank as soon as it opened.

When he and Jennifer reached the airport, they went on stand-by. Hawkman had learned a long time ago that it worked well, not to mention much more economical. They were on their way by nine o'clock.

Hawkman had requested a special car at the rental car agency and drummed his fingers on the counter while they waited. When the attendant finally drove up in a dark green Ford, his face lit up.

Jennifer glanced at him with skepticism. "What is it?"

He crinkled his face into a mysterious expression. "I'll tell you later."

After finding a motel, Hawkman called Grolier and set up a meeting for the next morning. When he finished, he turned to Jennifer. "Where do we go for your appointment?"

She unfolded a street map and pointed. "It's clear across town."

He glanced at his watch. "We'd better get going. The commute traffic has already started."

They stopped and started through miles of bumper to bumper congestion. Jennifer raised and dropped her shoulders. "I've never seen so many cars in my life. Why, this is worse than the Bay Area."

Two hours later, Hawkman pulled into the parking lot of the publishing house. Jennifer grabbed her briefcase from the floor board and glanced at her watch. "Good thing we left when we did." She jumped from the car and dashed toward the entry.

Hawkman poked his head out the window and yelled. "How long do you think you'll be?"

"Probably not over thirty minutes," she called over her shoulder. Waving, she disappeared inside.

He drove to the fast-food place he'd seen down the block and bought a couple of sodas. Jennifer's meeting lasted close to an hour. When she finally emerged from the building, her stride and big smile told him things had been successful.

She climbed into the car, her eyes sparkling., "They want to see more of my work. I'm to send them a synopsis for each of the first five books in the series. Isn't that great?"

He reached over and gave her a big kiss. "Congratulations." Holding up their sodas they toasted her success.

She took a long draw on the straw and sighed. "Now, where are we going?"

"To meet some very interesting people. Remember earlier I told you I had an idea? Well, now I'm going to see if it works."

She raised an eyebrow and grinned. "Okay, I'm game."

He turned onto Binkley Street and pointed out Tonia Stowell's house to Jennifer. He parked in front of the house next door and grinned to himself when he noticed the pulled back drape. He took Jennifer's arm and guided her up the porch steps. The curtain had dropped back into its original position and before he had a chance to knock, Ellie Mae had the front door ajar. Holding Cyclone in her arms, she smiled and pushed open the screen door.

"Mr. Casey, what a pleasant surprise."

Hawkman introduced Jennifer and the two women hit it off immediately.

"Well, Ellie Mae, have you had any more unusual visitors?" Hawkman asked.

"Just a couple of men from the FBI. They asked questions about Tonia's past." She shook her head. "But, I couldn't help them. I didn't know her back then."

Jennifer thoroughly enjoyed the spirit of the older woman and the antics of Cyclone, the cat.

Hawkman glanced at his watch. "Ellie Mae, hate to cut this visit short, but we have another appointment."

When they were back into the car, Jennifer looked at him in puzzlement. "What appointment?"

"You'll see." He drove around the block and pulled into the alley. Maneuvering the car into the right spot, he turned off the engine and glanced toward the street with concern. "Sure hope he hasn't changed his schedule." A big grin creased his face when he spotted the three-wheel bicycle with balloon tires swerve into the alley right on time, heading straight for the big blue dumpster.

Jennifer sat up straight and stared at the man. "Oh, my word, who is that?"

"Elliot Cleaver Washington." Hawkman stepped out of the car and walked toward the man who already had his head buried below the rim of the large container.

"Mr. Washington."

The old man jerked up and squinted his eyes. When he finally focused on Hawkman, he stepped back.

"Do you remember me? I talked to you about the lady who'd been murdered."

"How could I forget ya with that eye-patch. You're a scary son-of-a-bitch. Did ya find the killer?"

"No, we're still looking."

Mr. Washington's gaze drifted to Hawkman's rental car. Suddenly, he yanked off his hat and ran past him. He pointed a crooked finger at the green Ford. "That's it. That's the car I saw parked here that night."

"Are you sure?" Hawkman asked.

"Well, I ain't sure it's the exact one, but that's what it looked like, color and all." Then he tapped on the back window. "See here, got them same funny marks right here on the glass." He scratched his head and stared at Hawkman. "What'd you tell me they was?"

"Bar codes."

"Yep." Then, the old man abruptly stepped back and put his hand to his beard. "Oh, my goodness, there's somebody in the car."

Hawkman motioned to him. "Come here. I'll introduce you to my wife."

Washington approached the side of the car, smoothed back his dirty hair, then held his hat in front of him with both hands.

"Very nice meetin' ya," he said, slightly bowing and grinning a big toothless smile. "You're much too pretty to be married to the likes of this ugly guy."

Jennifer stifled a laugh. "He's not as bad as he looks."

Hawkman walked Mr. Washington back towards the dumpster and handed him a ten dollar bill. "Thanks again for your help."

The old man's eyes lit up and he scratched his head. "Did I tell ya ten bucks worth? What'd I say?"

Hawkman turned toward him before getting into the car. "You confirmed that this was the same kind of car you'd seen the night of the murder."

"Glad I helped ya." He crammed the bill into the pocket of his grubby pants, then immediately continued his dig through the garbage.

Hawkman drove out into the street and glanced at Jennifer. "Now that I've talked to Mr. Washington twice, I'm convinced the murderer parked in the alley."

"You think he had a rental?"

"I'd bet on it. The bar codes left quite an impression on Washington."

"It should be easy enough to track through the records."

"Yeah, I've already done that. Damon McElroy rented a car and turned it in at the airport the night of the murder."

Jennifer blinked her eyes. "Who's Damon McElroy?"

"Jack Gilbert's associate."

"Oh." She looked thoughtful and turned quiet.

After several minutes of silence, Hawkman asked. "What's on your mind?"

"What wonderful characters Mr. Washington and Ellie Mae will make in one of my stories. I'll definitely find a place for them."

Hawkman threw back his head and laughed. "I thought you would." But then his face grew solemn as he thought about Jack Gilbert and Damon McElroy being in Los Angeles at the time of Tonia Stowell's murder.

CHAPTER FIFTEEN

Leaving Jennifer asleep, Hawkman slipped out of bed early and went straight to the police station. Possibly, Grolier could help him sort out some of the problems of this case. He looked forward to working with the detective and hoped he felt the same way.

Grolier glanced up when Hawkman entered his office. "Casey, good to see you." He stood, offering his hand.

"Same here. How's it been going?"

"Busy." He motioned toward a chair. "Have a seat."

Hawkman moved it up to the desk and sat down. "Anything new on the Stowell case?"

Grolier raised his bushy eyebrows and scowled. "Not a damn thing. The lab's doing some forensic testing on those leather gloves, but I haven't received the results yet."

"What's the latest on Harland? Did he die innocent of Tonia's murder?"

Grolier snorted in disgust. "Yeah, he's clean. We finished checking out the party guests and the majority confirmed his trip to the liquor store. And to make it even tighter, some gal had her eye on Drew. She actually pinpointed the exact time when he left and when he returned. So his alibi is damn tight." Grolier placed a cold cigar between his teeth and continued. "Got the autopsy report yet?"

Hawkman shook his head. "No. But my inside source says

Harland died from an overdose. Heroin injected into his intravenous feeding tube."

Grolier looked thoughtful and chewed on the unlit stogie.

Hawkman leaned forward and put his arms on the desk. "You know, I've got a gut feeling that Tonia Stowell's murder is connected to Drew's death."

Grolier looked him in the eye. "Sounds as if you've got something brewing under that cowboy hat."

"Just a hunch. I'll let you know if it pans out. By the way, you been tailed by the Feds lately?"

Grolier laughed. "So, you've spotted them."

"Hell yes. Their techniques haven't changed in years. If they're not tailing me, they're standing on the corner waiting."

The detective chuckled. "Guess now that Drew's gone, the boys figure Nancy knows where that money's hidden." He pointed a finger at Hawkman. "And since you're her hired hand, you're the next target."

Hawkman grinned. "Well, I'll keep them busy and make them earn their pay. I've lost them a few times, but they always manage to make it back to my office." Then he changed the subject. "Are you free to leave?"

Grolier stood and shrugged into his jacket. "Sure. Where to?"

While walking to the car, Hawkman explained. "First, I want to check the motels close to the airport. Jack Gilbert and his associate, Damon McElroy, flew down to Los Angeles on September fourth and rented a car. They returned it at midnight, September sixth, and caught the late flight back to Medford."

Grolier raised an eyebrow. "What does this McElroy have to do with Tonia's murder?"

"Probably nothing. It could've been a coincidence that he and Jack were down here at that time."

"Jack Gilbert? You think he might be involved in Stowell's murder?"

"Not sure. But, I'm giving him a closer look."

"We'll check the court dockets. But since we're closer to the motels, let's start there first." Grolier motioned for Hawkman to turn at the next corner. "Lawyers like fancy places, so let's hit the big expensive ones."

They stopped at three with no results, then entered the Marriott Inn. Grolier showed his badge to the clerk behind the front desk. After the detective explained what they wanted, the clerk brought the dates up on his computer.

On the fourth of September, Damon McElroy had checked in and made special arrangements with the hotel management to keep his room beyond the normal check out time the evening of September sixth.

"Do you know Mr. Damon McElroy?" Hawkman asked.

"No, sir."

"How about Mr. Jack Gilbert?"

"No, sir."

"Would you know if two people shared the same room?"

"If the name doesn't registered on the computer, there's no way I'd know."

"Were you on duty either of those days?"

"I don't recall. I'd have to check the work roster."

"Who else might have seen these two men?" Grolier asked.

"There are the bell hops," the clerk suggested. "Also the maids. There are housekeeping quarters on each floor You could check their duty rosters for those nights."

"Thank you." Grolier turned to Hawkman as they headed for the elevators. "Got a picture of either of these guys?"

"No, but I think the description of Damon McElroy will serve nicely. He's not one you'd easily forget."

"Well, let's give it a try."

They rode to the third floor and found the maid's work area. One of the women responsible for that wing remembered McElroy because of his limp and kind disposition. She didn't recall seeing anyone with him.

Later they questioned the bell boys. One remembered McElroy.

Walking back to the car, Hawkman shook his head. "I'm sure Jack Gilbert accompanied him. It's strange no one saw or remembered him."

Now that they were outside, Grolier stopped to light his cigar. "Maybe he's got a girlfriend and stayed with her."

Hawkman shrugged. "Anything's possible in this business.

When I get back to Medford, I'll talk to McElroy and see what I can find out."

After Groiler had a few puffs off his stogie, he put it out in the ashtray, then they drove to the court house and checked the September docket. Groiler pointed a stubby finger. "There they are. Counselors Jack Gilbert and Damon McElroy, September fourth through the sixth."

With that information confirmed, they headed back to the police station. "Jennifer's here with me. How about joining us for dinner tonight?"

"I'd like that. It'll be interesting to meet the little woman who married the likes of you," Groiler said, with a twinkle in his eye. He got out of the car and lit his cigar again.

Hawkman leaned toward the window. "Got any suggestion on a good place to eat?"

"The Blue Velvet Restaurant over on Hollywood Boulevard is real nice. Food's good and service isn't bad. Your wife will like it."

"How about we meet you there at seven?"

"Sounds good."

Hawkman smiled to himself as he watched Groiler go slowly up the station steps, puffing his cigar. When he got back at the motel, he found Jennifer relaxing in a chair with her feet propped on the bed, thumbing through a magazine. He gave her a peck on the cheek. "Hope I didn't wake you this morning."

"No, I didn't hear a thing. I feel like I'm on a mini-vacation." She stood and slipped her feet into her shoes. "Did you have any success?"

"Not much. Some of the employees at the Marriott recalled Damon McElroy but we didn't find anyone who remembered Jack Gilbert. However, the court docket showed they were both here trying a case."

"Maybe Jack didn't stay at the Marriott."

"You sound like Groiler."

"How?"

"He figures Jack might have a girlfriend down here."

Jennifer screwed up her face. "For Nancy's sake, I hope that's not true, but it's definitely possible."

"But wouldn't you think if two lawyers were trying a case together, they'd want to confer with one another?"

She shrugged her shoulders. "All depends on what kind of case and how much preparation they need before each session."

"You've got a point. Looks like I've got some investigating ahead of me. Thank goodness, Grolier's willing to help. Oh, by the way, I've invited him to join us for dinner."

"Splendid. I'm looking forward to meeting him."

"You want to go to the bank with me and see if there's anything in Tonia's safe-deposit box?"

Her hazel eyes sparkled. "I wouldn't miss it."

On the way, Hawkman kept an eye on his rear view mirror and made several out of the way turns.

"Why are you doing this?" Jennifer asked.

"Just being cautious. Making sure we're not being followed."

"Who do you suspect would tail us here in Los Angeles?"

"The Feds for one. And this case has taken so many twist, I don't want to take any chances." He finally pulled into the bank parking lot. "When we get inside, I want you to stay out in the lobby while I go into the vault. Keep your eyes open for anyone who looks suspicious."

Jennifer walked in with him, but hung back, pretending to be interested in the brochure display. Hawkman went to the counter and showed his identification along with the Power of Attorney to the clerk. She told him that Mrs. Gilbert had called and alerted them to his arrival. Before going around the petition and into the vault, Hawkman glanced at Jennifer. She gave him the okay sign as he followed the woman.

Hawkman took the safe-deposit drawer into one of the small rooms where he could inspect the contents privately. Fully expecting the box to be empty, it surprised him to find a large bulky sealed brown envelope wedged inside. Several smaller envelopes were tucked along the edge. He worked the large envelope back and forth, until it finally came loose and he could lift it without tearing the brown wrapping. Nestled underneath he found Nancy's mama's Bible.

After he put everything into his briefcase, he stepped out of the room and motioned for clerk. Handing her the empty box, he met her back at the counter, turned in the key and closed out the account.

Jennifer joined him in the center of the lobby and they returned to the car. "That didn't take long. It must have been empty."

"On the contrary. And guess what I found on the very bottom?"

"I haven't the vaguest idea."

"Nancy's mama's Bible."

Her eyes widened. "Let me see it."

"Wait until we get back to the motel." He again, kept his eye on the rear view mirror as he drove.

Jennifer glanced out the back window. "Have you spotted anyone yet?"

"No, haven't seen one Fed today. They're harmless, just doing their job and anxious to find Drew's stashed loot."

"But Drew's dead."

"True. But Nancy is his ex-wife and I'm her hired investigator. They're not about to leave any stone unturned."

Back at the room, he spread the items out on the table. He picked up the large bulky envelope and ran his hands over the outside, as if trying to feel what the contents might be. "I won't be looking inside this, unless Nancy gives me permission."

Jennifer raised a brow. "Why?"

"He pointed to the bold letters scrawled across the front: "For Nancy Gilbert—Personal"

He gently picked up the King James Bible bound in soft leather. It showed wear and sticking out around the edges were remnants of pressed flowers. He flipped through the pages, coming across hand written recipes, poems and personal cards tucked between the pages. The aroma of the old musty items lingered in the air.

Fascinated with its contents, Hawkman sat down at the small table. He started with Genesis and leafed through the Bible, one page at a time, being careful not to disturb any of the mementos.

Jennifer lay across the bed and silently watched her husband. Suddenly, he turned to her and held up a small envelope.

"This looks interesting." He opened the flap and a key dropped into his palm.

Jennifer sat up cross-legged in the middle of the bed. "Good grief, that looks like it belongs to a safe-deposit box. How many did that woman have?"

"I doubt this one belonged to Tonia.

Her eyes sparkled. "You think that's why Drew wanted the Bible?"

"I'd bet on it. He entrusted Tonia to save it for him."

"I don't like the sound of that. Do you think they had something going?"

Hawkman shrugged. "Hard to say. But it wouldn't surprise me to find the stashed loot in the box this key fits."

Jennifer squinted and pointed at the envelope. "What's written on the outside."

He turned it over and glanced at the writing. "Psalm 23." Flipping to the scripture, he read it out loud. "Well, what do you think?"

"I think it's a clue."

"I'll deal with that later. Right now I want to see what else is here." He put the Bible aside and picked up an unsealed letter. "This is interesting. It's addressed to 'Mrs. Nancy Harland', from some attorney in Los Angeles."

Jennifer slid off the bed, went behind him and peered over his shoulder. He pulled out the single sheet from the envelope and they read together.

"Oh my God," she whispered, putting a hand to her mouth.

Hawkman glanced up at her. "You can say that again. Want to bet Nancy doesn't know about this. But we can see that Drew did. Look." He pointed to the notation at the bottom of the letter that stated a copy had been sent to Drew Harland in prison. "This is another reason Drew was so intent on reaching Nancy. He wanted her back."

Jennifer picked up the envelope and knitted her brows into a frown. "This is postmarked two years ago. Wonder why Tonia didn't forward it?"

"Your guess is as good as mine," Hawkman snickered. "But I've got my suspicions about our little Ms. Tonia Stowell. I don't think her ambitions and goals were too pure. My gut tells me she tried her bit at blackmail." He tucked the letter back inside. "It will be interesting to see Nancy's reaction to this letter."

"Who would Tonia blackmail. Drew?"

"I"m not committing myself yet. Want to do some more research."

Jennifer ran her fingers over the bulky envelope. "Can we open this?"

"No, it's sealed with Nancy's name. It would be illegal to open without her permission."

She threw her hands in the air. "Men! How can you stand the suspense? It would kill me." She looked at him with pleading eyes. "Can't we just take a peek?"

Hawkman could barely suppress a smile, as he shook his head. "Jennifer! Shame on you."

She rolled her eyes. "Well, it would drive me nuts not knowing. Especially if I thought I might never get to see what's inside."

He laughed. Wanting to get her thoughts away from the sealed items, he slipped everything back into his briefcase, then glanced at his watch. "We're meeting Grolier at seven so we should leave here no later that six thirty. You better get ready."

⊱✶⊰⊱✶⊰⊱✶⊰

After dinner, Hawkman leaned back in his chair and groaned. "Detective, you were right about the food here. It's excellent and I ate too much."

Grolier nodded. "Thought you'd like it."

Hawkman motioned for the cocktail waitress and ordered a round of after-dinner cocktails. He then opened his briefcase and pulled out the letter he'd found in Stowell's safe-deposit box and handed it to Grolier. "Take a look at this. Think you'll find it interesting."

Grolier took a pair of half reading glasses from his vest pocket and pushed them on his nose. When he finished, he glanced at Hawkman and tapped his finger on the letter head. "I recognize the name of this lawyer. The firm he used to be with got into a heap of trouble several years back."

"Oh?"

"Looks like Nancy is one of his victims."

"What'd they do?"

"Took money from young naive women who wanted quickie divorces. They promised they'd go down into Mexico and take care of everything. But hell, once they got their money, they didn't do a damn thing. When the authorities finally caught up with the them, each lawyer was given orders to notify their clients and let them know they were not legally divorced."

"Do you remember when this all came to a head?"

Grolier looked up at the ceiling and wrinkled his forehead. "Time goes by so fast. Let me think. I'd say somewhere around four to six years ago. I can't remember the name of the law firm, but you could easily find it in one of the older Bar Directories at the library under this Paul Bradley's name."

"Might be worth checking," Hawkman said thoughtfully.

"The firm's seniors were pretty sleazy and the Judge sentenced a couple of them to jail. I'm sure all of them were disbarred. Does Nancy know about this?"

Hawkman rubbed his chin. "I don't think so. She's never mentioned it."

"Well, she'll have a handful of litigations to go through since she's remarried." He waved a hand in the air. "But hell, she's married to a lawyer. It should be a piece of cake." Grolier picked up the envelope. "This is to Nancy. You found this in Stowell's box?"

"Yep."

"Why the hell didn't her sister forward it? This seems mighty suspicious," he mumbled.

Hawkman leaned forward putting his arms on the table. "You know, we've been wondering where Tonia Stowell got her money. We better dig a little deeper into her past."

"It might be well worth our time," Grolier said, nodding. "You could start by looking up Tonia's former supervisor. The company she worked for is located right off the road on your way to the airport. You could stop on your way home. Give me a call tomorrow before you leave and I'll give you directions."

Hawkman leaned over to get the Bible out of his briefcase when Jennifer placed a hand on his arm and whispered. "Hawkman, have you noticed those two men sitting at that table against the wall? They've sure been watching our table."

"Grolier raised his eyebrow, shot a look across the room, then glanced back at Jennifer. "What'd you just call him?"

She laughed and explained to the detective how Tom Casey had become known as Hawkman.

Grolier shook his head and pointed a stubby finger. "You'd never know by looking at that big ugly guy that he'd have a soft place in his heart for birds."

Hawkman chuckled while slyly slipping the key from between the pages of the Bible into his pocket. He then put the book on the table.

"What's this?"

"Remember I told you about Drew's interest in Nancy's mother's Bible. Nancy thinks it's lost. Well, I found it in the safe-deposit box."

Grolier picked it up. "Anything interesting inside?"

"Oh yeah. A key to a safe-deposit box. But since we're being watched, I'll give it to you later."

Grolier nodded. "Sounds like a plan."

Jennifer leaned forward and whispered. "On the outside of the envelope someone wrote: 'Psalm 23'."

"I memorized that chapter as a kid." Grolier said, and began reciting the verse. "Yea, though I walk through the valley of the shadow of death, I will fear no evil; for thou art with me; thy rod and thy staff they comfort me."

Jennifer grabbed his arm. "Is there a bank or savings around here that has any of those words in their name?"

Grolier's eyes lit up. "I'll be damned, Valley Federal" Jennifer, you're a genius."

"Not quite. I just know my Bible verses too."

They all laughed.

Suddenly, Jennifer nudged Hawkman's leg with her foot. He glanced at the two men approaching their table. "We have company coming."

Grolier twisted his head around. "Figures."

The tall lanky man spoke first. "Mr. and Mrs. Casey, Detective Grolier, please excuse our intrusion. We're from the Federal Treasury. . ."

"Yes, yes, we know," Hawkman interrupted.

"My name is Frank Collins. This is my partner, Mike Monahan."

"Okay, Collins," Grolier said. "What's the problem?"

Collins looked down at the Bible, then picked it up and flipped through the pages, dislodging some of the pressed flowers, causing them to fall onto the table. "What are we having here, a Bible class?"

"Well, it certainly doesn't hurt to have the Big Guy on your side." Grolier proclaimed.

"Is this a joke?" Collins asked..

"Quite the contrary, Mr. Collins. It helps us in what we do."

The two agents glanced at each other. "We're looking for the money that Harland and Coty stole. We feel Drew stashed it. If you have any leads, we'd like to be informed."

Grolier raised a hand. "We wouldn't think of holding back information. We'll let you know if anything comes down."

Collins dropped the Bible back on the table and the two men stalked away.

When they were out of ear shot, Grolier turned back to Hawkman. "I'll find out which Valley Federal has the box and get a court order to open it. Be at the station at nine thirty tomorrow morning. You know those two will be on one of our tails. So if the hundred grand happens to be in that box, we'll turn it over to them."

Hawkman nodded. "I'm sure they won't let me out of their sight until the Bible mystery is solved."

Grolier chuckled. "I deal with these guys on almost every bank robbery. They'll hound you to death if you let them."

They finished their drinks and left the table. Hawkman brushed against Grolier as they walked out the door, slipping him the key. They said their farewell in the parking lot and before the detective got into his car, he turned and waved. "Nice meeting you, Jennifer. Good night, Hawkman."

⊹⊱✦⊰⊹⊱✦⊰⊹

The next morning, Hawkman and Jennifer had breakfast in their room before signing out. They met Grolier at the police station, then followed him to the Valley Federal Bank. Strolling toward the front doors, Grolier nudged Hawkman and thumbed toward the parking lot. Frank Collins and Mike Monahan were just pulling up.

Grolier took command when they got inside and presented the bank manager with the court order. Just as they started for the vault, Frank Collins and Mike Monahan walked up behind them.

Hawkman checked his watch. "You guys are late."

CHAPTER SIXTEEN

The bank manager and Grolier went into the vault first. After a few minutes, they reappeared and the detective motioned for Hawkman, the two FBI agents and Jennifer to follow. The manager led them into a private office where he set the large deposit box on the desk. Then he left, closing the door behind him.

Grolier surveyed each person in the room, a slight grin twitching the corners of his mouth. "We'll know in a few minutes if this is where Harland stashed the loot. Hope you boys brought the serial numbers."

Collins and Monahan stood silently with their arms crossed in front of them, but when Grolier's gaze rested on them longer than necessary, they both nodded and patted their vest pockets.

The detective slowly lifted the lid. All stared at the brown paper sack jammed inside. Grolier took hold of the open end with both hands and ripped the paper bag down the middle.

The two agents, big grins cutting across their faces, stepped forward. They stared at the bundled money bulging from the drawer. Collins took the list of serial numbers from his pocket and started checking them against the stashed bills. It only took a few minutes before he glanced up at Hawkman and Grolier.

"They match."

Grolier moved a chair up to the table. "Let's count it."

Hawkman and Jennifer each took several parcels and helped. It didn't take long before the group tallied up the total and found the stash to be short only five thousand of the hundred grand.

Grolier stood and dusted his hands together. "I think you boys can feel lucky that we've recovered ninety five thousand dollars of the stolen loot. That's better than average."

Collins extended his hand to Grolier. "I think we can take it from here."

The detective nodded. "No problem with me. How about you Hawkman?"

"Sounds good."

Hawkman, Jennifer and Grolier left the bank, leaving Collins and Monahan in charge of the stolen loot.

"Now, maybe they'll leave us alone so we can get on with the murder investigation," Hawkman said, as they walked to the car.

Grolier snapped his fingers. "Glad you mentioned that." He stopped and groped in his suit vest pocket until he drug out a crumpled piece of paper. "Here's the address of Tonia's workplace. The turn off is right before a huge 'Claremoor's Electronics' sign. You can't miss it."

"Thanks," Hawkman said. "We're headed for the library right now. How far is it from here?"

"Follow me. It's on the way back to the station."

Hawkman and Jennifer quickly found the reference section and selected a stack of Bar Directories dating back five years and lugged them to one of the tables. Sitting opposite each other, they began their search.

They'd poured over the big ledgers for an hour and were about to give up when Hawkman leaned over and whispered, "I've found something."

She walked around the table and sat down beside him. His finger tapped softly on a name under the firm of 'Bradley, Horn, Stack & Associates'. Her eyes grew wide. "Jack Gilbert! An associate of that firm?"

"Sure looks that way."

"The plot thickens," she said.

After writing down the information and Jack's old address, they returned the books to their proper stacks. Hawkman studied his notes while walking back to the car. "Let's drive by this address if it isn't too far away."

Jennifer located it on the map. "We're close."

When they approached the area, she pointed out a large apartment building with the numbers inscribed on the front. "Looks like the typical first apartment. He'd probably just gotten out of law school when he lived here."

Hawkman made a U-turn and headed back the way he'd come. "I'd lay odds that he and Nancy met through the law office when she filed for a divorce. The timing seems right."

"Are you going to try and interview anyone around here?"

"No, it'd be fruitless. Too many years have passed. Let's go on to Tonia's company."

Jennifer accompanied Hawkman into the business office of 'Claremoor's Electronics'. He flashed his badge and asked to speak with the supervisor of the late Tonia Stowell. While the woman sent out the message, Hawkman turned and smiled at Jennifer. Flashing his badge had worked again. Within a few minutes, a professional looking woman walked toward him with her hand extended.

"Hello, I'm Jessica Johnson. I was Tonia's supervisor. I'm absolutely devastated by her murder."

He introduced himself then turned to Jennifer, introducing her as his partner. "Do you think you could spare us a moment of your time? I'd like to ask you a few questions about Tonia."

"Certainly, Mr. Casey. Come with me."

They walked down a long corridor before they turned into an office. A young woman sat in the reception area. "Ms. Carrington, see that we aren't disturbed." She then led them into an inner office and closed the door.

"Please, have a seat." Ms. Johnson took her seat behind the desk. "Now, how can I help you?"

Hawkman sat forward in his chair. "I've read the police reports and realize you've already been interviewed. However, I'm more interested in getting some insight on Tonia's character. It might help us find her murderer."

"Fire away. I'll answer whatever I can if it will help."

"Can you give me some idea of her personality."

"Everyone here liked her. She always attended the office socials. And always had a good time."

"I take it she was a good worker?"

"Absolutely. There's a big void here without her."

"What about her disposition? Did she appear moody, despondent, or angry?"

Jessica shook her head. "No more than anyone else. We all have our bad days, but I'd say she had fewer than most. Her spirits were high, always pleasant to be around."

"Did you ever meet Tonia's sister, Nancy?" Jennifer asked.

"Yes. She'd moved in with Tonia after some marriage difficulties and applied here for a job, but unfortunately we weren't hiring at the time."

"Did they seem close?"

"Well, I think Nancy tended to be more fond of Tonia than vice-versa. Nancy was the older and quite the beauty. I think Tonia held a tad of jealousy in her heart." She smiled. "But they seemed to get along quite well. That is, until Nancy stole Tonia's boyfriend and ended up marrying him. That caused a bit of friction."

Hawkman's eyebrows rose. "Tell me about it."

Tonia's boyfriend, Jack, worked as an associate at a law firm at the time. He introduced Nancy to this lawyer who promised to get her a quickie divorce. I can't remember his name."

"Paul Bradley?" Hawkman asked.

"Yes, that's it. He handled Nancy's divorce. Then one thing led to another and before I knew it Tonia told me she'd lost Jack. . . gee, why can't I remember his last name."

"Jack Gilbert," Hawkman prompted.

She put a finger in the air. "Yes, of course. Thank you. Anyway, Jack and Nancy married and took off up north some place. Tonia didn't like losing him, especially to her sister. But time passed and healed her broken heart. Before long she appeared to forget about it, and got on with her life."

Hawkman stood. He'd found out all he needed to know. "I want to thank you for giving us this much time."

When he and Jennifer returned to the car, he noticed her excellent spirits. "Did you hear something that I didn't catch?"

"Nope. Just glad you've finally recognized me as your partner."

Hawkman chuckled as he started the car and headed for the airport. After they arrived home, he tried to call Nancy, but received no answer.

⊹⊱⊹⊱⊹⊱⊹⊱⊹

Thursday morning, Hawkman decided he better have that chat with Damon McElroy. But before leaving, he again dialed Nancy, letting the phone ring several times. It puzzled him that the answering machine never picked up.

He finally gave up and left for Jack Gilbert's office. After he parked he glanced around the lot, but didn't see Jack's white Cadillac, which pleased him. He preferred to speak with McElroy alone.

When he entered the office, the receptionist glanced up and spoke in a southern drawl. "May I help you?"

"Yes, I'd like to speak with Damon McElroy."

"Do you have an appointment?"

"No."

"Your name, please."

"Tom Casey, Private Investigator."

Her eyes quickly revealed that his name sounded familiar. "Just a moment, Mr. Casey. I'll see if Mr. McElroy is available."

She left her desk for a few minutes then returned and pointed to the office on her left. "He'll see you now."

McElroy stood and extended his hand, then gestured for Hawkman to have a seat. "What can I do for you, Mr. Casey?"

"I'm investigating a murder and would like to ask you some questions."

"Local?"

"No. One in Los Angeles. I'm checking out people who were registered at the nearby motels and hotels. You were at the Marriott Inn, September fourth through the sixth. Is that correct?"

"Let me check our roster." McElroy pulled a large ledger toward him and flipped open the pages. "Yes, Mr. Gilbert and I were there on those dates."

Hawkman pretended to check his notes. "That's strange. Why wasn't Mr. Gilbert's name recorded on the hotel's register."

"Because I made the reservation."

"Did you also rent a car?"

"Yes."

"What kind and color?"

McElroy closed his eyes in thought. "A dark colored Ford. Green, I believe." He closed the ledger. "Mr. Casey. Before you go any farther. What's this all about?"

"A witness reported seeing a dark colored rental car in the vicinity of the murder."

"What time did the homicide occur?"

"Early evening, between six and seven."

"Well, I worked at the courtroom most of the day, retired to my room afterwards and called for room service. Which can be checked."

Hawkman fingered his notebook,. "Did you both use the car?"

"Yes."

"When did Mr. Gilbert drive it?"

"Why are you interested?"

"Because the murder victim happened to be Mr. Gilbert's sister-in-law."

McElroy's face registered a trace of surprise, then settled back into his lawyer's mask. "I see. He used it the last night we were there."

"Where did he go?"

"All I can tell you is that court adjourned early that day and he dropped me at Marriott's around five. Said he had a meeting with a client." He shifted uncomfortabley in his seat. "I feel these questions are out of line, Mr. Casey. If you're interested in Mr. Gilbert's movements, I think you should be asking him, not me."

"I intend to do just that, Mr. McElroy. What time did he return?"

"Around nine. Maybe later."

"Did he come back to Medford that night?"

"Yes. We came back on the same flight."

"Thank you, Mr. McElroy. I won't take up any more of your time."

On his way out, Hawkman stopped at the receptionist desk and read the name placard. "Becky Titus. Are you Mr. McElroy's, or Mr. Gilbert's assistant?"

She put on her business smile. "Actually I work for both."

He tipped his hat. "Have a good day, Ms. Titus."

When Hawkman pushed open the door, he noted the reflection of Damon McElroy standing in the hall.

Once inside his truck, he jotted down the name, 'Becky Titus' in his notebook. An interview with her might prove worthwhile.

⸭⸭⸭⸭⸭⸭⸭

Back in his office and after two hours of studying the Gilbert file, Hawkman leaned back in his chair. Had Tonia Stowell been blackmailing Jack? He also sensed a strong connection between Tonia and Drew while he and Nancy were married. Did Tonia make up to both these men while they were married to her sister? Would she go that far to seek revenge? Hawkman let out a long breath and readjusted his eye-patch. Tonia Stowell did not appear to be a loving sister. Was Nancy so naive that she couldn't see it? He rubbed a hand across his face. Things were getting mighty nasty.

He stretched his arms, then pulled the phone book toward him. He searched the T's and found B. Titus. After he dialed the number, he heard a southern drawl message come over the line, which satisfied him that he'd reached the right number. He wrote it down along with her address for future reference.

Just as he shoved the phone book back to the corner of his desk, the office door flew open. Jack Gilbert stormed toward him, his eyes flashing and his finger punching the air. "Why the hell are you questioning my associate about my whereabouts?"

Hawkman didn't move. "I have a job to do."

Jack leaned over the desk so close that Hawkman could smell the garlic on his hot breath. "Does my wife have anything to do with this?"

Hawkman stared at him. "That's confidential."

Jack shook his finger at Hawkman's nose. "I'm warning you. Don't go near my office or my wife again. Do you understand?"

Hawkman stood, his gaze never leaving Jack's face. "Tell me something, Mr. Gilbert. Why were you at Tonia Stowell's house on the evening of September sixth?"

Jack sucked in his breath and his face drained of color. "What the hell are you talking about?"

"How come you never mentioned you were in Los Angeles at the time of her murder?"

Jack's eyes narrowed. "I had a trial in Los Angles."

"I think you better tell me where you were the night of September sixth."

"That's none of your damn business," Jack said through clenched teeth.

"The police are going to be very interested in where you were that night. If you have a witness that can verify you weren't at Tonia Stowell's house, I think you better produce him."

"My client's names are confidential and I don't have to reveal anything to you. If it comes down to the police, I'll deal with that when it happens."

"That's your option but I'd definitely give it some serious thought."

"What are you trying to do anyway? Pin Tonia's murder on me?"

"No, Mr. Gilbert. I'm going to prove it."

Jack glared at him, turned abruptly and stormed out of the office.

Hawkman released his clinched fist, walked over and closed the door. He then crossed the room to the window and watched Jack drive out of the parking lot. He went back to his desk and made a notation of the visit. In block letters, he wrote, 'VERY AGITATED' underscoring it several times.

It reminded him that he had yet to get hold of Nancy, but he wouldn't tell her about Jack's visit. This time when he called, she answered.

"I've been trying to reach you," Hawkman said.

"My machine broke down and I had to buy a new one."

"I have the contents of the safe-deposit box."

"It had something in it?" Her voice revealed surprise.

"Yes, several items."

"Oh dear, I can't pick them up right now. Can I call you in the next few days and set up an appointment."

"That's fine."

After hanging up, he glanced at his watch. It was five fifteen. He dialed Becky Titus' number.

"Hello, Ms. Titus, this is Tom Casey, Private Investigator. Remember, I stopped by the office today and spoke with Mr. McElroy."

"Oh, yes."

"I'd like to ask you some questions."

She paused before answering. "I don't think so, Mr. Casey. It could put my job in jeopardy. Your visit has already caused quite a turmoil at our office."

After she hung up, he chewed on the end of a pencil and stared at the phone. Obviously, Jack had been pretty verbal when he found out he'd spoken to McElroy. More than likely he'd yelled at the whole office staff and she wasn't about to take a chance at loosing her job. He tossed the pencil on the desk, stood up and stretched. Time to go home.

❖❖❖❖❖

Early Friday morning, when Hawkman entered his office he found the message light flashing. He punched the play button and started to remove his jacket, but froze in the spot when he recognized the southern drawl of Becky Titus.

Her message instructed that she would meet him at the single's club, off of Interstate Five, just past the Bear Creek Golf Course at nine o'clock tonight. What a surprise. He wondered what had changed her mind.

Nancy also called, wanting to meet him at a little restaurant off Highway Sixty-Two near Poplar Square. Now, he puzzled over how he'd present the items from the safe-deposit box. He wanted her in his office when she opened the big envelope, not at some cafe where she'd just take it home. Knowing Nancy would be shocked over the letter, it would probably be best if he picked out only a couple of things and not give her the whole packet at once. Then he'd try and convince her to come to the office for the rest.

CHAPTER SEVENTEEN

Hawkman left his office a few minutes before twelve to meet Nancy for lunch. When he pulled into the parking lot of the small restaurant, he spied her silver Mercedes and half-way expected to see the Cadillac, but it was no where in sight. Inside, Nancy hovered in a booth at the far corner of the dimly lit room. He slid into the seat opposite her.

"Where's Jack?"

She frowned. "In Ashland. He won't be home until late this afternoon."

"You look worried. Is there a problem?"

She slumped back in the booth. "Something's bothering him, but he won't tell me what."

Hawkman picked up the menu and pretended to study it. He knew full well what bothered Jack. "Maybe he's having trouble with a case."

She waved a hand in the air. "I hope that's all it is."

Dropping the menu, he reached into his briefcase and removed the Bible, placing it on the table in front of her. "Maybe this will make you feel better."

Her face broke into a radiant smile and her hands gently caressed the worn leather. "I'd given up finding it."

"Thought you'd be pleased."

She glanced at him with a puzzled look. "You found this in that safe-deposit box?"

"Yes, along with a few other things." He told her about the key in the Bible and how they discovered it belonged to a safe-deposit box in Drew's name. That's where he'd stashed the stolen money. He leaned back, crossing his arms and studied Nancy's face. "Why do you suppose Tonia had the key."

Nancy's chin quivered and she avoided his gaze.

He knew from the look on her face, that she hadn't leveled with him from the beginning. His suspicions had been correct. "Can you explain it?"

Taking a tissue from her purse, she dabbed at her eyes. "It's personal."

"So you're not going to tell me?"

She clutched the Bible to her chest. "No."

He decided to leave it alone and brought out the letter from the lawyer. "This was also in the box."

She took the envelope from his hand and glanced at the address. Her expression changed from distress to puzzlement. "This is addressed to me."

He pointed to the round circle on the front. "Yes, postmarked several years ago."

She frowned as she pulled out the letter. Hawkman watched her rosy cheeks turn pale. Letting the paper drop to the table, she covered her face with her hands. "This can't be," she whispered, shaking her head from side to side.

Hawkman realized, the news had definitely shocked her, so he kept his voice low and calm. "I'm afraid it's true. I checked it out. You and Drew were never divorced."

Tears flowed down her cheeks. She banged her fist on the letter. "Why did Tonia not send me this?"

Hawkman reached across the table and took hold of her wrist. "Look, Drew's dead. Your husband's a lawyer. He can take care of this problem discreetly and no one will ever know the difference."

Horror flashed across her face. "No. Jack mustn't know. I'll take care of it myself."

He dropped her hand and leaned back. "Why not tell Jack?"

She turned her head and stared across the room.

"Nancy, doesn't it seem suspicious that Jack was in Los Angeles the night of Tonia's murder?"

She jerked her head around and glared at Hawkman. "How dare you insinuate such a thing. He and Mr. McElroy had court dates."

Hawkman returned her steady gaze. "Did you ever have Jack deliver things to Tonia when he made these trips?"

"Sometimes. But not that trip. They were going to be too busy."

"Why does he have a separate answering service?"

She shifted uneasily in her seat. "Why are you asking me all these questions? You're making it sound like Jack murdered Tonia."

Hawkman met her gaze in silence. She obviously didn't know about the extra service, he thought. If so, she's a damn good liar."

She put the Bible and envelope into her purse. "I think I'd better go." She scooted out of the booth and left her lunch untouched.

His gaze followed her until the door closed.

⊹⊱•⊰⊹⊱•⊰⊹⊱•⊰⊹

Returning to his office, Hawkman worked until the time rolled around to meet Becky. He arrived at the single's bar a few minutes before nine. Not seeing her in the half-filled room, he ordered a beer and carried it to a small booth on the opposite side of the room, which allowed him a clear view of the entry. He put his briefcase on the floor beside his feet and waited.

When he saw her enter, he reached up and flipped on the voice activated recorder in his shirt pocket. She spotted him and approached the booth.

"Hi. Sorry I'm late. Hope you haven't been waiting long."

Hawkman indicated the seat across from him. "No problem. I've been enjoying the band."

Becky smiled. "Yeah, they're good."

"I appreciate you meeting me. I just have a few question so I promise not to keep you long."

She peered at him anxiously.

"Let me get you something to drink first." He hailed a waitress and they both ordered. Then Hawkman leaned back in his chair.

"The things I'm going to ask you may seem personal, but they don't involve you at all."

She smiled. "I understand."

"How long have you worked for Jack Gilbert?"

"It'll be three years in March."

"Do you like your job?"

"Very much. Mr. Gilbert pays well and is a considerate boss."

"That certainly makes it more pleasant."

The waitress delivered their drinks. Becky took a sip, staring at Hawkman over the rim of her glass.

"When did Mr. McElroy come into the firm?"

"He's only been there about six months. He's an excellent lawyer and has really helped lighten Mr. Gilbert's case load."

Hawkman leaned forward and rested an arm on the small table. "Does the firm have a lot of out-of-town cases?"

"No, not really. Just a few, and Mr. Gilbert usually handles those. He goes down to Los Angeles once or twice a month."

That answer certainly sounded rehearsed. He'd bet that she'd been prepped. "Do you make his airline reservations?"

"Most of the time, but every once in awhile he'll make his own."

"Do Mr. Gilbert and Mr. McElroy ever try cases together?

"Sometimes."

He watched her face closely. "When was the last time they both served on the same one?"

"Last month in Los Angeles."

She's too quick with her answers, he thought. Someone had definitely prepared her for this interview and rehearsed her well. "Do you think both men are honest?"

"Definitely."

Hawkman shifted his position and crossed one leg over the other. "Do you ever do any personal work for Mr. Gilbert?"

Her hand stopped short as she started to take a chip from the dish. "Huh, what do you mean?"

Now why did she respond like that? Hawkman wondered. He casually waved a hand in the air. "Oh, things like writing out checks for bills, personal errands, make dental or doctor appointments. Things that aren't work related."

"Oh," she said, her tone relieved. "No, I don't. Both men are very private. Especially Mr. Gilbert. He's very strict about any of us using the office for our personal business. However, I've seen him put personal stuff into his safe. But he's the boss and I don't ask any questions."

Hawkman raised a brow. That slipped out. Jack certainly wouldn't want anyone to know he used his vault for anything but business. "Who takes care of the calls that come in on his answering service?"

Becky tilted her head slightly and looked straight into Hawkman's face. "Mr. Gilbert."

"Do you open the mail?"

"No. I just sort it."

"Have you ever noticed anything out of the ordinary?"

She shrugged. "I don't know what you mean by 'out of the ordinary'. We get lots of advertisements and lawyers often get disgruntled mail from people when they've lost a case. However, there's so much mail that comes into the office, I don't pay that much attention."

Hawkman placed a twenty dollar bill on the tray for their drinks, picked up his briefcase and stood. "Thanks for your time, Ms. Titus. I'll leave so you can join your friends."

She glanced up at him with a startled expression. "That's it?"

"Have a good evening."

Hawkman strolled out of the club. He nonchalantly reached up into his pocket and turned off the recorder. Once in the 4X4, he glanced into the rear view mirror and grinned. It figures, he thought.

Jack Gilbert had parked two rows back in his white Cadillac. Hawkman gunned out of the parking lot while keeping an eye on the white car through his mirrors. When he'd gone a couple of blocks without being followed, he turned around and went back. Jack no longer occupied his car, so Hawkman pulled into the shadows alongside the building and killed the engine.

Soon, Jack came out of the club with Becky on his arm and they drove off in the Cadillac.

Hawkman gripped the steering wheel. Yes, Ms. Titus your job is secure. He's very interested in finding out what I know. Where'd you hide your recorder?

CHAPTER EIGHTEEN

Nancy stood back and inventoried the boxes stacked inside her garage. She'd finally finished sorting Tonia's possessions, saving only a few items for keepsakes which she'd stored in the attic. The rest would be hauled off to the Charity for their flea market. I hope Jack will be happy having the garage clear again, she thought.

She'd started back into the house when she noticed a Federal Express truck stopping out front. The courier approached her, carrying a large box. "Mrs. Nancy Gilbert?"

She furrowed her brows. "Yes."

"Sign here, please."

She grasped the box with both hands and carried it into the kitchen, where she plopped it down on the table. Her eyes riveted on the return address and a cold shiver went down her spine when she read, David Harland. Maybe she should just toss the whole thing into the trash without opening it. But curiosity got the best of her. She removed a knife from the butcher block and cut the tape, pulling back the cardboard flap. She gasped, as her gaze met a picture of herself.

She quickly removed it and found a letter from David tucked underneath. Feeling weak in the knees, she sat down at the kitchen table as she unfolded the piece of paper.

Dear Nancy,

Before Drew died, he told me where you lived
and that you two weren't legally divorced. Since
you're his next of kin, I've packed all his stuff
and am sending it to you. I don't know if they'll mean
anything to you or not but I don't want them.
The only thing I kept was a picture.

Sincerely, David

Oh, David, why? she sighed. After all these years you know I
don't want any of Drew's things, legally divorced or not. She blew out
a puff of air, making strands of hair flip out of her face. Laying the
letter aside, she began digging into the box. Picking up clothes with
two fingers and making a face, she piled them on the floor along with
rodeo programs and several trophies. When she reached the bottom,
her hand closed over a wooden chest the size of a small jewelry box.
She lifted it out and discovered it was secured with a small padlock.

Turning the box upside down, she searched for the key, then
went through the pockets of the clothes in the pile. She even checked
the bottoms of the trophies, but found nothing. In desperation, she
took a screwdriver and removed the hinges. When the latch fell away,
she closed her eyes and lifted the lid.

Taking a deep breath to build her confidence, she looked inside.
Letters filled the box. She flipped through the first few envelopes
and noticed they were from David while Drew was in prison. Digging
deeper, she pulled out another and her mouth went dry when she
thought she recognized the handwriting.

Her fingers trembled as she pulled out a single sheet of paper.
Her gaze traveled down to the signature and she quickly covered her
mouth to stifle the agonizing cry that ripped from her throat. Her
tears blurred the words as she read.

Drew,

You son-of-a-bitch. Don't threaten me. I'm not
afraid of you. I'll have the cops on your ass faster
than you can blink an eye. Remember I have the key to

your future.

Don't write me again.

Tonia

Nancy folded the letter and wiped her cheeks. Suddenly, her grief turned to anger. She hurled the trophies, clothes and rodeo stuff back into the large box and cried, "I can't stand much more of this. And Tonia, how could you do this to me?"

Sobs tumbling from her throat, she slapped the flap down and hauled the box outside to the trash can. "I hate you! I hate you! Drew Harland. You murderer! You scum! You killed my sister! You bastard! You deserved to die!"

She pushed and shoved the box with all her might to the bottom of the large round trash can.

Still choking on her sobs, she mashed the lid onto the receptacle until it snapped tight. She straightened and wiped the tears from her face, then took several deep breaths as she walked back into the house. She gathered up the letters strewn across the kitchen table and shoved them back into the small box. She then took it to her bedroom and hid it in one of her dresser drawers.

Glancing at the bedside clock, she moaned. "Oh no, I'm supposed to be at Mr. Casey's office in thirty minutes to collect the rest of the stuff Tonia had in her safe-deposit box. But I can't leave until the Charity stuff has been picked up." Disheartened and frustrated, she sat down on the edge of the bed and called Tom Casey.

⊹⊱⋅⊰⊹⊱⋅⊰⊹⊱⋅⊰⊹

Hawkman found himself relieved that Nancy couldn't make it until Friday morning. It gave him time to investigate a few more items on his list. He hoped to convince her to stay in the office so he could witness her opening the big brown envelope. His gut feeling told him that packet held the key to this case.

Tapping a pencil against his hand, he punched on the speaker phone and called Stan.

"I need the ballistics report on Alphonso Vernandos and Alvero Rodreges."

"Okay."

"Also, see if they have the report on the bullet they dug out of Drew."

"Why do you want that?" Stan asked. We already know it came from Jack's gun. You got something up your sleeve?"

"Not sure yet. Did the police confiscate his Smith & Wesson?"

"No. No charges were filed."

"I'd like to have some tests run on that gun and check it against the ballistics reports we already have. Is there some way we can get it?"

"Let me see what I can do," Stan said. "I'll fax the reports to you as soon as I collect them all."

"Thanks, Stan."

⊹⊱•⊰⊹

After dinner, Jack promised Tracy a story in the television room while her mommy cleaned the kitchen. They'd no more settled on the couch when the doorbell rang.

"I'll get it," Nancy called, drying her hands. She opened the door and stepped back in shock to see a policeman on her stoop.

"C-Can I help you?" she stammered.

"May I speak with Jack Gilbert, please."

"Just a moment." Frowning, she stood at the den door.

Jack glanced up. "What is it, honey?"

She motioned for him to come into the kitchen.

He handed the book to Tracy. "You hold daddy's place and I'll be right back."

"There's a policeman at the door," Nancy whispered. "He wants to talk to you."

Nancy followed and stood a short distance back and listened.

"Jack Gilbert?"

"Yes."

The policeman showed his identification and a warrant. "I'm Sergeant Ben Rice. I have orders to confiscate the Smith & Wesson .38 caliber hand gun you own."

"I don't understand, There were no charges filed." Jack kept his voice controlled.

"We're aware of that, sir, and apologize for the inconvenience. But we need to conduct some tests." Nancy noticed Jack's jaw tighten. His eyes blazing, he turned and charged down the hallway toward their bedroom. Returning with the gun, he stared hard and cold at the officer as he dropped it into the plastic bag he held open. "I want a receipt and I want my gun back soon."

"I'll relay your request." Officer Rice held out a clipboard for him to sign the release. "Thank you, sir." He then ripped off a copy, handed it to him and left.

Jack headed back toward the den and hissed at Nancy in passing. "I think your damned private investigator is behind this."

She grabbed his arm. "Why do they want your gun?"

He glared at her hand on his arm. "Damned if I know." Then he yanked himself out of her reach and stormed back into the study to Tracy.

◦⫶◦⫶◦⫶◦⫶◦

Tuesday morning, when Hawkman got to his office, the fax machine was printing the ballistics reports. When it finally finished, he took the papers to his desk and studied them. The bullet from Drew's body came from a Smith & Wesson .38 revolver and had smashed against the bone, leaving no distinguishable markings.

On both Vernandos and Rodreges, a Glaser Safety Slug had been used and no distinguishable barrel marks were available. But both slugs came from a Smith & Wesson .38 revolver.

Hawkman hit his fist against the desk, "Dammit! Everyone owns a .38."

Also included was the report on the bullet he'd dug out of Drew's old gray car. It came from the gun found on Alphonso Vernandos' body.

Stan had written a note at the bottom of the page. "Sergeant Ben Rice picked up Jack Gilbert's gun last night. I'll let you know what they find out. Stan"

Hawkman leaned back in his chair, tapping his pencil on the edge of the desk. He knew the barrels on that particular Smith & Wesson revolver could be switched at random. And it wouldn't surprise him to find nothing on Jack's gun that would even come close to resembling the marks found on the bullets that killed Vernandos and Rodreges.

Later that day, Stan called and confirmed his suspicions.

"Gilbert's gun had been fired but the technicians couldn't match the markings with anything we have."

"Damn," Hawkman swore. "Those guns are notorious for barrel switching. I'd sure like to know if Jack has the Dan Wesson Pistol Pac."

It frustrated Hawkman that he didn't have any concrete evidence under his belt. He grabbed his briefcase and went to the library, where he sat at a microfilm machine and examined the Los Angeles Times papers dating back ten years. It took a couple of hours of research before he finally found the article he wanted. "Security Guard Killed In Armed Robbery". Which led to the follow-up articles telling how Drew Lawrence Harland and William 'Coty' Masters were apprehended. Hawkman made copies of the stories and slipped them into his briefcase. The features didn't provide a lot of information, only some dates he needed.

One of the columns stated that the two men were tried separately for different offenses: Harland, armed robbery and Masters for murder. Masters went by his middle name, 'Coty', because he'd always carried a gun. This caused his downfall when he used it to murder the security guard.

Back at his office Hawkman made a call to the "Inmate Locator Line" where he found out that William 'Coty' Masters made his home at Soledad. He made a quick decision to go visit Coty. Grabbing the duffel bag that contained an extra set of clothes for this very purpose, he grabbed his briefcase, locked up the office and headed for his truck.

⟨‡⟩∗⟨‡⟩∗⟨‡⟩∗⟨‡⟩∗⟨‡⟩

When Hawkman reached the prison, he showed his identification and checked his gun at the registration desk. After he signed in, a guard showed him to the room where cubicle-like stalls lined the walls. Each one was equipped with three sides and a thick pane of glass separating visitor and prisoner. A phone-like instrument sat in the corner. The guard indicated a cubicle for

Hawkman, then left.

He soon returned with a man about forty years of age, dressed in gray prison clothes. The prisoner's dark hair, speckled with gray, hung limp around his ears. His lean shoulders drooped slightly.

Sitting down in the cubicle opposite Hawkman, he stared through the glass with cold gray eyes. Both men picked up their receivers.

"Who are you?" Coty asked.

"Tom Casey, Private Investigator. I'm looking into the murder of Drew Lawrence Harland."

"So, what's that got to do with me?"

"I want to know why you put a contract out on him?" Hawkman asked.

The man turned his head and pretended to spit

"My sources informed me that you sent Alphonso Vernandos to find Drew Harland. But when he failed, you had him killed," Hawkman lied.

Coty's throat muscles twitched and he looked up at the ceiling. "Never heard of him."

"I've also been told that Drew hid the stash, but never told you where."

Coty's gaze came down off the wall and narrowed on him.

Hawkman returned the glare. "This time you'll get the death penalty."

Never taking his cold eyes off Hawkman, Coty stood and replaced his receiver on the hook, cutting Hawkman off. 'I'm through," he yelled to the guard.

Hawkman left the prison, knowing he'd hit pay dirt. He found a motel in Soledad and made a call to Detective Grolier, explaining his plan. Grolier sounded excited about the progress in the case. He promised to find Master's wife and check out her finances.

⫷•⫶•⫷•⫶•⫷•⫶•⫷•⫶•⫷⫸

Hawkman arose early Thursday and drove back to Medford. He arrived late in the afternoon and stopped off at his office to check his messages. The one from Grolier, he returned immediately.

"Grolier, you found something already."

"Hey, nothing slow about me. I found Master's wife. She living in the same house and working at the same job she's had for ten years."

"Wish they were all that easy."

"You can say that again. Got her financial records and discovered two hefty fifteen thousand dollar deposits made into her savings account within the past three weeks. I talked with the clerk at the bank. He said she'd inherited the money. Which, of course, we know is a bunch of bunk."

"Couldn't say it better," Hawkman smirked.

"Another thing. Got the test results back on the leather driving gloves. There's enough material for DNA testing. I've called the hospital for Harland's samples, but I need something of Jack's."

"Okay, I'll see what I can do."

After talking with Grolier, Hawkman paced the office in deep thought. How would he obtain something of Jack's that would have enough DNA for testing. He knew Nancy wouldn't give him anything that might incriminate her husband. Suddenly, he stopped in the middle of the room and snapped his fingers. Jack wore driving gloves, he'd seen them on him more than once. But does he leave them in the car?

Hawkman checked his watch. He didn't have much time before Jack would be leaving for home. Snatching his jacket, hat, and briefcase, he charged out of the office. Cruising by Gilbert's office complex, he noted the white Cadillac still parked at the back of the lot under a big shade tree.

He pulled around the corner and parked, then jogged toward the lot. He waited until a couple of cars pulled out of the complex before he stepped over the shrubs that lined the area. Just as he slipped around to the driver's side of the Cadillac, a familiar voice pierced the air.

He ducked below the window, then taking a chance, sneaked a peek through the glass. "Damn, it's Jack and one of his clients," he hissed to himself. He frantically looked for an escape route, but breathed a sigh of relief when Jack headed back into his office and the other person walked around the corner of the building.

He spotted Jack's driving gloves on the front seat. The window had been left open a tad, but his hand was to big to fit through the small crack. He'd have to use his lock picks. The minute he jimmied the lock, the alarm would sound. He'd have to work fast.

Keeping a wary eye, the minute the alarm sounded, he snatched the gloves, jumped the shrubs and ran like hell toward his truck.

Driving out of sight of Jack's office, he pulled over to the side of the road and dropped the gloves into a paper sack he'd taken from his duffel bag of supplies. He held it up and swung it from side to side. "Now, I'm going to nail you for murder, Jack."

Back at his office, he poured himself a cup of coffee and indulged in the donut he'd grabbed from the shop below. He then settled at his desk and called Detective Grolier.

"Hawkman, about time you returned my call."

"Had to get you something for the DNA match."

"Christ, I'm not going to ask how you got it. Just send it."

"I'll mail them off first thing in the morning," Hawkman said.

"I'm questioning Serene Masters this evening," Grolier said. "See if I can find out more about this inheritance hog-wash."

"Let me know what you find out."

"Will do."

Hawkman hung up and downed his last bite of donut, then packed the gloves into a box so he could mail them off early in the morning before Nancy came to view the contents of the big brown envelope.

CHAPTER NINETEEN

After seeing his client out, Jack stopped at Becky Titus' desk, to confirm his appointments for the next day. Suddenly, the sound of a car alarm pierced the air and Jack frowned, recognizing the sirens of his own car's warning system. Stepping outside, he saw the driver's door of the Cadillac standing ajar and he raced across the lot, swearing.

Becky chased after him, holding her hands over her ears until he disengaged the alarm. "Should I call the police, Mr. Gilbert?"

He examined the interior of the car then glanced at Becky and shook his head. "No, Looks like the only thing missing are my driving gloves. Probably some kid. Damn, can't keep anything in your car anymore."

He silently examined the door lock area and realized it had been opened by a professional. More than likely, Tom Casey. He re-locked the car and returned to the office. While gathering up the papers on his desk, he wondered why Casey would want his gloves. That seemed a peculiar thing to steal. What did he know?

The room seemed to close in and perspiration popped out on his forehead. He shoved the papers back into a file folder and put on the head phones to listen to Becky's interview with the private investigator for the second time. He wished she hadn't mentioned his personal safe. But too late to worry about that. The damage had been done. Turning his chair toward the open vault, he tossed the cassette inside, then chose a key from his ring and opened the small inner compartment. He pulled an envelope from underneath the desk blotter and slipped it inside, then locked it. Pushing the heavy safe door closed, he whirled the outer knob, then folded his suit jacket over his arm and left the office for home.

He breathed a sigh of relief when he pulled into the driveway and saw that Nancy had finally gotten rid of Tonia's junk. He'd hated coming home every evening, only to be reminded of that woman.

Before getting out of the car, he sat for a moment pondering over Nancy's attitude change. She used to consult him before making any decisions, but now she just took matters into her own hands.

It also bothered him that if that damned private investigator happened on to any evidence that connected him with Tonia, it could really mess up his run for the senate, not to mention his marriage. He couldn't allow that to happen. The political ambitions he had in mind included having his beautiful wife help promote his career.

He stared into space, drawing a mental picture of how she would look as a senator's wife. Smiling to himself, he could imagine how people, especially the men, would ogle over such a beautiful woman. Nancy held the looks department a head above her sister. That, he noticed a long time ago.

Then his insides tensed again, thinking of how their relationship had changed. Maybe with Drew dead, things would get back to normal. Suddenly, his thoughts were interrupted by a tap on the car window. He turned and looked at the smiling face of his daughter peering at him through the glass.

He grinned, thinking, and you, my lovely daughter, will also help your daddy along. Opening the car door, he lifted Tracy into his arms. "Hello, my little sweetheart,"

They came into the kitchen, singing nursery rhymes. Nancy glanced up and smiled, even though her eyes were tearing from the onion she'd just cut up. To the child's delight, Jack wrinkled his nose and swooned. He set her down and scooped the peelings into the garbage, blinking against the onion's strong aroma "Whew, that is a strong onion. Come on, Tracy, let's get this out of here for mommy."

Tracy insisted they skip to the trash can. Laughing, Jack opened the lid and started to toss the sack inside when he noticed the large squashed cardboard box addressed to "Mrs. Nancy Gilbert from

David Harland." Puzzled, he pulled it up and realized the contents were still inside. He opened the flap and saw the rodeo trophies, his jaw tightened. What the hell? he thought, and shoved the box back down into the can and replaced the lid.

Later, after Tracy had been put to bed, Jack helped Nancy clear the table. He noticed her unusual quietness. Taking hold of her arm as she brought a stack of dishes to the sink, he gazed into her eyes. "Why did David send you Drew's junk?"

The plates slipped from her hand, breaking into pieces as they hit the enamel sink. She quickly turned away and picked up a kitchen towel to wipe her hands.

He grabbed her shoulders and turned her toward him. "Why didn't he keep his damn brother's stuff?"

Nancy's eyes filled with tears. Slumping into a chair, she dropped her head into her hands. "Because I'm Drew's next of kin," she whispered.

"What the hell are you talking about?"

"Oh, Jack," she cried. "I can't believe all this has happened."

"Nancy, I don't understand what you're talking about. Explain it to me."

After a tearful description of the lawyer's letter found in Tonia's safe-deposit box, she looked up at him. "Jack, we're not legally married. I'm going to Los Angeles next week to see if I can get our marriage legalized. Mr. Casey thinks since Drew's dead, it shouldn't be a problem."

Jack's eyebrows shot up. "So Casey knows about this?"

"Yes. He read the letter." She picked up the towel again and wiped her eyes. "Oh Jack, all I can think about is little Tracy. What kind of an effect will this have on her later in life?"

Jack pulled her up into his arms and held her close. His eyes focused on the wall. "Honey, I'm a lawyer, remember. You don't have to go to Los Angeles. I'll fix it so Tracy will never know." He kissed her cheek and had her sit back down. "I'll make us a drink."

"Oh, Jack, I've caused you so much grief."

He dropped ice cubes into the glasses. "I knew that damn bunch of lawyers were incompetent, But I didn't anticipate how they'd affect my life down stream." He sat down at the table opposite her. "Once I left that firm, I thought I'd be rid of that whole crew."

"I'm so sorry for all the pain I've caused you." She reached across the table and touched his hand. "If Tonia had told me about the letter, I could have taken care of this problem years ago." She glanced up into Jack's face. "I wonder if she ever planned to tell me?"

He avoided her gaze and stared up at the kitchen wall clock. Hell no, he reflected, unless I quit paying her each month. "You know how head-strong she was about things."

"Yes, and I remember how often you'd get angry with me for defending her. But after all, she was my sister."

Your sister would have dealt us misery for the rest of our lives, Jack thought as he patted Nancy's hand. "Look, let's not worry about this anymore. I'll handle this marriage problem discreetly and we can get on with our lives." He stood and headed for the TV room. " By the way," he called over his shoulder, "get rid of Casey. We don't need him anymore."

⊹⊱•⊰⊹⊱•⊰⊹⊱•⊰⊹

Friday morning on his way to the office, Hawkman mailed the gloves to Grolier. He sat at his desk listening to the taped interview with Becky Titus when the phone rang.

"Hawkman, Detective Grolier. Talked with the Masters woman last night."

"What'd she say about the deposits?"

"She says her husband inherited the money."

Hawkman flopped back in his chair. "Come on, give me a break. We didn't just fall off a turnip wagon."

"She doesn't give a damn where the money came from. It's cushioning her account."

Hawkman let out a chuckle. "You're right there. Did Coty negotiate the transaction?"

"I'd guess he's behind it. I checked the bank video for who made the deposits, but couldn't tell other than it looked like the same man both times. Had a hat pulled down low over his face with shades on and never looked into the camera.

"Our man thinks he has all ends covered. Well, I'm going to find his weak link," Hawkman stated.

"Keep me posted."

"Will do."

He hung up, finished listening to the Titus tape and put it away, assuming Nancy would be there any minute.

⊹⊱⊰⊹⊱⊰⊹⊱⊰⊹⊱⊰⊹

Nancy, still in her robe, sat at the kitchen table sipping coffee. She enjoyed the peace and quiet, plus Jack had instructed her to relax and offered to drop Tracy off. But before leaving, he'd made a definite point of telling her to get in touch with Tom Casey and pay him off. He didn't know she had an appointment with Mr. Casey this morning.

She took a deep breath, letting it out slowly. Her intuition had warned her against telling Jack about the other envelope in the safe-deposit box. Why did she feel so apprehensive? She really knew the answer but didn't want to believe it. Tonia had betrayed her more than once and she feared what might be in that other envelope. Dear God, she thought. I don't think I can handle much more and keep my sanity.

Then an idea struck her. Why not just let Mr. Casey open the damned thing? After all, that's why I hired him. But, maybe he won't without me being present. She wrestled with what to do and glanced at the clock. Going to the sink, she rinsed out her cup and stared out the window for several moments. Then she turned abruptly and headed for the phone. She'd made up her mind.

⊹⊱⊰⊹⊱⊰⊹⊱⊰⊹⊱⊰⊹

When the phone rang, Hawkman glanced at his watch and knew Nancy would be on the other end of the line.

"Mr. Casey, I don't think it will be necessary for me to come to your office, I'm going to give you permission to open that envelope and handle whatever problems might be involved."

Hawkman felt silently overjoyed at her decision. "For legal purposes I need to record your instructions. Would you mind repeating it?"

"Not at all."

He punched the record button. After she finished, he flipped out the tape and smiled to himself. "I'll get back to you as soon as I go through the items."

But before he could sign off, she blurted. "I told Jack our marriage wasn't legal."

His brows shot up. "I thought you told me you weren't going to tell him. What made you change your mind?"

"I received a box from David yesterday, packed full of Drew's belongings. He said Drew had informed him that we were still married. I guess he figured the items belonged to me. I threw the stuff in the trash and Jack spotted it. He approached me on the matter and I told him everything."

"How'd he react?"

"He said he'll take care of the problem discreetly. I'm so relieved. So, we won't need your services anymore."

Hawkman straightened in his chair. "You don't want me to continue with the murder investigation?"

"No. The police can handle that. Tonia stumbled and fell. It must have been an accident."

Hawkman's jaw tightened. "Nancy, you don't believe that. She had bruises on her face and arms where someone hit her hard enough to cause her to fall against the table. Whether you want to accept it or not your sister was murdered. Remember too, her house had been searched twice. "

"Please, Mr. Casey. I don't want to think about it anymore. Thank you for your services. Send me an invoice."

"You realize I'll have to bill you separately for the job you have me on right now?"

"Yes. I'll take care of it later in person."

"You're sure that you and Jack don't want to open this envelope together?"

"No." I don't want Jack to know about anything else in that safe-deposit box. Nor do I want him to know that you're still in my employment."

Hawkman decided not to press it any farther. "Okay, I'll get right on it."

"Thank you, Mr. Casey."

He hung up and cleaned off the top of his desk. Then, he removed the sealed brown envelope from the deep drawer on the side and laid it in front of him. Not wanting to be disturbed, he locked the office door. Carefully, he cut through the tape on the brown envelope and slowly dumped the contents.

Several hours later, he leaned back in his chair, drumming his fingers on the arm rests. His eye scanned the stacks of pictures, papers and videos that lay in front of him. Reaching across the desk, he picked up the phone.

"Detective Grolier Please."

CHAPTER TWENTY

Detective Grolier stood at the terminal window watching the activity on the runway until the arrival of Hawkman's plane. When the passengers flooded out the gate, he searched over the top of their heads and soon spotted the familiar cowboy hat swaying above the crowd. He waved his newspaper to get Hawkman's attention, then motioned toward the front entrance. The two men jumped in an unmarked patrol car and headed for the police station.

The detective led Hawkman into a conference room dominated by a large round table surrounded by chairs. A coffee maker sat at the far end of the room and the aroma of fresh brew wafted through the air. A large chalk board rested against one wall and a phone rested quietly in the middle of the big table. Grolier removed his coat and rolled up his sleeves. "We have everything at our fingertips. Let's get started."

Hawkman glanced around, an expression of satisfaction settled on his face as he placed his briefcase on the table. "This will do great." He shrugged out of his leather jacket and tossed it on a nearby chair along with his cowboy hat.

"You hungry?" Grolier asked. "Want to order a pizza or something before we start?"

"No, thanks. I'm fine. But how about you?"

"Maybe later." Grolier clenched his unlit cigar between his teeth and took a pair of reading glasses from his pocket. "I'm ready to dig in."

Hawkman's expression remained serious as he dumped the contents of the briefcase onto the table. "Here's the new evidence I told you about on the phone."

The detective let out a short whistle, then raised his bushy eyebrows and reached for a small floral decorated book. "Is this what I think it is?"

Hawkman nodded. "Tonia Stowell's diary. The entries date back to Nancy Gilbert's wedding to Jack."

Grolier flipped through the pages. "Refresh my memory on how you came onto all this stuff?"

Hawkman repeated the story, then added. "Nancy kept putting off opening this envelope and I gathered she had a wary feeling about it. It's probably a good thing she gave me the permission to open it. I don't think she could have handled what's inside very well."

"Anything we need before we get started?"

Hawkman picked up a video tape from the table and glanced around the room. "I see the television and VCR over in the corner. Looks like we're set."

Grolier raised a brow. "We have a movie?"

"Yep. Tonia thought of everything."

The detective picked up the diary again and thumbed through the pages. "This may not take as long as we thought. Where do you suggest I start?"

Since Grolier seemed particularly interested in the small book. Hawkman shrugged. "Start with that. It's as good as any. It will give you a sense of the time element plus some background information. We'll view the video later."

Grolier made himself comfortable while Hawkman sorted through the items on the table, placing them in chronological order.

The detective glanced up from the diary and pointed his unlit cigar at Hawkman. "Once Jack became the brother-in-law, sure made it convenient for him to drop in on Stowell whenever he traveled to Los Angeles."

Hawkman shook his head in disgust. "You'll see where Jack renewed his relationship with Tonia after Nancy got pregnant."

Grolier scowled. "What a bastard."

"However, later on the relationship cooled off. Either Jack felt guilty or lost interest."

"Huh," the detective sneered. "I doubt he felt guilty about anything."

"Tonia knew him pretty well. From what's in this envelope, I gather she suspected this would happen and wanted to make sure she had enough stuff on him to keep the money coming."

Grolier furrowed his brows. "But it appears her scheme backfired."

Hawkman rolled his shoulders. "Yep, she got greedy. To fuel her demands, she hid a camera in the bedroom and recorded their sexual encounters. Not only that, the camera had audio and caught their conversations. One session even involved an argument about Nancy."

"Man, she sounds like quite a wench," Grolier said. "When did she start blackmailing him?"

"I'd say she had her claws deep in him for about three years. Hard to pinpoint exactly in the diary, but she does allude to the fact that she enjoyed the extra money. But what really struck me odd was the hatred she portrayed toward her sister. Nancy may have suspected some jealousy, but nothing like what Tonia speaks of in that diary. Yet, on the other hand, she spoke very fondly of Tracy. I think the woman had a real psychological problem."

Grolier placed his cold cigar in the ashtray. "You'd think she'd resent the child. Maybe she felt a bond to her because of Jack."

"Hard to say. But I do believe, regardless of how much it may have hurt the little girl later, Tonia would've told Nancy about the affair with great satisfaction if Jack failed to make a payment. The vengence toward her sister overpowered everything else."

Grolier snorted and shook his head. "Boy, it takes all kinds."

Hawkman shuffled through some of the papers then handed him Tonia's phone bill. "You'll notice I've high-lighted a number. That's Jack's answering service. He installed this line three years ago and I believe he installed it for the sole purpose of keeping in touch with Tonia. She used it at least once a month."

Grolier took note and scanned the paper, then glanced up at Hawkman. "What did her bank statements show?"

"A hefty amount of money deposited each month with a sizable increase every six." Hawkman pushed those across the table. "She really socked it to him."

"How the hell did he get by, paying out that much money without Nancy or his office getting suspicious?"

"Good question. I figure he paid her in cash since I found no receipts. However," Hawkman held up a small thin black book. "This little baby is where Stowell recorded each payment."

Grolier raised a brow. "Wonder where Jack's little black book is hidden?"

"If he kept a record, it would more than likely be in code. He's got too much at stake."

The detective chewed on his cold stogie. "How the hell did he get it to her? No one would send this much cash through the mail,"

"I thought about that. So, when I spoke with Becky Titus, Jack's secretary, she confirmed that Gilbert made a trip to Los Angeles at least once a month."

"Anyone ever see him make a delivery?"

"Ellie Mae Williams, Tonia's neighbor, saw Jack come by and drop something into the front door mail slot several times. A simple and safe method, even after their relationship cooled. Ellie Mae knew Jack and thought nothing of his monthly visits. She assumed he left messages to Tonia from her sister."

Grolier picked up a sheet of paper from the table. "So where does this letter about Nancy and Drew fit in?

"Tonia and Drew were the only ones aware of the divorce never getting finalized until Tonia told Jack, adding fuel to her blackmailing scheme." Hawkman waved his hand over the table strewn with evidence. "However, when Drew Harland got out of prison early, it threw a bomb shell into her plans."

"How's that?"

"Well, as you know, she had the key to Drew's safe-deposit box. She didn't expect his early release and didn't have time to set her plan against him into action."

"Good Lord," Grolier said, shaking his head.

Hawkman held up a bundle of letters tied together by a string. "These are letters sent to Nancy from Drew in care of Tonia's address. Tonia never forwarded them, but read every last one. No telling what she had in mind for Harland. Also, in this bunch is a letter Drew wrote Tonia."

"What'd he want?"

"He probably found out through David that Nancy no longer lived with her sister and that she'd gotten married. He wanted Nancy's address and new name. But since Tonia wanted to keep him under her power, she never gave him that information."

Grolier picked up a pen and pulled a pad of paper toward him. "I better make a note to get a subpoena for Drew's personal possessions."

"To late. David sent them to Nancy and she heaved everything into the garbage."

He threw the pen down. "Great. We've probably lost some important evidence."

"Hard to say. Nancy described a cardboard box full of trophies, clothes and a few pictures. Can you imagine all your worldly possessions wrapped up in one small cardboard box?"

The detective let out a sigh. "That's pitiful. What did Jack say about the box of stuff?"

"After he spotted it in the trash, she confessed to him that they weren't legally married."

"Guess that shook him."

"Well, he told her he'd take care of everything. He also instructed her to fire me, that they no longer needed my services. I have a suspicion I make him mighty nervous."

The detective pulled the cigar butt from his lips and chuckled. "I can understand that."

Flashing a sideways glance, Hawkman grinned. "However, there is one thing he never found out about."

Grolier's blue eyes sparkled. "Yeah. What's that?"

Hawkman held up the empty brown envelope. "This. I always had it in my possession and Nancy never told him about it."

"How the hell did she keep that information from him? I'm surprised she didn't tell him at a weak moment."

"Like I said earlier, this package worried and frightened her. She somehow convinced him that the Bible and the letter were the only two things in that safe-deposit box."

The detective's gaze scanned across the table. "Well, I can see that she has every right to be scared."

"Jack knew Tonia had some pretty good evidence on him to keep up the threats." Hawkman waved his hand over the table. "This is what he searched the house for, after killing her. When he didn't find it, he figured it must be in one of the safe-deposit boxes. So he's breathing a little easier at this moment."

"Ha!" Grolier scoffed. "Jack Gilbert is in for one hell of a rude awakening."

Hawkman picked up the police file on Tonia's murder case. "He's one son-of-a-bitch I'd like to see behind bars."

The two men worked silently for two hours before Hawkman stood and stretched. "Think I need a cup of coffee."

Grolier glanced up from his note pad. "Found any hard evidence yet?"

He shook his head. "Everything's circumstantial. I'm convinced with Elliot Washington's and Damon McElroy's testimony that Jack visited Tonia's house the night of the murder. But there's nothing's concrete here. No eyewitnesses or written proof, it's all just hearsay. A lawyer will have one hell of a time convincing a jury."

"Let's keep digging." Grolier got up and refilled his cup. Blowing on the hot brew, he glanced at Hawkman. "You know, I'd sure like to know what really happened that night."

"I've been trying to piece the picture together with what evidence we have. Let's say that Jack went to Tonia's to deliver the monthly pay-off. Considering the position of her body and the cause of death, I'd say they had an argument. She might have threatened to call Nancy or even the police. He grabbed the phone from her, and she attempted to get it back. They scuffle. Then he smacks her with it, knocking her off balance, causing the fall against that sharp edged table which killed her."

Grolier nodded in agreement. "Sounds plausible."

Hawkman dropped his hands to the table. "Yeah, but a good lawyer will get him off."

The detective held up his index finger. "We can prove the driving gloves were his. Which would at least prove he'd been at her house. Pass me that file you have."

Hawkman's face lit up as he scooted the folder across the table. "DNA?"

Grolier held up a piece of paper. "Yep. The gloves we found on the coffee table at her house, matches the ones you sent me. Both sets were worn by Jack and no other human DNA was present."

"Well, that gives us something. Unfortunately, it doesn't place him at the house that night. Those gloves could have been left during any of his previous visits. I'm also running into the same problem placing him with Alvero Rodreges and Alphonso Vernandos at the time they were killed."

"Do the ballistics reports help?"

Hawkman frowned and scooted them toward Grolier.

After reading them, he looked up and grimaced. "What a clever bastard."

"I need to find grounds to search Jack's house and office. I think what I need is in his office safe." Hawkman then went over to the TV and rolled it toward the center of the room. "Right now, this is about the closest we have to any hard evidence of Tonia's and Jack's relationship." He handed Grolier the remote control, slipped in the cassette and flipped off the lights.

Both men sat silently for a few moments as the film began. "My God," Grolier blurted. "Does this woman have no scruples? She knows the video is running, yet, look at what she's doing to him. It doesn't appear she gives a damn."

Hawkman shook his head. "She wanted it to look as bad as she could make it."

Suddenly, a conversation began and Grolier hit the volume button.

"Bet Nancy never made you feel so good?"

Jack jerked away from the folds of her arms. "Keep Nancy out of this."

"Why keep that bitch out of anything. She took you away from me, but one of these days she'll regret it."

Jack sat up and threw his legs over the edge of the bed, his naked body revealed in whole to the camera. "You ever mention our times together and you'll never get another dime from me."

Tonia climbed out of the bed, her oil covered, naked body glistening in the light of the bed lamp. She took a cigarette out of a pack and thumped it on the top of the dresser before lighting it. Blowing smoke into his face, a sly grin etched the corners of her mouth. "Don't worry, darling. As long as you're a good boy, my wretched sister will never know that you seek your sex fantasies with her little sister."

Jack grabbed her arm. "Shut up, Tonia."

Snuffing out her cigarette, she worked herself between his legs, closing the gap between them. She rubbed her hands over every inch of his body, smearing it with some sort of oil until you could see his breathing deepen. He wrapped his legs around her and pulled her upon the bed atop him.

"I think I've seen enough," Grolier said, punching the off button. "What a bitch."

Just at the moment Hawkman flipped on the lights, the phone rang. The detective answered it and handed it to Hawkman. "For you."

He listened intently, his expression grim. When he hung up, he turned to Grolier. "Something's coming down."

CHAPTER TWENTY ONE

That same day, Nancy finished the family's laundry and headed for her bedroom to put away the last of the folded clothes. When she attempted to put her underwear into the dresser drawer, they wouldn't fit. "That's odd," she said aloud and reached inside to shift things around. Her hand bumped something hard and she pulled out a wooden box. "Oh my gosh. I forgot all about these letters." She dropped the clothes into the drawer and glanced at the clock.

Jack wouldn't be home for another hour and a half. She sat cross-legged in the middle of the floor and slowly opened the lid. Taking a deep breath, she put Tonia's letter aside then proceeded to thumb through the ones from David. Using the postmarks as a guide she stacked them in order of date. Her hands trembled slightly when she pulled the first letter from it's envelope.

After an hour, with a dismal expression on her face, she returned them all to the box and carried it to the kitchen. Fearful that Jack might walk in any moment, she slid the small chest into a paper sack and stuck it up in the cabinet.

She reached for the phone, but the minute the familiar click came over the line, she hung up quickly. Shoving her hair behind her ears, she stood for a moment in thought, drumming her nails on the cabinet. She glanced up at the clock and calculated she didn't have to pick up Tracy for another forty-five minutes, but Jack could be home within the next fifteen. Grabbing her purse, she yanked the sack from the cabinet and raced for her car. She sped toward Tom Casey's office, checking her rear view mirror periodically. Then, suddenly she spotted the white Cadillac round the corner, two cars behind her.

She hit the steering wheel with the palm of her hand. "Damn him." Trying to think, she remembered seeing pay phones located inside one of the stores at the mall and quickly pulled into the underground garage.

Checking over her shoulder to make sure Jack hadn't followed, she hurried inside and ducked into the store where she'd seen the phones. She kept her eyes on the front entrance while dialing.

Shocked by the female voice that answered, she almost hung up. "Tom Casey, Private Investigator, May I help you?"

"Uh, this is an emergency. I need to talk to Mr. Casey."

"Nancy, is that you?"

"Yes."

"This is Jennifer. He's out of town for a couple of days. Can I help?"

Nancy felt the panic rising in her chest. "No, I really need to talk to him."

"There's a possibility he'll be in late tonight. I'll have him contact you first thing in the morning."

"No! He mustn't call my house. I'll call him."

Jennifer's voice remained calm. "That's fine, I'll let him know you want to get in touch."

Nancy hung up, gnawing her lower lip. Still looking for any signs of Jack, she moved away from the phone area and entered the interior of the store. She picked up an item from the shelf and went through the check out counter.

❧·❀·❧·❀·❧·❀·❧

Hawkman hung up and turned to Grolier. "Jennifer just got a call from a frantic Nancy Gilbert. Said she needed to talk to me immediately."

Grolier gestured toward the phone. "Give her a call."

"Can't. She left instructions not to contact her home. Jack must still be recording her conversations."

The detective tapped his pencil on the table, his expression serious. "We've done about all we can for now. Why don't you take off and find out what's going on. Anything she has to add can only help."

Hawkman rubbed the back of his neck. "You sure you don't want me to stay and help wrap it up?"

"No. This could be very important and you need to contact her as soon as possible. I can handle this end. I'll get in touch with Detective Brogan in Medford, get the paperwork done here and fly up on Saturday. We'll be ready to make our move no later than Monday morning."

Hawkman held out his hand. "It's been a pleasure working with you."

"Same goes here. Grab your coat and hat. I'll take you to the airport."

⟨⊹⟩⋈⟨⊹⟩⋈⟨⊹⟩⋈⟨⊹⟩⋈⟨⊹⟩

Hawkman flew home that night and arrived in his office Friday morning at nine o'clock. While hanging up his hat and jacket, the phone rang.

He reached across the desk and pushed the speaker button. Nancy's urgent voice came over the line. "Mr. Casey, thank God you're back. Jack's out of town and I desperately need to see you."

"I'll be here."

Fifteen minutes later, a soft knock sounded on his office door.

He discretely closed the Gilbert file and placed a piece of paper across the identifying label. "Come in."

When Nancy entered, he motioned toward the chair in front of his desk. "Have a seat."

He watched her unsteady stride and noticed her ashen face, along with the small box she held so tightly that her knuckles had turned white. She sat down stiffly.

"Jennifer told me you'd called."

She lifted the lid off the box and tilted it toward him.

Hawkman gazed at a bunch of envelopes stuffed inside. "What are those?"

"Letters sent to Drew while he was in prison."

Puzzled, he looked up at her. "Where'd you get them?"

"They were in Drew's stuff that David sent me. I hid the box and truly forgot about them until yesterday."

Hawkman furrowed his brow. Letters sent to Drew, this could be the link that ties these people together, he thought. "I'm listening."

"I read every one of them and am convinced that after Drew received his letter from the lawyer, he had David find out where Tonia lived. He wrote her for my address, not knowing that she'd already read the letter to me about the illegal divorce." She pulled one of the envelopes from the box and handed it to him. "Tonia told him in so many words not to bother her."

Hawkman read it and let out a whistle. "Doesn't appear she was about to tell him anything."

Nancy shook her head. "No. But Drew asked David to keep an eye on Tonia's place." She paused and took a deep breath.

Hawkman held up his hand. "Wait, I'm confused. I thought David wanted nothing to do with Drew's personal business."

"Oh, I doubt Drew leveled with him or he wouldn't have done anything to help him." Then she hesitated, her voice caught as she glanced down at her hands in her lap. "In a couple of the letters David mentions Jack going to Tonia's house."

Hawkman noticed the tears rimming her eyes.

She looked up at him. "I wanted to get through this without crying."

"Take all the time you need," he assured her.

Taking a deep breath, she proceeded. "I haven't been completely honest with you, Mr. Casey. My sister and Jack had an affair shortly after our marriage, or I should say, continued their affair."

He knew this, but asked. "How can you be so sure?"

She again stared down at her hands. "I had him followed."

Hawkman leaned back in his chair. This wasn't coming easy for her. "I see. Once you found out, what did you do?"

"Being pregnant at the time, I decided to wait and see if things improved after Tracy was born."

"Did they?"

"Yes. Our personal relationship got better and I had a feeling the affair had ended so I never approached Jack about it. Shortly afterwards, I noticed our bank balance growing smaller."

He continued to probe her gently. "What did Jack say about that?"

"That his clientele had dropped off, plus the mortgage had gone up. Even though I let him think I believed his story, I became suspicious of a blackmailing scheme by Tonia."

"What made you think it was Tonia and not some other woman?"

"She began to buy very expensive things. Like the house, a brand new car and started wearing designer clothes. Like I told you, she knew how to budget, but I knew she didn't make that kind of money. Putting two and two together, I figured she'd been blackmailing Jack for a long time. Then, after she died, I discovered she didn't owe a dime on anything. It pretty well confirmed my suspicions."

It relieved Hawkman that Nancy had sorted this out, even though he knew it had hit her hard. Because it wouldn't be long before he had to tell her things that would truly break her heart. The more she could decipher for herself, the better.

"Did you ever approach Jack on the subject?"

She shook her head. "No. I figured since I'd end up with her property and money, we'd get most of it back, so no big deal. But it just isn't working out like I thought it would, Mr. Casey. The heartache of the affair is over. But now that she and Drew are dead, my life will never be the same."

Hawkman leaned forward, picked up a pencil from the desk and held it between his two hands. "No it won't be, Nancy. And there are things I have to tell you that aren't going to make it any easier. One thing is that Jack has known for a long time that your marriage is not legal."

Astonishment showed on her face. "I don't believe you. He would have done something about it."

"His hands were tied. Tonia held the original letter and used it as part of her blackmailing scheme. Drew held the other one and thought he'd be able to woo you back. But now Drew's dead and you have the original letter. So, move ahead with whatever needs to be done."

She sat up straight and put her hands on the edge of the desk. Her eyes reflected that things were coming together. "Jack's a lawyer. He could have gone to the county and gotten a copy of the letter if he so desired."

If anyone ever underestimated this lady, they were wrong, Hawkman thought, dropping the pencil onto the desk. "You're right. He could have handled it other ways."

She looked him in the eye. "There's something else you're not telling me." Her voice dropped to a whisper. "The safe-deposit box, right?"

"Yes." Hawkman nodded.

"The stuff inside proved what I've just told you, didn't it?"

"Yes. And more."

She slumped back in the chair. "I knew I didn't want to open that big envelope." Looking down, she began shredding the tissue she had in her hands. Tears started running down her cheeks. Her speech softened. "At first, I really thought Drew killed Tonia, but not anymore. I'm afraid Jack murdered her."

"Why Jack? He has too much at stake."

"I saw Jack's hatred for Tonia growing after their affair ended. He'd even leave town when she came to visit." She sobbed softly. "Tonia had a way about her. Once she got her hold on you, she could torment a person with a look or a laugh. There were times when I spotted her bitterness toward me for taking Jack away from her."

"But animosity doesn't always drive a person to murder." Hawkman said, pushing steadily for her to relate as many of her suspicions as she possibly could unload without breaking.

"I know. Maybe I'm jumping to conclusions and it worries me constantly. But look how strange he's been acting." She threw her hands up in question. "He records my phone calls and follows me. Why is he doing it?"

"Because he's afraid of what I'm finding out. That's why he'd like me out of the picture."

She nodded. "You're probably right on that."

"You realize there's more to this than just the letter about your divorce? Tonia started on Jack long before that ever arrived. He hoped to call her bluff, but the items she threatened him with would have destroyed his political career."

Nancy let out a long sigh and dabbed her eyes. "Now I'm beginning to understand why he insisted on going through all the boxes and the drawers in her furniture. When I questioned him, he told me he was just curious." Then she sat up straight and pointed a finger at Hawkman. "He wanted the things in that envelope, right?"

"Yes."

"Oh dear God." She slumped back into her chair. "Now I know why it frightened me." Searching Hawkman's face, she asked. "Do I want to see them?"

Hawkman's gaze dropped to the small box now on his desk. "I'm not sure, Nancy. But right now, they're in the custody of the police."

She stiffened and her eyes widened with fear.

CHAPTER TWENTY TWO

Saturday morning, after Hawkman picked up Detective Grolier at the Medford airport, they went straight to the police station where they met Detective Brogan who'd been assigned to the case. After introductions and a quick run through of plans, they headed for Jack Gilbert's office, followed by two patrol cars and a crime van with a specialized crew.

Surprised to find the door unlocked, Brogan poked his head inside and called out, "Police."

Damon McElroy limped out of his office with a puzzled look on his face. "May I help you?"

Brogan stepped forward. "Mr. McElroy, we have a warrant to search the premises."

McElroy's expression changed to surprise. "What for?"

"Police business."

"Does Mr. Gilbert know about this?" McElroy asked.

"I doubt it," the detective said. "Which office is Gilbert's?"

He pointed toward Jack's door.

"Just have a seat out here. We won't be long."

Nervously, McElroy sat down at Ms Titus' empty desk and watched the officers troop past him. A couple of the uniformed men stopped in the reception area, one at the door and one at the entry of the hallway as Brogan, Grolier, Hawkman and the crew disappeared into Jack's office.

While the men worked in front of the safe, Hawkman and Grolier went through Jack's desk. Brogan started with the wall shelves and flipped through the pages of every law book in sight.

"I've found nothing in the desk that applies to this case," Hawkman said.

"Neither have I," Grolier answered.

The locksmith, part of the specialized crew, stood and faced Hawkman and the detective. "There you go," he said opening the door to the vault. "This is an old baby and the tumblers were easy to hear. Made it a lot easier." He glanced inside the safe and held up his hand. "Hold on a second. I see this has one of those inner compartments, let me get that open too."

Within a couple of minutes, he straightened. "It's all yours."

He backed away as Hawkman and Grolier slipped on gloves and knelt in front of the opened vault. Grolier soon held up a couple of papers between his thumb and forefinger. "Here are two receipts that definitely implicates him with the money deposited into the Master's account."

Hawkman nodded and continued filling a box with papers. Then his face lit up. "Here's the barrel pac. I figured it'd be in here."

They were soon finished and left the office as quickly as they'd come.

⋅⊰×⊱×⊰×⊱×⊰×⊱×⊰×⊱⋅

Early afternoon, Jack, Nancy and Tracy returned from the outskirts of town where they'd attended a political fund raising picnic.

"I need to run by the office and pick up some papers before we go home," Jack said.

Nancy frowned. "I hoped we'd be able to relax and spend the evening together."

"Sorry, honey, but I have court Monday morning and have to get the brief ready."

When he pulled into the complex and saw the police cars out front, he quickly sped past his office and went out the back exit of the parking lot.

Nancy's face registered surprise. "Don't you think we should stop and see what's wrong?"

Jack's jaw tightened and he gripped the steering wheel, his knuckles glazed white. "I don't want to stop with Tracy in the car," he whispered.

When he reached their house and pulled into the driveway, he didn't kill the engine. "You and Tracy go on inside, I'll be back shortly." He impatiently thumped his thigh with the heel of his hand while Nancy got Tracy and her toys from the backseat of the car. "Hurry up, I want to get back to the office and see what's going on."

As soon as Nancy shut the car door, Jack backed out of the driveway and took off. He pulled into the complex just in time to see the police van round the corner out of sight. Jumping from his car, he dashed into the building. Damon McElroy, his shoulders slumped, stood at Jack's office door staring at the opened safe.

Jack brushed past him. "How the hell did they get it open?"

"A locksmith from the specialized police force," McElroy said.

"They have no right to come in here and open my private safe." Jack knelt down and examined the interior. "Damn," he mumbled. "They've taken everything."

McElroy didn't move, his gaze fixed on the interior of the large square box. "I'm sorry Mr. Gilbert, I couldn't do a thing. They had a warrant. But tell me. Why would they crack your safe?"

Jack's mind focused on what the police had confiscated and his thoughts churned over his legal rights. Somehow he'd get his personal belongings back. Then he glanced up, realizing McElroy was patiently waiting for an answer. "I'll handle the problem. It doesn't concern you, so don't worry about it."

With his hands in his pockets, the young lawyer followed Jack into the outer office. "I'd like to know what's going on. If it has something to do with the firm, it does involve me."

"It's all personal stuff and has nothing to do with the firm." Jack rubbed his hand over his chin and paced the floor. "Look, McElroy, I need to think. Why don't you go on home and I'll talk to you later."

⊹⊱⋆⊰⊹⊱⋆⊰⊹

Nancy stood at the kitchen sink fixing Tracy a snack. When she glanced out the window, her stomach turned into a knot. A police van and two patrol cars had stopped in front of her house. She recognized the silhouette of Tom Casey getting out of one the cars and knew something had gone wrong. Her heart skipped a beat. She dropped the dish cloth into the sink and glanced down at her daughter. Should she flee out the back door with Tracy or stay there? Before she had a chance to make a decision, the doorbell rang and Tracy jumped off her stool.

"I'll get it, Mommy."

She grabbed the child and set her back on the seat. "No, Tracy, you stay right here. Mommy will answer the door."

The first thing that met her eyes was the search warrant held up by one of the police officers. His voice sounded far away. Her vision blurred as she stared at the troop of men filing past, she thought she was going to pass out. Shaking her head, she leaned against the wall just as Hawkman walked through the door. She grabbed his arm. "Mr. Casey, what's going on?"

He looked down at her. "I'm sorry, Nancy, we've got to search the house."

"But I thought you had everything you needed in the envelope?"

"Unfortunately, it's only the tip of the iceberg."

She felt her blood turn cold in her veins as she dropped her hand from his arm and watched him move down the hallway behind the two detectives.

⊱･❖･❖･❖･❖･❖･⊰

Grolier opened every door, peering into each room and closet. Soon, his eyebrows arched when he came to what appeared to be an office. "I think this is where we want to start."

"I'll go to the Master Bedroom," Brogan stated, and continued down the hall."

Hawkman and Grolier put on rubber gloves, and with extreme care, removed all of Jack's guns and ammunition from the gun case. They wrapped each weapon separately, then an officer carried them to the police van. Once they emptied the gun case, they turned to the desk and removed anything that might be pertinent to the investigation.

In the master bedroom, Brogan had discovered some shirts with suspicious looking stains in Jack's closet. He placed them in plastic bags, along with several pairs of shoes.

Meanwhile, Nancy hurried into the kitchen and picked up the phone, only to be stopped by an officer. She stared at him when he took the phone from her hand and hung it up. "Sorry m'am, you can't call anyone until we're through."

Panic gripped her. She lifted Tracy into her arms, who by now had sensed her mother's fear and started to whimper.

"Shh, honey, it's okay. Tell you what, let's go get an ice cream." She headed out the kitchen door, but before she could get into her car, she was stopped again by an officer posted outside.

"Sorry, m'am, you can't leave right now."

Frustrated and frightened, she fled back into the house and searched the rooms for Hawkman. When she finally spotted him coming out of Jack's office, she stepped in front of him. "Mr. Casey, I need to get Tracy out of here, but there are police all over the place and they won't let me leave."

Hawkman glanced at Detective Brogan coming down the hall, his arms loaded with plastic bags. "Go watch television or read your daughter a story, Mrs. Gilbert. We won't be much longer."

A chill ran down her spine when she recognized Jack's personal belongings inside the clear plastic bags. Her breath came in ragged spurts as she carried Tracy into the den. An officer guarded the door and watched her nestle the child close beside her on the couch. Determined to remain strong, in spite of her trembling insides, she patted the child's arm and forced a smile. "Mommy will read you a story and everything will be all right."

⊹⊱∗⊰⊹⊱∗⊰⊹⊱∗⊰⊹

When Jack rounded the corner and saw the host of police cars at his house, his grip tightened on the steering wheel. He whirled into the driveway, bounded from the car and dashed into the house. Two officers immediately brought him to a standstill.

"What the hell's going on?" he yelled.

"There's my daddy," Tracy cried, climbing off the couch.

Nancy grabbed her. "Just a minute, honey, mommy will go with you."

Grolier packed the last of the stuff into a box and groaned as he got to his feet. "Not as young as I used to be." When he heard Jack's booming voice, he threw a hard look at Hawkman. "Our boy is here."

Hawkman nodded. "Yeah, I hear."

Grolier shifted his weight and started toward the kitchen, his unlit cigar clenched between his teeth. Detective Brogan walked in the front door after depositing his evidence in the van. The detectives entered the kitchen together and the two officers stepped away from Jack, allowing Nancy and Tracy to move closer to his side.

Grolier took the warrant from one of the officers and displayed it. "Mr. Gilbert, we have a search warrant that includes your office, home, and car. May I have the keys?"

Jack glared at him. "You're invading my privacy. I'm not giving them to you."

"Mr. Gilbert, I'd advise you to cooperate, because you're in a heap of trouble." The detective held out his hand. "The keys, please."

Jack threw them on the floor. Grolier scooped them up and handed them to one of the officers. "Take one of the technicians with you."

"I want to know what's going on," Jack demanded. He glanced around the room and spotted Hawkman. His eyes narrowed. "And what the hell are you doing here?"

Hawkman returned his stare, but remained silent.

Detective Brogan stepped forward. "Mr. Gilbert, you're under investigation for murder. I'd advise you to seek counsel. And do not, under any circumstances, leave town."

Nancy felt her knees buckle and the blood drain from her face. Jack grabbed her as she swayed against him. He glared at Hawkman who also reached out to catch her. "I'll take care of my wife."

Fighting for control, but still dazed, Nancy groped for her daughter's hand and stumbled out of the room with the child in tow. No officer stopped her this time.

Once they were out of ear shot, Jack whirled around and faced the detectives. "Murder! And just who the hell did I murder?"

Brogan stared into his face. "Tonia Stowell, Alphonso Vernandos and Alvero Rodreges."

For a split second, Jack's mouth twitched. "Why the hell would I kill my wife's sister? And I've never even heard of the other two." He glanced nervously out the kitchen window. Neighbors had gathered in their front yards, gaping at the police activity. Turning around, he glared at Hawkman and asked in a low voice, "Why are you doing this to me? Just look out there." He waved his arm toward the front yard. "My neighbors think something awful has happened."

Hawkman glared at him. "It has. It's called murder."

⊹⊱⊰⊹⊱⊰⊹⊱⊰⊹

After the police and their vehicles finally left, Jack found himself alone in the kitchen. He walked aimlessly down the hall and went into the room he used as his home office. The sight caused his gut to tighten. His gun cabinet stood naked against the wall, its doors ajar. The desk had been gutted and the drawers left open. Letting loose a string of obscenities, Jack stormed from the room, slamming the door behind him. He leaned his head against the jamb for a few moments, then pushed away and moved toward the master bedroom.

When he turned into the room, his gaze went immediately to his closet. Glancing at the floor, he noticed several pairs of shoes missing. He frantically pushed hangers to one side and soon discovered two of his shirts were gone. "What the hell," he swore, shoving the sliding closet door shut with a bang.

He whirled around to see Nancy standing in the doorway watching him, her eyes wide with fear.

"Jack, what's happening?"

Brushing past her, he spat out, "Nothing."

She followed him down the hallway and into the kitchen. Standing back, she watched him fling open one of the cabinet doors and grab a glass. Without a word, he filled it with ice cubes from the freezer, then headed for the liquor cabinet. He poured the glass full of Scotch, took a large gulp and walked into the television room, where he plopped down on the couch beside Tracy. "Can daddy watch the program with his little sweetheart?"

"Sure daddy," she said, climbing into his lap.

He looked up at Nancy, whose eyes seethed with anger. She reached a hand out toward Tracy. "Come on, honey, it's time for your bath."

"Oh, not now, mommy," she whined. "Daddy's going to watch television with me."

"Maybe another night. It's getting late."

Reluctantly, Tracy slid off the couch and took her mother's hand. Halfway down the hall, Nancy called over her shoulder. "I'll talk to you later, Jack."

Suddenly, he jumped up. Not seeing his car keys on the cabinet, he grabbed the extra set off the key holder and dashed outside. He opened the trunk of his car and stood staring at the interior. He closed his eyes and leaned his head heavily against the metal edge. "Damn, they even took my tire jack."

He let the lid drop back into place and sauntered back into the house. Tossing the keys onto the coffee table, he went back into the television room and sank down into the couch. Picking up his drink, he took long gulp and stared at the screen.

CHAPTER TWENTY THREE

Hawkman and the two detectives waited in a small conference room inside the police lab for preliminary test results. They indulged in small talk and cups of coffee to help pass the time.

Soon, a lab assistant brought in a stack of papers and placed them on a round table in the center of the room. Detective Brogan picked up the first report and sat down.

Grolier, his unlit cigar clenched between his teeth, put on his reading glasses, picked up the next report and took a place at the table. Hawkman did the same. An hour passed before anyone spoke.

Finally, Brogan leaned forward, placing his elbows on the table. "Mr. Casey, we've got a problem."

Hawkman glanced at him. "What's that?"

"Putting Jack Gilbert at the scene of any of these crimes."

Hawkman tapped his pencil on the table. "I know. I've been thinking about that."

Detective Grolier started to speak when one of the technicians came scurrying into the room carrying a file box.

"This container came from Mr. Gilbert's car trunk. Thought you might be interested in what's inside."

The three stood as the man placed the box on the table. His hands protected by latex gloves, he scooted several file folders aside and tilted the box toward them.

Hawkman let out a low whistle at the sight of the Smith & Wesson .38 revolver.

"Put this gun as top priority," Brogan ordered. "Go over it thoroughly, then send it to ballistics."

Grolier stepped toward the technician. "Before you go, may I see one of those files?"

The man handed the detective a pair of latex gloves from his pocket. After tugging them on, Grolier examined one of the folders, then took another from the box. Hawkman and Brogan looked on with puzzled expressions.

After flipping through several, Grolier ripped off the gloves and sat back down at the table. "You can take them away now."

"What was that all about?" Hawkman asked, slipping into the chair next to him.

"Those files are not only old, they're not even Jack Gilbert's. They're a worthless bunch of prop material."

"It looks like Mr. Gilbert thought himself pretty clever hiding an identical gun in his trunk," Brogan said, shaking his head. "Hasn't he been a lawyer long enough to know that we'd eventually find it?"

Hawkman stared at the center of the table, rubbing his chin, then suddenly snapped his fingers.

Grolier jerked his head around. "I think a light bulb just went off under that cowboy hat."

"You're right," Hawkman said, coming out of his chair. "Excuse me for a few minutes. I've got some phone calls to make."

After twenty minutes, he strolled back into the room, his face grim. "I should have checked this out some time ago."

"What?" Grolier asked.

"I had a hunch and contacted my attorney friend. There hasn't been a lawyers' convention anywhere in the states for the past six months."

"What are you talking about?" Brogan asked, his forehead creased.

Hawkman thumped a forefinger on the table. "Jack Gilbert told Nancy and me, that he had made plans to attend a lawyers' convention back east. There was no way I could talk him out of it. I even saw the airline tickets and a rental car packet at his home. Unfortunately, I never questioned him on it. He not only fooled me, but lied to his wife. I've got a suspicion that Jack made a trip to Los Angeles instead. Jennifer is checking with the airlines right now. She'll call as soon as she finds out anything. If they won't give her the information, we might have to get a court order."

"Why would he go to Los Angeles?" Brogan asked.

"Jack Gilbert wanted Drew Harland dead. But he didn't want to do the job himself. Since I had surveillance on his house twenty four hours a day, he had to come up with some believable distraction that would keep us off his tail. That's where Coty Masters figures in. Jack knew the robbery story and after a few contacts with the inmate, discovered that Coty could supply a hit man on the outside. But, first, Jack had to deposit the money agreed upon into Mrs. Masters' account. Once that was accomplished, Coty set up the contact from inside the prison walls. Then Jack had to meet the hit man in Los Angeles to make the arrangements."

Grolier carefully placed his cigar butt on a saucer. "We found two deposit slips in Gilbert's safe, each for fifteen thousand dollars. The numbers matched Serene Masters' bank account. We also discovered the Soledad prison phone numbers on Jack's bills. He'd made several calls from his office. However, like Casey says, Gilbert's a lawyer and could be representing Coty in a case or any number of the prisoners. So again, some defense lawyer could tear that apart."

"Why two fifteen thousand dollar deposits?" Brogan asked.

Hawkman faced him. "Vernandos failed in his attempt to assassinate Drew. Then, when Jack's bullet didn't do the trick, he had to pay Masters another fifteen thousand for the set up at the hospital. We all know from the autopsy, that somebody pumped Harland full of heroin."

"Did anyone ever talk to Coty Masters?" Brogan asked.

"I tried," Hawkman said. "Not cooperative. He's in for life and doesn't want to jeopardize his contacts outside the walls. So, I doubt we'll ever get anything out of him."

"That's going to make it hard to prove Jack set this whole thing up," Brogan stated.

At that moment, an assistant from the lab poked her head in the door. "Mr. Casey, you have a phone call."

Hawkman returned within a few minutes and slapped his hands together. "It took Jennifer a little while, but she finally contacted someone who agreed to check the records of the airlines. Jack Gilbert made a flight to Los Angeles on the same day he was supposed to have gone back east. He returned two days earlier than he told Nancy. Just as I suspected."

"Okay, so we might have something going there," Brogan said. "What's our next move?"

He had to rent a vehicle when he returned. Also, he had to stay some place where he wouldn't be seen or recognized. So, we need to check the car rental agencies here in town. And do a run down on the motels."

"I'll get some men on that immediately. Maybe we can find something," Brogan said. "But how do we convict him of these other murders? I realize we're closer on Stowell's case than any, but even a good lawyer could prove her death accidental."

Hawkman gave an audible sigh and shook his head. "Yeah, I know. It's not going to be easy.

"How do you think he got Vernandos to that alley? Brogan asked.

"I assume Jack conned him with a pay off. Of course, we have no proof. Vernandos had all of twenty dollars in his pocket."

Then, there's the Rodreges deal," Hawkman said. "Jack hired a migrant worker to tail me. The guy didn't know nada. Afraid he might spill the beans of where he got the extra money, Jack got rid of him. Our only hope is that the lab can match up the impressions they took of some shoe prints at the scene, with a pair we confiscated from Jack's closet. Also the tire prints in the area. We hope to connect them to the Cadillac. That report should come out soon. Now, I'm hoping this other gun might help."

"Not to mention the barrel pac we found in Gilbert's safe," Grolier interjected. "However, we can't depend on ballistics. All the bullets were in pretty bad shape."

Detective Brogan glanced at his watch. "We have our work cut out for us. So, this is a good time to take a break and get a bite to eat."

⟨·‡·⟩⊷⟨·‡·⟩⊷⟨·‡·⟩⊷⟨·‡·⟩

After Nancy tucked Tracy into bed, she went back into the den where she found Jack slouched in the over-stuffed chair, his eyes glazed as he stared at the television. His drunken condition fueled her anger. She folded her arms and stood in front of the screen, blocking his view.

"Hey, you got a problem?" he slurred. "Get the hell out of the way. I'm trying to watch a program."

"I don't have a problem, but you do." She reached behind her and turned off the the set. "You're about to be arrested for murder, yet you're sitting there drunk."

"For God's sake, Nancy, I haven't killed anyone."

"That's not what the police think. Do you have a lawyer lined up?"

"I don't need a lawyer. Remember, I am one. Anyway, I haven't done anything wrong."

She stared at him hard and long. "Why do the police think you killed Tonia?"

"They're crazy, that's why." A sly grin curled the corners of his mouth as he got up, shook his head, and staggered into the kitchen.

Nancy followed him. "Why didn't you tell me that you knew our marriage wasn't legal."

"Now, how the hell would I have known that?" he asked, fixing himself another drink.

Nancy leaned against the counter and glared at him. "Because Tonia told you."

Without answering, he stuck his finger in his drink and twirled the ice cube.

She continued her tirade. "You had an affair, or I should say "picked up where you'd left off," with Tonia when I became pregnant."

He brushed by her and headed back into the den. "Good Lord, Nancy, who's been feeding you that garbage? Your private investigator?"

She clenched her fist as she trailed behind him. "No, Jack. I hired an investigator in Los Angeles when I got suspicious of you two."

He whirled around and shook a finger in the air. "Ah, ha! So, the truth is out. You didn't trust me?"

She took a deep breath and brushed wisps of hair out of her

face. "No, I didn't. But, after Tracy's birth, things seemed to get better, so I decided to forget about the affair so we could get on with our lives. Until I started noticing our bank account growing smaller. Tonia started blackmailing you, didn't she?"

He shook his head, swaggered out of the den and headed for the bedroom. "Shit, you don't know what you're talking about."

Nancy gritted her teeth and hissed. "Jack, we need to talk. Don't turn your back on me."

"I don't have anything else to say," he yelled over his shoulder.

Nancy put her hands on her hips and stood at the head of the hallway. "Well, that envelope that Tonia had in her safe-deposit box sure must have said a lot, because the police are certainly interested in you."

He raced back and grabbed her arm, squeezing it hard. "What envelope? What the hell are you talking about?"

She winced. "Stop it, you're hurting me."

His eyes narrowed. "You never told me there was anything else in that box."

She met his stare and yanked her arm from his grip. "You never asked. But yes, there was more.."

He stepped closer. "How the hell did the police get it?" His voice curled with contempt.

Nancy rubbed her arm and backed away. "I gave Mr. Casey permission to open it. I didn't want to be hurt anymore."

His eyes ablaze, he slapped her hard. "You bitch! How could you do that to me?"

Stunned and shocked, she stumbled backwards, tears rolling down her cheeks. "How dare you lay a hand on me after what you've done," she gasped.

He stepped toward her. She put her hands up in defense and retreated toward the kitchen. "Don't touch me."

As she passed the stove, she grabbed a long butcher knife from the wooden block and flicked it back and forth in front of her body. "Stay away from me."

He stopped and put his hands up in surrender. "I'm sorry, honey, I lost control. I've had too much to drink. You know I don't go for that sort of thing, so put that knife down. It's dangerous."

She gripped the handle even harder.

His voice softened. "If you'd only told me, we could have opened the envelope together. Now, we don't even know what it contained." He cocked his head and narrowed his eyes. "Or do you?"

Her chin trembled and she shook her head. "No. And I never want to know."

"There could be some incriminating evidence inside it."

She stopped moving the knife, a puzzled expression crossed her face. "What kind of evidence?"

"Something that might make me a prime suspect to Tonia's murder. It could ruin my future. I never intended to kill her, only scare her a bit."

Her eyes wide, Nancy stared at him in disbelief.

CHAPTER TWENTY FOUR

Jack stepped toward Nancy with his arms out-stretched. "Honey, you have to believe me, I didn't mean to kill her."

She stood rigid and brought the knife up in a threatening manner. "Stay back."

He dropped his hands and turned away. "Tonia got greedy. She kept wanting more of our money. I couldn't stand it anymore." He faced her again, his eyes pleading. "I told her the blackmailing had to halt. She laughed in my face. Then, she threatened to call you. When she picked up the phone, I grabbed it away from her, but she came at me, clawing the air with those horrible long red fingernails. She looked like some sort of a witch. That's when I hit her."

Nancy stared at him as he emulated his actions, his eyes darted around the room.

"It wasn't a hard blow, but it knocked her off balance and she stumbled backwards. She fell over the ottoman and didn't get up." He stopped a moment and rubbed his temples, then looked back at Nancy. "I yelled at her and told her to quit play-acting, but she didn't make a sound. I went over to help her up and that's when I realized she'd hit her head on the corner of that damned glass table. I thought at first she'd just been knocked out until I saw the puddle of blood under her head and those glassy orbs."

Even though Nancy's heart ached, she never took her gaze off Jack. "Why didn't you call the police?" Her voice caught. "At least they wouldn't think of you as a murderer." When Jack looked at her, she noted how waxy and dull his eyes appeared.

"I couldn't let the police come in there and find all the stuff she had on me. I had to find it first. So I went through that house with a fine tooth comb. I didn't find a damn thing and couldn't figure out what she'd done with it."

Nancy couldn't take her eyes off him. "I don't understand. What did she have that was so damaging?"

He looked at her blankly as if he hadn't heard a word she said. "There's no way the police can prove I killed her."

Her eyes filled with tears. "My only sister. My last living relative." she whispered. "Killed by my husband."

He reached toward her, but she jerked out of her inner thoughts and flashed the knife. "Stay away from me, Jack."

"Honey, don't you realize Tonia hated you? She detested your beauty, your hair, your body and most of all, she loathed the idea that you had the daughter she wanted so badly. The woman wrapped herself in jealousy and greed."

Nancy wiped her eyes with the back of her hand and lowered the knife. "I don't believe you. She loved coming here to see me and Tracy."

He shook his fist at her. "Don't you understand what I'm saying. Yes, Tonia loved Tracy." Then, he poked his thumb into his chest. "And me. That's what she told me, Nancy. Your sister was sick."

A chill ran up her spine. And you're not? she thought. Jack Gilbert, you're a very sick man.

"Then to make matters worse, that stupid Drew got out of jail early and made our lives miserable." Jack rubbed the stubble on his chin. "How the hell did you ever get mixed up with that creep?"

Goose bumps lifted on her arms. "What does Drew have to do with Tonia's murder?"

He continued as if never hearing her question. "Just think of all the problems he'd have caused if he was still alive. Not only did he want you back, but he'd have tried his hand at a bit of blackmail." He pointed a finger at her. "Just think about it. An ex-husband, ex-con. The minute he learned I wanted to go into politics, he'd sure as hell have taken every bit of my money to keep quiet. And I wouldn't have had a dime left to cover my campaign expenses."

Nancy's mouth dropped open. "You killed Drew?"

He looked at her with glazed eyes. "I couldn't let him live."

"Jack, we need to find some help for you."

He rolled his head back and laughed. "Sure, so you can hire more private investigators." He advanced toward her with his palms up. "Now, if Mr. Casey uncovers the rest of this damn mess, I'll end up in jail. Then, my little wife, where would that put you?"

Startled by his movement, she stepped back and held up the knife. "Don't come any closer."

He waved his hand in front of him. "Put that damn thing down. I'm not going to hurt you."

Her stomach cramped in knots. "Jack, what more could Mr. Casey uncover?"

"Like that first idiot who drove around our house looking for Drew. He didn't have any brains and Casey's crew got suspicious."

She furrowed her brow. "But you weren't even in town. You were back east at the lawyer's convention."

He waved a hand in the air and shook his head. "I didn't go to any damned convention. I made that up so you wouldn't run to your investigator."

She felt the perspiration beading on her forehead. "So where did you go?"

"Los Angeles."

"Why?"

"To meet the contact Coty had arranged." A grin twitched the corners of his mouth. "You remember Coty, don't you?"

She felt the blood drain from her face. "Drew's partner in that robbery."

"Yep," he nodded. "But that guy turned out to be an idiot too, just like the rest. He fired one shot at Drew and figured that scared him off. So when he wanted to collect his pay, I shot him through the head. No mess, no noise. Except, the police took the shirt I'd worn that day that had his brains splattered on it." He turned his back to her and stared at the wall. "Damn, I should have thrown it away or better yet, burned it."

Nancy tasted bile in the back of her throat and swallowed hard to keep the waves of nausea from coming up. It occurred to her, that in his state of mind she should choose her words carefully so as not to trigger him to turn against her. Then her repulsion turned to fear and her heart pounded loudly in her ears. Even though she'd not taken her eyes off him, she jumped when he suddenly slapped his thigh and turned toward her.

"Then there's that migrant worker. You know why I hired him?"

She didn't even know what he was talking about, but silently shook her head.

"Because of your damn private investigator."

When he suddenly took a step toward her, Nancy stiffened and held the knife out. "Back off."

He drooped his shoulders and motioned for her to lower the knife. "My sweet and beautiful Nancy, I wouldn't hurt you. Just looking at you is sheer heaven. Why, with you at my side, I could be president in a few years. Just think of the throngs of people that would vote for this handsome couple." He threw his shoulders back and winked at her. "Tell me, how would you like living in the White House?"

She ignored his question. "What did a migrant worker have to do with Mr. Casey?"

Jack put his hands on his hips and glared at her. "Hell, to keep track of him. But he didn't know shit either. You can't hire good help anymore. He bungled everything and then blabbed it. So I told him to meet me out on a certain country road and I'd pay him off. He drove out to the meeting place all by his lonesome. I walked up to the side and 'pow', gone. Easy."

She almost gagged and put her hand over her mouth. This couldn't be the man she loved. "Jack, you just can't go around killing people because they don't suit your needs."

His eyes darted back and forth.

Suddenly, Tracy meandered into the room rubbing her eyes. Fear grabbed Nancy's heart and swept through her every fiber. But before she could reach the child, Jack swooped her into his arms.

"Ah, my little sweetheart," he crooned, "what are you doing up? It's way past your bedtime. Did you have a bad dream? Well, Daddy will rock you back to sleep."

Nancy started to raise her hand in objection, but decided surely he wouldn't hurt his own daughter, and it would be best to humor him at the moment. She followed to the den door and watched him sit down on the couch and cuddle the child in his arms. He slowly began rocking back and forth, singing in an eerie voice about how one day he'd be president and they'd live in the White House.

Nancy quietly stepped backward toward the phone. She could see Jack and Tracy through the hinge crack in the door. Laying the knife down, she dialed Hawkman's pager and keyed in the emergency number, 911.

She turned to lay the receiver down, when suddenly, Jack's hand reached around her and picked up the butcher knife. Whirling about, she gasped, "You startled me."

"Who were you talking to?"

Swallowing the lump in her throat, her hand on her heart, she stuttered. "I—I—don't know. I kept saying hello, but no one answered. Did it wake her?"

He smiled, then looked down at the child in his arms. "I think I'll rock her some more." He carried Tracy back into the den, the butcher knife dangling from his fingers. Once settled on the couch, he glanced up at Nancy with a far-a-way look. "When she's asleep, we'll talk some more."

CHAPTER TWENTY FIVE

After dinner, Hawkman and the two detectives strolled back into the conference room. The growing stack of papers in the center of the table caught Hawkman's eye and he immediately sat down. Detective Grolier hustled to his chair, pushed his glasses up on his nose and got busy reading. Brogan grabbed a cup of coffee and joined them. The room remained quiet for over an hour.

Suddenly, Hawkman hit his fist on the table. "Damn, I'd hoped the Dan Wesson Pistol Pac would give us some evidence that Jack had switched barrels, but the test revealed that the Pac was never used."

"Maybe he found it to complicated and didn't want to mess with it." Grolier said.

"You're probably right." Hawkman plopped the report on the stack of read papers. He thumbed through some of the sheets then turned to Brogan and Grolier. "Either of you seen the report on Jack's gun purchases?"

Detective Brogan shuffled through some of the papers, then handed it across the table. "Yeah, here it is."

After a few minutes, Grolier glanced at Hawkman. "Find anything interesting?"

Hawkman shook his head. "Looks like his father gave him the hunting rifles and shotguns. He's had the Smith & Wesson for two years. The one just discovered in the box was purchased six months ago in Los Angeles." He tossed the paper back to the center of the table and leaned back in his chair. "All bought legally."

Brogan let out a long sigh. "Why do I feel like I'm hitting my head against a brick wall? Let's try another avenue. Fill me in on Tonia Stowell's connection with Jack Gilbert."

"They were lovers," Hawkman stated flatly. "And continued their relationship after Jack and Nancy were married. There are tapes and videos that we assume she used to blackmail him with when the affair ended."

Detective Grolier leaned forward. "DNA on the driving gloves we found at the Stowell house matched Jack's DNA. However, a good lawyer could convince a jury they'd been left at the house during a previous visit."

Brogan grimaced and slapped his hand down on the table. "Damn. Do we have anything concrete?"

Grolier shifted in his seat. "We had the lab go back over everything again. The phone was used as the weapon and proved to be a crucial piece of evidence. A partial palm print, plus hair and flesh fragments from Stowell's head were found on the surface. Hawkman snatched a drinking glass Jack had used and we compared the prints. They matched. Again, a lawyer could state Jack had used the phone on numerous occasions and the print never got wiped off."

"Let's see the video," Brogan instructed. After the viewing, he raised his eyebrows. "That film would definitely give Jack Gilbert or any other man a reason to kill her."

Hawkman flipped on the lights. "Not only that, he had political dreams and wouldn't want the opposing party to get their hands on that tape."

Brogan rubbed his chin. "I get the feeling that Tonia, knowing the camera was running, tricked him into arguing about Nancy. She was definitely a devious woman."

Hawkman put the cassette back in the evidence box. "No question about that."

Brogan stood and paced the floor. "Unfortunately, the film only proves they had an affair and Jack frequented her place. His prints are all over that house. Any good lawyer hired by Jack could tear this case apart."

Grolier fidgeted with his cold cigar. "The ballistics reports are useless. Let's hope we get something off that gun found in the trunk of his car."

Hawkman got up from the table. "We didn't find any Glasers in his gun case. Did you find any in the bedroom, Brogan?"

"A box with four bullets missing, but that doesn't prove a damn thing."

"Well, it means something to us. But it wouldn't convince a jury, unless we can prove the missing four were fired from his gun." Hawkman shook his head. "And with that type of ammunition, it's impossible."

Grolier punched his finger in the air. "We know a jury would rule that Jack shot Drew to protect his wife against an ex-con who threatened her with a gun. They'd never buy the alternative motive that he aimed to kill Drew."

Hawkman leaned against the wall and let out a sigh. "We do have Jack's shirts with blood spots on them. If the lab can prove that the DNA is either Vernando's or Rodreges', we might have something."

Brogan picked up a pencil and ran it through his fingers, then thoughtfully looked at Grolier. "When Gilbert made those deposits into the Master's account, is there a chance that anyone could identify him?"

Grolier shook his head and chewed on his cigar. "I took a picture of Gilbert along with several mug shots of criminals that resembled him into the bank and no one could positively identify him from the group. He covered his face up pretty damned good. I can certainly give it another go around and maybe trigger someone's memory."

"Looks like we're in trouble," Hawkman said.

Brogan clasped his hands together on top of the table. "About the only thing we can do is arrest him on suspicion of murder and hope the District Attorney can do something with what we have."

Suddenly, Hawkman yanked the pager from his belt, read the message, and stiffened. "Nancy's in trouble. Let's hit it."

The three men ran out the door, Brogan shouting orders over his walkie-talkie. They climbed into Brogan's unmarked car and the detective flipped on his radio and barked out, "Code 10-40."

They squealed around the corner as Grolier rolled down the

window and slammed the red light on top of the car. Two other patrol cars brought up the rear. They came to a halt in front of the Gilbert home. Hawkman leaped out of the car then stopped dead in his tracks and stared at the house. Grolier stood beside him.

"It's awfully quiet," Hawkman said

"Brogan joined the two men. "Makes me nervous about what might be going on inside."

❖-»«-❖-»«-❖-»«-❖-»«-❖-»

While Jack carried the sleeping Tracy back to her bedroom, Nancy pondered her next move. Taking advantage of the moment, she discreetly unlocked the deadbolt on the front door. She heard the cars outside and looked out the kitchen window.

When Jack came into the room, flashing red beams were hitting the interior walls. He yanked the cord on the blinds, causing them to drop in front of Nancy's face. He turned on his heel, headed for the living room and closed the drapes. Nancy followed.

"What are you doing?" she asked.

He moved to the den, closed the curtains, then stopped at the couch where he'd been rocking Tracy and pulled out the butcher knife from between the cushions. Nancy stepped back in horror, her hands at her throat. "Jack, what are you going to do with that?"

A loud knock sounded at the front door. She whirled around and started to dash for the entry, but Jack grabbed her. He encircled her neck with one arm, then wrapped the other hand with the knife around her waist, keeping the point upward toward her chest.

She struggled in vain against his strength. "Jack, let me go," she cried.

"You bitch, you called the police, didn't you?" he hissed through gritted teeth.

She felt his spit hit her ear, but before she could respond, Hawkman's voice resonated from the other side of the door. "Everyone okay in there?"

"Answer him," Jack whispered harshly, gripping her tighter.

"We're fine," she called in a low and quivering voice.

Hawkman slowly opened the door a few inches, but stopped when he saw the pair. "Take it easy, Jack."

Jack waved the knife in front of Nancy's face and bellowed. "What the hell are you doing here?"

Hawkman slowly edged inside. "Just thought I'd stop by and say hello."

Jack's eyes narrowed. "That's a bunch of crap. There's a whole raft of you police out there. I saw the red lights. She called you, didn't she?" He placed the knife across her chest. "You come one step closer and I'll carve up her pretty face."

Hawkman stopped in his tracks and kept his voice as soothing as possible. "Jack, things aren't as bad as they seem."

"Hell they aren't. If it weren't for the two of you, I wouldn't be in this mess."

Nancy shifted her weight and Jack flexed his arm around her throat. "Jack, you're hurting me."

"Shut up," he spat, then pointed the knife at Hawkman. "Put your gun on the cabinet. But don't try any funny stuff or she's had it."

Nancy's chin trembled. "Mr. Casey, please do what he says."

Hawkman slowly drew back his jacket exposing his shoulder holster. Then with both hands exposed, he used two fingers of his right hand and placed the gun on the counter.

"Now, get the hell out of here," Jack demanded.

Hawkman eased out the door and closed it.

Jack walked Nancy toward the cabinet and picked up the gun. When he had it safely in his hand, he shoved her away. She backed up against the wall.

He kept the gun aimed at her as he threw the dead bolt on the front door. Grabbing her arm, he dragged her behind him into the den. "Just remember if you try to escape, I still have Tracy."

"Surely you wouldn't hurt our little girl," she cried.

A twisted grin formed on his mouth. "Don't push me."

‹╬›‹╬›‹╬›‹╬›‹╬›

When Hawkman returned to the police car, he explained the hostage situation. Brogan immediately put in a call for the SWAT team.

Grolier gnawed on his cold stogie. "Any ideas?"

Hawkman rubbed the back of his neck. "I'm just trying to imagine what's going through Jack's mind."

"Yeah," Grolier said. "How did he look?"

"If I'd made a false move, he'd have used that knife on Nancy right then and there."

"Dear God. Where's the child?" Brogan asked.

"I didn't see her. She's probably in bed."

Grolier nodded. "Sure hope so."

"But what worries me," Hawkman said. He's going to use Nancy and the little girl as hostages."

"How's Nancy holding up?" Grolier asked

"Scared but seemed fairly stable." He glanced up at the house. "Does anyone remember where the child's room is located?"

"Yeah, I do," Brogan said. "It's on the other side. Her window overlooks the play area."

The three men quietly walked around, keeping their distance from the house so they wouldn't increase Jack's fury. Grolier pointed out the closed drapes in all the windows. But when they came to Tracy's room, a small shaft of light penetrated through the closed curtains. The window looked partially opened.

"We need to get the child out of there," Brogan said in a hushed voice. "When the SWAT team gets here, we'll devise a plan."

They returned to the police van. "As far as we know, we confiscated all of Jack's personal guns and ammunition," Hawkman said. "But, he forced me to leave mine inside, so if he starts shooting, count off six rounds and it's empty."

"That won't help much with a kitchen full of butcher knives," Grolier interjected.

Hawkman let out a long breath. "You're right."

Brogan reached inside the van and handed Hawkman a gun. "Here's a loaner."

"Thanks," Hawkman said, checking it, then slipping the weapon into his shoulder holster.

When the back up police arrived, Brogan ordered them to cordon off the block and evacuate the immediate neighbors, worried there could be a gun battle. He sketched out the house plan for the SWAT team and pointed to the child's room. "We're assuming the little girl's in bed. We've got to get her out of there. So keep a tight watch on her window."

The team scattered to their assigned areas. Two sharpshooters positioned themselves on neighboring roofs so they'd have Tracy's windows in their sights. Two other men were assigned to the ground on each side of her window. The rest singled off to strategic points around the perimeter.

❖≫❖≫❖≫❖≫❖

Inside the house, Jack's strange behavior amplified Nancy's fear. He'd put a dining room chair in front of the front door and forced her into it, then he tied her hands behind her."

"Will they be surprised if they come charging in that front door. You'll be the first to get it my pretty little wife." His high pitched laugh sent chills down her spine.

"Jack, please don't do this," she pleaded. "I promise I won't try to get away."

"Sure, sweetheart," he snarled. "Just like you wouldn't think of calling the police."

He tightened the rope around her wrist, then crossed over to the dining room window and peeked out the side of the curtain. "Well I'll be damned. They've even called in the SWAT team."

Nancy closed her eyes and fought back tears, knowing she was about to die. How could she save her daughter?

But, at that moment, and to her horror, Tracy came dashing into the room crying, "Mommy! mommy!" She climbed into her mother's lap and wrapped her arms around her neck.

Nancy immediately detected the child's soaking wet garment.

"Mommy, I didn't mean to go pee pee," Tracy sobbed. "I had a bad dream."

"It's okay, honey," Nancy replied calmly.

Jack stormed toward them. "What the hell's she doing out of bed?"

"She's had an accident," Nancy said. "Let me get her cleaned up."

He snatched the child from her lap. "I'll do it."

"No! No!" Tracy cried, reaching out for her mother. "I want mommy."

"Jack, she's embarrassed. Undo my hands. I'll fix her bed and get her some dry clothes. She'll go right back to sleep."

He reluctantly set the girl down. "Dammit," he said, crouching down and untying the ropes binding Nancy to the chair. When he threw the last one to the side, he hissed in her ear. "Don't try anything stupid.".

Tracy stared at her dad as he released her mother. "Daddy, why did you have mommy tied up?"

Nancy stood up and rubbed her wrist. "It's okay, honey. We were just playing a game." She picked up the girl and hastened down the hall to the child's bedroom. Jack followed.

But Tracy slammed the door in his face. "No, daddy, stay out. I'll call you in a minute."

Her mind churning, Nancy put her finger to her lips and whispered in Tracy's ear. "We're going to play hide and seek with daddy."

Then she quietly pulled the curtains back and opened the window wider.

⊹⊱⊹⊱⊹⊱⊹

The sharpshooter stationed on the neighboring roof, spoke into his walkie-talkie. "Something's happening. The light in the child's room just came on." He focused his scope. "Woman opening curtains."

"Jack Gilbert in sight?" Brogan asked.

"No. But she's lifting the child through the window."

"One of the team should be there."

"Yep, he just got her."

A harsh whisper interrupted their conversation. "I've got the child. Taking her to safety."

Suddenly, the sharpshooter shouted. "Gilbert just burst through the door with a gun."

"Take him out if he starts shooting." Brogan commanded.

⊹⊱⊹⊱⊹⊱⊹

Nancy had one leg out the window when Jack lunged through the door. "No Jack!" she screamed, holding up one hand in front of her face. Suddenly, she felt her body being pulled through the opening.

The man on the roof watched through his scope, keeping Jack in his sites.

Nancy yelled at the man who practically dragged her around the corner of the house. "My daughter! Where's my little girl?"

"She's safe." He then stopped, still holding on to her arm and spoke into his walkie-talkie. "The woman's okay. We're on the south side of house."

Hawkman hurried toward her.

Nancy fell into his arms sobbing. "Mr. Casey, where's Tracy?"

He half carried and half led her to Jennifer's van where she enveloped the child in her arms.

"Mommy has daddy found us yet?"

"No dear," she whispered.

Suddenly, a single gun shot echoed through the stillness of the night.

Nancy jerked her head around and stared at the house.

Hawkman dashed across the lawn to where the two detectives stood. Brogan with the walkie-talkie close to his ear.

"What happened?" Hawkman asked.

"Jack Gilbert just shot himself."

"Jesus!"

⟨⋅⟩⋈⟨⋅⟩⋈⟨⋅⟩⋈⟨⋅⟩⋈⟨⋅⟩

After the coroner's van took Jack's body away and the SWAT team evacuated the area, Nancy sat in Jennifer's van, staring into space while cuddling Tracy and stroking her hair.

Jennifer touched her arm. "You can't stay here tonight, so why don't you two come home with us."

Nancy wiped the tears from her cheek and nodded. "Thanks."

Jennifer informed Hawkman that she was taking Nancy and Tracy to Copco Lake. He agreed that she should get them out of there as soon as possible.

Once the van had left, Grolier walked over to the unmarked

police car, removed the red emergency light from the top and climbed into the back. Brogan started the car and Hawkman slid into the passenger seat. The team drove slowly away from the silent house.

THE END